NO GOOD DEED

NO GOOD DEED

Barbara Block

severn House

This firs[t] ... [pu]blished in [Great Britain by]
SEVER[N] ...
9–15 Hi[gh] Street, Sutton, Surrey S[M1 1D]
This firs[t] ... [pu]blished in [the] ...
SEVER[N] [HO]USE PUBLISHERS I[NC. of]
595 Ma[d]... [i]n Avenue, New York, [N.Y. 10022]

Copyright © 2007 by Barbara Bloch.

British Library Cataloguing in Publication Data

Bloch, Barbara
    No good deed. - (A Robin Light mystery)
    1. Light, Robin (Fictitious character) - Fiction
    2. Women private investigators - New York (State) - Syracuse - Fiction
    3. Pet shop owners - New York (State) - Syracuse - Fiction
    4. Syracuse (N.Y.) - Fiction
    5. Detective and mystery stories
    I. Title
    813.5'54 [F]

ISBN-13: 978-0-7278-6464-2

All Severn House titles are printed on acid-free paper.

Typeset by Palimpsest Book Production Ltd.,
Grangemouth, Stirlingshire, Scotland.
Printed and bound in Great Britain by
MPG Books Ltd., Bodmin, Cornwall.

To Leslie Seamon
Thanks for everything

My heartfelt appreciation to the usual suspects
for your help and your patience with my endless stream of
questions. I couldn't have done it without you.

One

When John Gabriellas got the call he was sitting up in bed watching TV with his goose-down comforter wrapped around him. He'd been hoping for a call from Trent apologizing for what he'd said earlier in the evening, so when the phone rang John picked up immediately.

'So, you've come to your senses?' he said without waiting to hear who it was.

The voice on the other end of the line chuckled. 'As far as I can tell I've never left them.'

John didn't say anything.

'So how are you and Trent getting along these days?'

John took a deep breath and let it out. 'Fine,' he lied. 'Just fine.'

'Glad to hear it,' the voice said.

'What do you want?'

The man on the other end of the line chuckled again. 'I thought you'd never ask.'

As John listened to what the man had to say he watched little pellets of ice hit his bedroom window and slide down the glass. It was not, he reflected, a good time to be outside. If the temperature went down another degree the rain would turn to black ice on the roads.

'I don't think what you're suggesting is such a good idea,' John protested when the man was done speaking.

The man laughed. 'Don't worry. She'll love it.'

'No. She won't.'

'You're wrong.' And the man began to tell him why he was.

John sighed. It was one thirty in the morning and he wanted to go to sleep or at least he didn't want to listen to the man anymore, but he couldn't hang up. Well, he could but it would be unwise to, so he kept listening even though he didn't want to.

He hadn't liked the suggestion when he'd heard it the first time and he liked it even less now. Unfortunately, saying no was going to be more difficult than he'd imagined. He kept finding polite ways of telling the man, but the man wasn't listening. He was good at not listening, John reflected.

'No, I really couldn't,' John said again. 'There has to be another way.'

'Of course you can.' The voice was quiet but determined and John couldn't help thinking that this was a man who got his way with whatever he set out to do.

John coughed. He was having trouble catching his breath. 'You still haven't told me why I'm doing this.'

'Do you want me to take care of your problem or not?'

'Of course I do.'

'Then don't question me.'

'It's not that I'm trying to make trouble. It's just that I don't feel comfortable doing this,' John protested. He should be asleep right now. He had to get up at six thirty to get to his job on time.

'Trust me, she's not going to mind. She'll think it's funny.'

'I wouldn't think it's funny.'

'She will,' the voice said firmly.

'No. She won't.'

'I know her better than you do.'

'You don't know her at all.'

The man didn't say anything.

John's eyes strayed to the ice sliding down the windowpane. 'It's a bad night to be out driving around.'

'It's not that bad.'

'She could get into an accident.'

'She could get into an accident on her way to her house.'

'I don't like this,' John repeated.

The man on the other end of the line cleared his throat and said, 'I asked you for a favor, one tiny favor, something that will just take a moment of your time. Considering what I'm going to do for you I don't think that's too much to ask, do you?'

'I suppose,' John said.

'You suppose?' the voice on the other end of the line said.
'You suppose?'

John reflected that the man sounded incredulous.

'She's a friend of mine,' John explained. 'A good friend.'
He knew it was an idiotic thing to say, but he couldn't think
of anything else.

'Why do you think I called you?' the man said.

'Can't you do it?' John asked.

'Stupid suggestion,' the man said.

John stared out of his window again. The branches of the
maple tree were coated with ice. They glistened in the reflected
glare of his neighbor's security light. He realized he was
clutching his comforter and eased his grip. He wished he'd
never gotten involved, but he had. He wished he could see a
way out, but he couldn't. The truth was he wasn't what his
dad liked to call 'a standup guy'. Maybe if he had more back-
bone. But he never had and he was too old to change now.
He wished it wasn't the case, but it was.

'It's just a joke,' the man said in a soothing voice.

'You promise,' John said.

'I swear,' the voice said. 'Boy Scout word of honor.'

'You were a Boy Scout?'

'I was an Eagle Scout. That's higher.'

'For real?'

'For real.'

Somehow that made John feel better. Eagle Scouts were
good people, weren't they?

'So you'll make the call,' the voice persisted.

For a moment John was silent as he thought over what
would happen if he didn't do what the man wanted. No. He
couldn't deal with that. Maybe he should be able to, but he
just couldn't. This was a joke, a practical joke, he told
himself. Robin would understand. He'd call her up and
explain afterwards. He'd buy her a drink to make up for
this or maybe take her out for barbecue. It would be fine.
Really, it would.

'Well?' the voice prompted.

'I'll call,' John said suppressing the voice in his head that
told him that this was a bad idea and that Robin wouldn't
like it at all.

'Now,' the man said.

'Now,' John agreed.

'And you'll ring me back when you have?'

'Yes,' John promised. 'I will.'

Two

We were getting ready to close up Shamus's for the night when Ian threw Chad Cutter out of the bar, and I do mean throw. Lucky for Chad that Ian was in a relatively good mood that evening, otherwise Chad would have been paying a visit to the ER. I could tell from Ian's face that he'd had enough of Chad.

I could see it in the way Ian's jaw tightened ever so slightly and his eyes went from dark brown to black. But those were the only signs. Unless you knew Ian you wouldn't be able to tell that he was really pissed. He wiped his hands on his apron. Two seconds after that he was heading around the bar. He was like a locomotive: large, fast, and implacable.

'Go get him,' Carmen yelled at Ian as he flew by her.

You wouldn't think a man of his size could move that fast, but boy could he ever. Before Chad had time to blink Ian was on him. He grabbed Chad's right arm, spun him around, and yanked his arm up till it couldn't go any farther without breaking. Chad bent over. He had no choice. His face was contorted with pain.

'I already told you once I don't want you doing your business in my bar,' Ian told him. His voice was dead calm.

'I was calling Manuel,' Chad whined. His words came out in little gasps.

'Really?' Ian looked at me. Manuel was a kid that worked for me in my pet shop, Noah's Ark. 'They know each other, Robin?' he asked.

'You think I'm lying?' Chad cried.

Ian ignored him. 'Well?' he asked me.

'They might.' It was conceivable. I hoped not, though. The last thing Manuel needed to be doing was hanging around with the likes of Chad Cutter.

'You ask him,' Chad insisted. 'Call him up and ask him.'

'It's too late,' I told him. 'I'll ask him when I see him at the store tomorrow.'

Ian jerked Chad's arm up slightly.

'That hurts,' Chad complained.

'It's supposed to,' Ian told him.

'You got no call to do this to me.'

Ian jerked his arm up a little higher. 'I most certainly do. I don't care if you're speaking to the Crown Prince of Yemen. You're doing what I told you not to. So let me repeat this one last time. I don't want you doing business in my place.'

'I'm not.'

'How stupid do you think I am? You were talking to Joe before. Now I want you to get your skinny Indian ass out of here.'

Chad grimaced in pain as Ian hurried him out. I heard a thud as he managed to bump Chad's head against the door-frame. Funny how that happened. None of the ten people in the bar moved off their seats to follow Ian and Chad outside. They'd all seen this particular show before. They'd wait to hear what Ian had to say. Instead Stuttering Sam clapped and pointed to his can. He wanted another PBR. I went and got it for him.

'He's a gan . . . gan . . . gan . . . gangsta,' Stuttering Sam said as I slid the can across the bar to him.

'No. Chad is a punk,' I told him. 'He just likes everyone to think he's tough.' I took Stuttering Sam's two dollars and put them in the register and moved back to the end of the bar.

Actually Chad was a low-level screw-up who couldn't get anything right. He'd been fired from every straight job he'd ever had and from what I heard he'd messed up a drug deal pretty badly. That's why I was having trouble believing he was involved in another. I couldn't believe that anyone would trust him with anything higher than a dollar bill. But there are a lot of morons out there.

I just hoped that he wasn't working a deal with Manuel. Manuel and I had been through a lot together. He was more like my kid than my employee. Usually he was copacetic, but occasionally the street called him back and that I didn't like because odd as it might seem to some people I don't want that kind of stuff in my life. I've found it always comes back and bites you in the ass.

I was thinking about what I was going to say to Manuel when I opened the store tomorrow as Ian walked back in. I watched him brush shiny little dots of hail off his shoulders. 'Crummy night,' he observed. The customers looked at him. They were waiting to hear what he had to say. This was their entertainment for the night and they wanted full value for the price of their drinks. Ian knew it too. In another life he was probably an actor. He didn't speak immediately. He went back behind the counter, put his hands on the polished wood, leaned forward, and smiled. But his smile didn't reach his eyes.

'Sorry about that, ladies and gentlemen, but it's been a long night and I'm just trying to keep this place nice for you.'

Which was a laugh because nice was not the word I'd be using to describe Shamus's. It was a local dive in a bad area of town. The building had an upper and a lower floor and it was tipping because there was a leak in the roof that had rotted some of the support beams, a leak that the landlord refused to fix. In the past year since I'd started part-timing here two days a week, I'd seen the angle get more and more marked. Ian had called Code Enforcement several times but the owner wasn't cited, possibly because he was a friend of one of the inspectors.

Someone who didn't live in the neighborhood would never walk in off the street to buy a drink. Shamus's looked like the kind of place where bad things could happen to people and in fact from time to time they did. The bars on the small rectangular window in front gave the place all the charm of the county jail. The paint on the outside was puckering and in the daytime it looked as if it had a rash.

Someone had tacked a sheet of metal over the front door, which was dented from people being thrown against it. When you walked in, after your eyes adjusted to the dim light, you caught the smell of cheap beer, old cigarettes, and bad luck. The walls and the floor were the nondescript grey-brown that places acquire when they haven't been painted for a long time.

The occupancy sign said it had the capacity to house fifty people, but I'd rarely seen more than twenty in here at one time and they were always the same twenty, the regulars who had no place else to go and nothing else to do. The bar owners might come and go, but the patrons remained the same. I was thinking about that when I noticed Bill had picked up his PBR and was nodding to it with his chin.

'Last one,' I told him as I took his two bucks and opened a new can for him.

I was surprised he could still drink let alone remain upright since he and his girlfriend Shelley had been here since five in the afternoon and it was now heading towards a little after one-thirty in the morning, but I guess that's what years of practice can do for you. The two of them looked like apple-core dolls that had been on the shelf for way too long.

Shelley wiped a drop of spittle off her jaw before she spoke to me. 'Those Onondagas are no damned good,' she said and she pounded her fist on the counter for emphasis.

I'd heard her say that before. Maybe she was saying that because she was Mohawk, or maybe she was saying it because she'd been married to an Onondaga twenty years ago. From the stories she told it hadn't been a match made in heaven.

Bill made shushing noises.

Shelley glared at him. 'All they do is lay around the Rez, drink and fight and steal cars. Then they torch 'em. Everyone knows that.'

Bill made another shushing noise and put his hand on Shelley's shoulder. She shook it off.

'It's true, isn't it, Robin?' She looked expectantly in my direction.

I put down the glass I'd been drying and tried to think of a tactful answer, but I was so tired my mind had gone blank.

'Isn't it?' Shelley insisted.

'Not in my experience,' I finally said.

'Chad is an Onondaga,' she said as if that clinched the argument. There was a slight slur to her words, which given the circumstances wasn't surprising.

'Chad is a punk,' Ian said. He pointed to his watch. 'You guys got to drink up and go. It's closing time.'

Bill belched. 'I don't got to do anything.'

Ian pretended he hadn't heard him and called a taxi from the bar phone. Even though Bill and Shelley didn't live that far away, they were too drunk to drive and it was too slippery for them to walk. Five minutes later the taxi rolled up and Ian escorted them out the door. Everyone else followed. As soon as the last person left, I poured a little beer into a bowl for my dog Zsa Zsa to drink. She was out of the backroom before I called her. Ian looked at her.

'I still don't think beer is good for dogs,' he said.

It wasn't but she didn't drink very much of it.

'And,' he continued, 'we already agreed she shouldn't be here.'

'It's just for tonight.'

'I could get cited.'

'Unlikely. The Health Department doesn't come around this time of night.'

'That's not the point.'

'I know.'

For reasons that escape me dogs are verboten in most restaurants and bars. However, stuff happens. In this case, I'd taken Zsa Zsa to my shop, Noah's Ark, earlier in the day. I figured I'd drop her off at home and grab a bite to eat before I came to the bar. However, I had a customer who couldn't decide whether he wanted a ball python or a monitor lizard and then my accountant called. He was going to come by and pick up tax stuff for this quarter.

By the time he got to the shop and left I didn't have enough time to take Zsa Zsa home, let alone eat anything other than a couple of chocolate donuts. I had to come straight to the bar and now I very much wanted to go home. Working two jobs was killing me. I didn't want to let go of my shop, but the way things were going I needed a second job to support it.

Zsa Zsa woofed and wagged her tail at Ian.

'You can't soften me up,' he told her as he leaned down and scratched between her ears before turning towards me. 'You think Chad is running a deal with Manuel?' he asked.

'No,' I said.

Ian folded his arms across his chest and gave me his 'how stupid are you?' look.

'OK. Maybe,' I allowed. 'I'll ask him.'

'And you think he'll tell you?'
I shrugged. 'He might.'
'No, he won't.'
'He will eventually.'
'After it's done.'
'That's what I just said.'
'Just watch your register.'
'Manuel wouldn't steal from me.'
Ian took one of his hand-rolled cigarettes from the package
he kept under the bar and lit it. He took a puff.
'Everyone will steal if the circumstances are right.'
'I don't believe that.'
'Fine.' Ian took another puff of his cigarette and tapped
the ash into a half-full beer can.
I started putting the chairs up on the tables. I was halfway
done when my cell rang. I went behind the bar and fished
it out of my purse. The caller ID read John.
'This is a little late for you to be up,' I said to him.
John coughed. 'That's one of the reasons I called.'
'You want me to sing you a lullaby?'
'Not exactly.' John paused. He coughed again. 'Ah . . . a
friend of mine saw Trent's car out at Benny Gibson's house
in Liverpool. At least he thinks it's Trent's car.'
'OK.' I waited to hear what was coming next.
'I know this is a lot to ask, but I was wondering—'
'Let me guess. You want to know if I could drive out and
check it out?'
'I would,' John said. 'But my car's in the shop. Please.'
I paused. I was so tired that my bones were aching. But
John and I had been trying to see if Trent was stepping out
on him with this guy for the past two weeks. We'd tracked
Trent to restaurants, gay bars, dance clubs, and private houses
without getting anything definite.
Some people would have given the whole thing up as a
bad job, but I kept at it. I kept at it because I knew what it
was like to always be wondering if your lover was unfaithful
to you or not. It was a knot in your gut that you carried
around wherever you went.
Or maybe it's because I've always been attracted to bad luck.
'All right,' I finally said.

'I'll buy you a dinner. A nice dinner.'

'You don't need to do that.'

'Yes, I do. You remember the address?'

'I think I do. One twenty-three . . .'

'One twenty-nine Winkinhauer Lane.'

'Close enough.' I'd remember what the house looked like anyway.

John said goodbye and hung up.

'I thought you weren't going to do this anymore,' Ian commented as I wrote the address down on a napkin before I could forget it. When I'm really tired numbers tend to fly out of my head.

I put the pen down. 'Follow Trent around?'

'Exactly.'

'Hopefully this will be the last time.'

'You know some people would call this stalking.'

'Don't be silly. I'm not stalking Trent.'

Ian snorted. 'What would you call it?'

'Information-gathering.'

Ian shook his head.

'Well, that's what it is,' I protested.

'I'm surprised this guy hasn't had an order of protection taken out against you and your friend.'

'He hasn't even seen us.'

'And you're sure of this?'

'Absolutely.' I stifled a yawn. 'Anyway, I'm just doing a favor for a friend.'

'I'm sure this Benny Gibson doesn't see it that way.'

'I just told you, he doesn't know.'

'I find that difficult to believe.' Ian held up his hand. 'But I'm not going to argue with you. Who is he, anyway?'

'Some business guy.'

'What kind of business?'

'Real estate.'

'So he has connections.'

'I don't have a clue.'

'Anyone who has anything to do with real estate in this town has connections.'

'All I know is that he has a house in Liverpool, he's married, and he's got a daughter who is living at home.'

Ian looked at me. 'I thought you said John thought this Gibson guy was going out with John's friend Trent.'

'I did.'

'And he's married?'

'Yes.'

'And he has a child?'

'Yes.'

Ian tapped his fingers on the bar. He kept them straight and did them one at a time as if he were counting them off.

'This is too weird for me.'

I bent down and scratched Zsa Zsa behind her ears. She made a low moaning sound.

'It isn't that uncommon,' I told Ian.

'It is in my circle.'

'You'd be surprised.'

'Yes, I would be.'

'You know . . .'

Ian put his hand out. 'Stop.'

'As in this topic is closed for discussion.'

'Why don't you finish wiping off the bar.'

I was when I remembered I had to put gas in my car. I just had enough to get home.

'Hey, can you lend me a twenty?' I asked Ian. My credit card was maxed out and I didn't have any cash on me.

'Why?'

'So I can get out to Liverpool.'

He reached over and picked up the napkin with Benny Gibson's address on it. 'I have a better idea. I'll drive. At least that way I know you won't get into an accident.'

'I'm not going to get into an accident,' I protested.

'Your eyes look like slits. You'll probably fall asleep behind the wheel. Then I'd have to find someone else to bartend while you recovered from your injuries.'

'Nice,' I said.

Ian laughed. 'That's one thing I'm not. Never have been, never will be.'

It took us twenty more minutes to close. When we were done Ian turned off the lights, clicked off the open sign, and locked the door. His pickup truck had a thin coat of ice on the window and it took him a moment to scrape it off. The ice made the street shimmer under the streetlight. As I got in the pickup I checked my watch. It was a little after two o'clock in the morning. I figured that with a little luck we'd be back in Syracuse in under an hour.

Boy was I wrong.

Three

Zsa Zsa was curled up in the back seat snoring as Ian and I drove along. As we wound our way through the city I reflected that early April was Syracuse's ugliest time of the year. If there was snow on the ground it was black with soot. If the snow had melted the ground was a muddy brown. Garbage, winter's flotsam, lay strewn over the city streets waiting to be picked up. As we went by Shonnard Street I noticed a couple of guys huddled in a doorway waiting to do business. It's nice to know that the entrepreneurial spirit is alive and well on Syracuse's West Side.

When we turned on to Route 81 the highway was deserted. You could have held a bowling tournament in the traffic lanes. The night hid the trash scattered on the sides of the road, while the rain reflected off the tarmac and made everything look bright and shiny.

It was the kind of night you wanted to be in your house, safely tucked up in your bed, and as I watched the buildings speeding by I couldn't help being envious of all the people who were home soundly asleep. Ian cleared his throat. I turned towards him as he was taking one of his cigarettes out of the pack he'd placed on the dashboard and lighting it. I actually think he smokes more than I do. He rolled down the window slightly to allow the smoke out.

'I don't get it,' he said.

'Get what?'

He picked a piece of tobacco off his tongue. 'This Trent thing.'

'What is there to get? John thinks Trent is seeing this other guy, but he wants to make sure before he says anything to him.'

'And you volunteered.'

'I didn't volunteer. He asked for my help and I gave it.'

'Because you have a soft spot for strays.'

'I can think of a worse thing to have a soft spot for.'

I must have struck a nerve because Ian was silent for a moment. 'And this Benny guy is married, right?'

'I already told you that he is.'

'So let me ask you a question. What the hell is Trent doing at his house this time of night?'

It was a good question, one I didn't have the answer to. 'I don't know. Maybe his wife's away on a trip somewhere.'

'And the daughter?'

'She's with the mother.'

Ian tapped his fingers on the dashboard. 'I have a cousin who lives in that development.'

I must have acted surprised because Ian said, 'What? You think I don't have any family?'

'I didn't say that.' But it was true. Maybe I thought that because he never talked about them.

'I have five brothers and fifteen cousins.'

'Really?'

'No. Not really.'

'Then how many do you have?'

'Two. Anyway,' Ian went on, 'that's neither here nor there. I went to Carol's house one time because I had to pick something up. Those houses are spaced close together.'

'I know. I've been there.'

'Then you should realize that someone would see this guy Trent going into Gibson's house.'

'Maybe it doesn't matter.'

'How could it not matter?'

I stifled another yawn. I could feel my eyelids starting to close. 'Maybe the people think they're just hanging out together. You know, two guys watching the game.'

'There is no game this time of night.'

'Then playing cards, drinking beer, doing whatever it is straight guys do together.'

'OK,' Ian conceded. 'But wouldn't this guy Benny be worried about the neighbors telling his wife?'

'Not necessarily. Maybe he's not worried because he's already told his wife that he and Trent are just friends and they're going to be hanging out together when she's gone. Maybe she feels relieved that he has company. Maybe they're fishing buddies. Maybe they bowl in the same league.' I curled my hands into balls so I wouldn't rub my eyes. 'Or maybe he and his wife have an understanding.'

'An understanding?'

'The don't ask, don't tell kind of understanding.'

Ian shook his head. 'That's disgusting.'

'Not to the people that have them.'

Ian sped up a little. 'I would have thought you would know all this stuff by now.'

'I don't think John wants to know.'

Ian snorted. 'No wonder you haven't been able to chase this guy down. You know what the first rule of tracking is?'

'And you know this how?'

'Because I taught a course in tracking and stalking for Eagle Scouts.'

I couldn't help laughing. 'For real.'

'For real.'

'OK. What's the first rule of tracking?'

'It's know your prey.'

Zsa Zsa woofed and I reached back and gave her a couple of pats.

'I'll bear that in mind.'

Ian nodded. He flicked his cigarette butt out the window and turned on his CD player. The sound of the Eagles filled the truck. I leaned back in my seat and closed my eyes. I could feel the bumps in the road. I was thinking that the truck needed new shocks when the next thing I knew Ian was nudging me.

'We're here,' he said.

I sat up with a start.

I'd been sleeping so deeply that for a second I didn't know where I was or who I was with. I'd been dreaming about a giant skull that was talking to me. I knew what it was saying was important, but I couldn't seem to concentrate on the words. They weaved themselves around one another in a river of sound. I knew I knew the language. I just couldn't remember what it was. Instead I kept on staring at the skull's eyes. They were pink diamonds that blinked. A sapphire floated in the hole where its mouth should have been.

A man was standing behind me. He had a monkey on his shoulder that was picking at my hair and telling me that everything was for sale. Then he asked me what I thought I was worth. For some reason it was important to me to make him understand that my car wouldn't run. He was screaming at me, telling me I was going to be deported to a pot, when Ian had nudged me in the ribs.

I shook my head to clear it. When I turned I saw Ian peering at me.

'You all right?' he asked.

I nodded. 'Just give me a minute.'

My head was filled with cobwebs. I opened the window a quarter of an inch to let some fresh air into the car. I took a deep breath. Then I reached in my pack for my cigarettes. Zsa Zsa stirred in the back and gave out with a little woof. I wondered if she'd been dreaming too.

'You don't look all right to me,' Ian observed.

'I will be once I have one of these.' And I held up a cigarette. That's why I don't like taking naps. I always wake up with a muzzy-headed, sick feeling that takes hours to go away. 'I don't suppose we can stop for some coffee?'

'Too late.' Ian pointed straight ahead. 'See. We're almost there.'

I had to squint to read the letters on the entrance to the development. *Maple Hills*. What a laugh. There wasn't a maple tree in the whole place. For that matter there weren't a lot of trees of any kind around. Just some young, small ones that they'd planted after they'd bulldozed the existing ones before building – it was easier and cheaper that way.

I lit my cigarette and inhaled. The fog in my brain began to clear.

'Have you ever noticed how developers name their places after things they've killed to make the development?' I observed.

'Very profound.'

'Do I detect a note of sarcasm?'

Ian snorted and leaned forward so he could get a better

view of the road. We drove through the curved metal arch with pretensions to Spanish wrought iron. There were two roads.

'Take the one on the left,' I instructed.

I was good for the next two turns, but after that things broke down a little. I'd been here twice before with John, but he was the one doing the driving. The place was like a maze, all winding roads that doubled back on each other. To add to the problem there were four styles of houses that repeated themselves endlessly.

Maple Hills was a planned community. You had to ask permission from the board if you wanted to put a basketball hoop in your front yard, let alone change the plantings, or paint your house a different color. I couldn't imagine living in a place like this, but evidently people liked it, because all the houses had been sold and they were building more.

The place was designed for the middle-middle class. Most of the houses went for $150,000. In other parts of the country that wouldn't even buy you a shack, but here it bought you a three- or four-bedroom house with a two-car attached garage, a den, and a laundry room on the main floor.

I guess that's one of the good things about living in a semi-depressed area. You can still, as people like to say, get a lot of bang for your buck. But I preferred living in the city of Syracuse. I liked the old houses, the ones built in the twenties, thirties, and forties, that still had hardwood floors and window sashes, stained-glass windows, dormers, and widow walks. The crime rate was higher but, hey, you can't have everything, right?

The houses outside the car looked ghostly in the darkness, white boxes that floated on a dark under-river. They must have unnerved Zsa Zsa a little because every once in a while she let out with a woof. Ian steered with one hand and dug the napkin with the address I'd written on it out of his back pocket with the other.

'Which way now?' he asked.

'Left, I think.'

'You're not sure?'

'No. I'm sure.' I'd just read the numbers on the mailbox in front of us.

'I hope so, because I don't want to be driving around here all night,' he groused. 'The last time I came here it took me twenty minutes to find my cousin's house and that was in the daytime.'

'Then you shouldn't have come.'

'And you shouldn't have either.'

I changed the subject. Sometimes there's no winning with Ian. 'What makes you think that Chad and Manuel have something going on?'

Ian raised the corners of his mouth slightly. 'They went to Canada last week.'

That was news to me.

'Manuel told me he went to visit his cousins in Buffalo.'

'Guess he lied.'

'They could have gone up to visit a friend.'

'They could have,' Ian said although his tone made it very clear that he didn't think they had.

'Why don't you believe them?'

'Because I had a visitor this morning. A large imposing gentleman. Someone with the name of R.J.' Ian stopped so he could build up suspense. 'He wanted to know if I knew the whereabouts of Jellybean.'

Jellybean was Chad's friend.

'What did you tell him?'

'That I don't know where he is.'

'Did he tell you why he wanted to speak to him?'

'Nope. Just that he wanted to talk to him.'

'So maybe this has nothing to do with Manuel.'

'Maybe,' Ian said.

But I knew that it had. Why else had Manuel lied? I realized I was biting my cuticles and stopped. Even worse I'd let Manuel borrow the van I use to make deliveries with for the trip because he'd told me his vehicle wasn't working and he had to go to his cousin's wedding. Way to go, Robin. This was not good. Not good at all. Manuel and Chad and Jellybean had probably gone up to Canada to get some weed and bring it back.

And Manuel had been acting squirrelly since then so

something must have happened on the way there or back. Obviously something had happened. Otherwise Jellybean wouldn't have gone MIA and R.J. wouldn't be trying to find him. The question was what. The only bright spot that I could see was that my van was back. I decided that the first thing I was going to do tomorrow was clean it up. In case the police came by. The last thing I needed was to have my van confiscated because the cops found traces of weed in it.

'Did R.J. say anything else?' I asked Ian

'He told me he was very, very interested in speaking to Chad.'

'Wonderful.'

'Not really.'

'I was being sarcastic.'

'I know that.'

Sometimes I really don't know about Ian. 'Take a right.'

We went up a hill and then around a turn. The road dipped down slightly into a valley and then began to climb again. I looked up at the sky but all I could see was dark gray. It was supposed to rain and/or sleet until tomorrow evening.

'Benny Gibson's house should be around the next turn,' I told him. When we got there I checked the street sign. 'Yup. This is it.'

Ian pointed in front of him. 'Lookee here.'

'What?' I asked. Then I saw what he was talking about.

'Police cars.'

From the number of red lights there had to be a lot of them.

'Maybe it's a raid,' Ian suggested.

'Or someone got hurt.' Given the number of official vehicles it was something fairly heavy duty. 'I hope they'll let us through,' I said. The thought of coming all the way out here for nothing did not make me happy.

Ian grunted and slowed down. 'Well, if Trent is here, he can't be very happy about this.'

'I wouldn't be if I were him,' I replied.

'I guess I should throw out the weed,' Ian said.

'What?' I yelped.

'Relax. I'm just kidding.' Ian turned towards me. 'So what do you want me to tell the cops when they ask why we're here?'

'How about the truth?'

'What are you, nuts?' Ian asked. 'You know how that sounds? I'm going to tell them we're lost.'

'Then why did you ask me in the first place if you're not going to take my suggestion?'

Ian shrugged. Now that we were closer I could see that there were four squad cars with their lights flashing, a fire truck, and an ambulance. One of the policemen was busy unrolling yellow crime-scene tape. Another one was talking to a plump-looking youngish woman in some sort of leisure suit. The rain had plastered her clothes to her body and she paused every now and then to wipe the rain out of her eyes.

But whatever had happened didn't have anything to do with Benny Gibson's house, it had to do with one of his neighbor's houses because, unless I was wrong, his place was two houses down.

'I wonder if Trent went wacko,' Ian said.

'I was thinking the same thing.'

We slowed down even more and then we stopped completely as a patrolman stepped out into the road. Ian rolled down his window as the patrolman came around to his side.

'Can I ask what your business is here?'

'We got lost,' Ian answered. 'I wanted to show this lady where I'm thinking of buying a house, but I took a wrong turn somewhere and we've been driving around for the last fifteen minutes trying to find our way out.'

The officer clucked sympathetically. 'Yeah, this place is bad enough in the daytime, but at night it's impossible.'

He began to give directions. He was halfway through when I noticed the woman in the leisure suit had approached my side of the car. The police officer she'd been talking to was right behind her.

She pointed at me. 'She's the one,' she cried. 'She's the one who's been following my father around for the last two weeks. Ask her what happened to him. Go on. Ask her.'

The policeman next to her approached my door. I could see he had his right hand resting on his gun handle.

'Ma'am, would you mind stepping out of the car,' he said. 'I'd like to have a word with you.'

Before I did Ian turned towards me and mouthed, 'What did I tell you?'

Four

The moment Benny Gibson's daughter opened her mouth I knew I was in big trouble. I figured Benny Gibson was dead. Had to be. Why else would all the cop cars be here? Then I figured that Trent had flipped out and gone off and done something like killed Benny in a fit of rage. Guess he shouldn't have been fooling around after all.

I didn't feel sorry for Trent or Benny Gibson, except in the abstract sense, because I didn't know them, I'd just met Trent once and Benny Gibson not at all, but I did feel bad for John. He loved Trent, he wanted to be with him, and now look what had happened.

But mostly I was sorry for me. All I wanted to do was go to bed and that didn't look like a possibility right now. I had a funny feeling it would be a long time before I got to see my bed again. The way things were going I'd probably be lucky if I got to go to bed at all today, considering that I had to open the store around eight in the morning so I could get my deliveries.

And then I got to thinking about what Benny Gibson's daughter had said and the more I thought about it the more disturbed I got. How did she know I'd been following her dad around for two weeks? Like I'd told Ian, I was reasonably sure the guy hadn't seen me. When John and I had gone out to his house, no one had been there. At least that's what I thought. But maybe she'd been in one of the bedrooms upstairs watching out the window. It would have been odd for her to have remembered me, though. John and I hadn't stayed that long. In fact, we hadn't stayed at all. We'd taken a look, turned around, and driven away precisely because there had been no place we could park my car inconspicuously.

The only other explanation was that Trent had known what we were doing and told Benny Gibson, who in turn told his daughter. Had he? Had he let John and me ride around making fools of ourselves? Had he been inside laughing at us? That didn't speak particularly well of him. But then neither did killing someone.

I was thinking that neither explanation made any sense to me while I was waiting to talk to the policeman in the back of his squad car. It reeked of sweat and pine air-freshener. Standing out in the rain and the sleet was beginning to look really good, but unfortunately I didn't have that option.

A few seconds after I got into the squad car another policeman came up and started leading Benny Gibson's daughter back towards her house. She went reluctantly. He had to tug on her sleeve a couple of times. When they were halfway there she slipped away from him, ran back, and started banging on the window next to where I was sitting.

'Why did you do this to me?' she cried, pressing her face and her hands against the glass.

'I didn't do anything,' I replied.

She pounded on the glass with her fists. 'You did, you did, you did.'

I was reminded of a child throwing a temper tantrum and pausing every thirty seconds or so to see if the parents were responding. Or perhaps she was in shock. A moment later the policemen ran forward to reclaim her just as you would a wayward child. As he pulled her away from the squad car she kept her head turned towards me. She kept it that way until she disappeared behind the curtain of flashing red lights, vehicles, and talking men.

As I looked into the distance I caught sight of Ian talking to an officer. The officer was writing something down, presumably Ian's statement. At that moment Ian turned towards me and we looked at each other. He shook his head slightly before going back to talk to the officer again.

I thought about the question the woman had just asked me. It was an odd question, one that made no sense to me, but then again none of this did. I sat there feeling as if I'd wandered into a play and no one had told me what role I was supposed to be playing. Maybe I was still asleep. I wanted to pinch myself but I didn't because I knew what the answer would be.

In case I had any doubts I could smell the detective's jacket as he settled into the car to take my statement. The rain had brought out its musty smell and it spread until it inhabited all the cracks and crevices in the squad car. He introduced himself as Detective Keene. I sighed and sat back in the seat. Something told me that the statement I was about to give was going to be the first of an endless number. I briefly entertained the thought of getting a lawyer but that would just make things longer and more than anything else I wanted to get out of there. Anyway, I hadn't done anything, right? What a laugh. Like that made a difference.

Keene took my name, address, and phone number. Then he asked me what I was doing there.

I explained. Given the circumstances I didn't have much of a choice. But I had to admit the explanation didn't sound good. Not even to me.

Keene stopped writing. He was a young guy and I got the feeling this was his first big case and he wanted to do well.

'So you and your friend have been following this guy, Trent,' he peered in his notebook to read the last name, 'Trent Goodwell around for the last two weeks?'

'Off and on.'

'And then your friend John . . .'

'Gabriellas.'

'Called you up tonight at one thirty in the morning and asked you to do him a favor.'

I nodded.

'Isn't one thirty a little late?'

'I work as a bartender at a bar over on the West Side two nights a week.'

The look on his face made it plain he disapproved of bartenders. When I gave him the bar's name his expression got even more disapproving. He made a clicking noise with his tongue as he wrote it down. 'So,' he continued. 'This John Gabriel—'

'Gabriellas,' I corrected.

Keene made an impatient gesture with his hand. 'This

Gabriellas got a tip that Trent Goodwell would be at Benny
Gibson's residence.'

'That's correct.'

Keene's leg started jiggling. He leaned forward slightly.
He looked like someone who was closing in for the kill.
'Who gave him the tip?'

'I don't know. He didn't tell me.'

'And you didn't think to ask?' I could tell from his expression that he thought he had me.

'It was late.'

'So?'

'I was tired.'

'And yet you hopped in the car and came out here?'

'He's a friend of mine.'

'Most of us don't have friends like you.'

'What can I say? I guess you're not lucky.'

He snorted. He wasn't buying my explanation, and I didn't
blame him because it was a pretty sketchy story. He asked
for John's address and telephone number and I gave them
to him. He wrote them down slowly and deliberately as if
that would counteract the motion in his leg.

'Stay here,' he instructed as he got out of the car.

Like I had a choice.

I spent the next twenty minutes looking out the car window.
The rain and sleet had stopped, but the officers still had the
collars of their waterproofs pulled up to their chins to protect
them from the wind.

I could see Ian was walking Zsa Zsa off on the side of
the road. She kept mostly to the pavement where possible
because she hated to get her paws wet, stopping here and
there to sniff something of interest. Ian started towards me
but an officer waved him away. He shrugged and continued
walking Zsa Zsa. When I looked again he was on his cellphone talking to someone. A couple of moments later the
officer who had taken my statement was back.

'This guy, John,' he said. 'He's not answering his phone.'

'Maybe he's asleep,' I suggested.

'We sent an officer over to knock on his door. No one is
responding.'

Which was odd since he'd told me his car was in the garage.

'Maybe he took a sleeping pill and didn't hear you.'

The officer began lightly slapping the tips of the fingers of his right hand against his thigh.

'Did he call you from his house?'

'I already told you he did. That was the reason I did this.'

'Tell me again.'

So I did. At that point I was thinking that maybe I should call my lawyer after all when they let me go. I don't think they would have if it weren't for George.

At first I couldn't believe I was seeing him. I spotted him out the squad-car window. He'd just gotten out of a big black SUV. He was wearing a heavy belted black leather jacket, a black turtleneck, and jeans. He'd shaved his head, which was something new. It looked good on him. Unfortunately. By my calculations it was a little over a year since I'd thrown him out of my house for two-timing me, but he still dropped by every month or so to say hello.

I tried to keep his visits short because I found them upsetting. I still wasn't at the stage where I could do casual. Maybe in a couple of years, but not now. He waved at me and I waved back. Then he went over and talked to Keene. A moment later one of the uniforms came and let me out of the squad car. George followed on his heels.

'Still getting yourself in trouble, I see,' he said to me.

'Once in a while.'

'Still think you're God's appointed savior?'

'I like to think of myself as one of his handmaidens.'

'I'm serious, Robin.'

'I know you are.'

'You should leave this kind of stuff to the professionals.'

'So you've said.' George had been a cop before he'd quit the force and gone to graduate school.

'Yes, I have.'

This was one of the constant arguments George and I used to have when we were living together. He thought I had bad judgment and I thought he had no compassion. As it turned out he was right. I did have bad judgment. About him. He was a womanizer and I should have thrown him out long before I did. I decided to change subjects.

'So how are your wife and the baby?'

'We're not married yet.'

'Sorry. It was just a figure of speech.'

George smiled. 'I got a tenure-track position at Oswego State.'

'Congratulations.' Up till now George had been working adjunct.

'Not bad for an ex-cop.'

'Not bad at all.'

'They probably had to fill their quota.' George was black. 'Hey,' he said when I didn't reply, 'you're supposed to dispute that.'

I shrugged. I wasn't in a playing-games kind of mood. 'You still look like a cop.'

George put his hand up to his head. 'Must be the shaved head.' He nodded towards Ian, who was sitting in his truck. 'Still working for the bar owner, I see. He's got a bad rep.'

'I don't care. You're the reason they're letting me go, aren't you?'

George shrugged. 'They would have done it anyway sooner or later. I just speeded things up a little.'

'It was good of you to come all the way out here at this time of the night.'

'I figured I owed you for the way I left. That wasn't very nice.'

'No. It wasn't.'

'I just want to apologize.'

'You already have.'

'I guess I need to keep doing it.' George shifted his weight from one leg to another and jammed his hands into the pockets of his leather jacket. 'I don't know if it matters, but I keep thinking about you.'

I put my hand up. 'Don't. We've played this game too many times before and I don't want to play another round.'

George nodded. 'I understand. All I'm asking is that you think about it.' He turned to go, then turned back around. 'One last thing. If I were you I'd get a lawyer.'

'I'm not sure I want to spend the money.'

'You always were cheap in the wrong ways,' George said. 'But you should. I have a feeling you're going to need one.'

I let that go.

'Did Ian call you?' It seemed unlikely but I couldn't figure out how else George had gotten here.

George shook his head. 'One of my buddies did. He bought a Haitian boa from your shop a couple of years ago. Then he came back and bought a gecko.'

'Does he still have them?'

'His fiancé made him get rid of them.' And with that George walked away.

He moved with the kind of grace big men who are confident of themselves have. He stopped to talk to one of the officers. I wondered if that was the guy who had called George as I walked to the truck. I wanted to thank him but this wasn't the time or the place.

Ian turned to me when I got in the pickup. 'Listen,' he began.

I interrupted. 'I don't want to hear it.'

But of course he couldn't resist telling me he was right.

'What don't you want to hear?' he asked me, ignoring my request. 'That I told you that what you were doing with John was sketchy. That I told you this whole thing was bad news. Is that what you don't want to hear?'

'Yes,' I said. 'That's exactly what I don't want to hear.'

'Good. Then you shouldn't listen. You never do anyway.'

'That is so unfair.' And I leaned over and turned on the radio.

Neither Ian nor I said anything until he dropped me and Zsa Zsa off at my car. We were both too tired to argue. It was a little after four o'clock in the morning when she and I got home. Zsa Zsa ran up the front steps and I was right behind her. I was wired and exhausted at the same time. Not a good combination. I decided it would be silly to go to bed considering that I'd have to get up again in two and a half hours.

Instead I poured myself a stiff shot of Scotch and sat down on the sofa in my living room and considered the evening's events. The more I thought about them the uneasier I got. I decided that at least I could attempt to straighten out one piece of the equation.

I got up and went over to the phone and tried John's

number. He didn't pick up. I got the answering machine instead. I left a message and sat back down. If I didn't hear from him by tomorrow morning, I'd drop by his house and see what was what. Then I watched the blue spruce across the street. It reminded me of a giant hovering over the street watching and waiting for a sign before it came to life.

The next thing I knew Zsa Zsa was licking my ear. Daylight was flooding in through the blinds of my living-room window, making bars on the floor. I glanced at my watch. It was seven thirty in the morning. I'd fallen asleep sitting up and hadn't even known it.

The handset to my cordless phone was lying on the sofa right next to me. I picked it up and dialed John's number again. After two rings, I hung up and went to take a shower.

Five

John Gabriellas couldn't believe what was happening on the TV screen. This isn't real, he told himself as he watched the footage. Finally he managed to get himself up and turn the volume down. With his eyes still glued to the screen he dialed the number. It was funny. Normally, he couldn't remember numbers, but this one he couldn't forget.

The man at the other end of the line picked up immediately. John thought he must be on his cell because he could hear mechanical noises and lots of voices in the background.

'I thought you said it was going to be a joke,' John said.

'It is,' the man replied.

'I'm watching the news. They're rerunning it. It doesn't seem like a joke to me.'

'I guess that depends on your sense of humor. She'll think it's funny.'

John swallowed. He felt vaguely nauseous. He hoped he didn't throw up. He hated throwing up.

'No. She won't think it's funny,' he protested. 'She won't think it's funny at all.

'She will later on.'

'I doubt that very much.'

John peered at the TV screen. Was that her in the squad car? Please God, no.

'I don't know,' the man was saying. 'She has a weird sense of humor.'

John swallowed again. Now he had a faintly bitter, metallic taste in his mouth. He didn't want to ask the next question, but he had to know.

'Tell me,' he said, 'did you have anything to do with what they're showing on TV?'

The man snorted. 'How can you even think something like that?'

John realized he was squeezing the phone and loosened his grip. If he were a better man he'd go over and beat the crap out of this guy.

'It's pretty obvious why I think that, isn't it?'

'I told you I didn't.'

He could tell the man was lying, he didn't know how he could, but he just knew he was. But he went on as if he believed him anyway. It was easier that way. He had to. To not believe him was to surrender to the shadows. 'I'm going to call her. I'm going to call and tell her what you did.'

The man chuckled. 'Tell her what I did? Ha. That's a laugh. If anyone did anything it's you. You're the one that made the call. You're the one that sent her out there. She already knows that you were part of this.'

John could feel his heart fluttering in his chest. He wondered if you could have a heart attack from something like this. His aunt always said you could. Maybe she was right. He wanted to say something but the words felt heavy in his mouth.

'How does she know?' he finally managed to get out.

'Don't be an idiot,' the man said.

John swallowed.

'She's going to try and get in touch with me, isn't she?'

'I would if I were her.'

'What can I say?'

The man laughed. 'Whatever you want.'

'I don't want to say anything.'

'Then don't.'

'But I have to,' John protested.

'That isn't my problem, is it?'

'I could make it your problem.' But it was too late. He'd already hung up.

John debated calling him back but he didn't have the energy. Instead he turned his attention back to the television. He watched with an appalled fascination. Now the station was showing a clip of the crime scene. John could see three or four police cars and an ambulance. One of the neighbors was telling the reporter what a nice family the Gibsons had been.

John thought that whenever anyone was killed the neighbors always talked about what a nice person the victim had been. He'd never heard anyone say, 'That so-and-so was a moron and he had it coming.' John rubbed his forehead with his hand. He felt hot. Maybe he was coming down with something. There was a lot of stuff going around.

All he wanted to do was sleep. But he couldn't. He had to think. He had to think about what he was going to say to Robin. He had to figure it out before he spoke to her. And the police. He put his hand to his mouth. He'd forgotten about them. Dollars to donuts they would be knocking on his door soon. He had to go somewhere quiet and think. He had to.

He'd just tried to do a good deed and look what had happened.

It just wasn't fair.

But as his dad always said, 'Life never is.'

Six

It was another gray Syracuse morning when I stepped outside my house. It was thirty degrees, and looking to the west I could see dark clouds massing, pregnant with snow. The sun gave them a luminous quality. According to the weatherman they were heading in our direction. I could hardly wait. The grass on my lawn was frozen from last night's rain and it crunched under my feet when I walked. I briefly thought about going back in the house and getting my gloves, but then I remembered I'd lost my last pair a couple of weeks ago.

'Spring will be here soon,' I told Zsa Zsa, but looking around it was hard to believe.

It was time to go to work, but I had a couple of things to do first. Like take the van to one of the car washes on Erie Boulevard. Maybe it wasn't strictly necessary, but given what had happened to me I was paranoid enough to want to make sure. The car wash I had in mind was one of those do-it-yourself ones that was slightly off the main thoroughfare.

I drove over and spent ten minutes vacuuming out the van. I also checked the glove compartment, under the seats, in the back, and under the luggage liner. As far as I could see everything looked the way it had when I loaned it out to Manuel. Then I made a pit stop at Dunkin' Donuts and ordered a large coffee with cream and sugar and three glazed chocolate donuts, all of which I shared with Zsa Zsa – she has to be the only dog I know that likes beer and coffee – after which I drove over to John's house and rang his bell.

No one answered. So where the hell was he? I really needed to speak to the guy and now he was nowhere to be found. I was angry and worried: this wasn't at all like John. He was an extremely responsible person. I tried peeking through his windows, but I couldn't see anything because the shades were down.

I was walking towards the garage when a man came out of the house next door and intercepted me.

'Can I help you?' he asked. His face was contorted in an expression of disapproval. I couldn't decide if it were of the world or of me.

'I'm looking for John Gabriellas,' I told him.

'He's obviously not home.' He tugged at the label of his overcoat with pudgy, pink fingers. He looked like the kind of man who would come knocking on your door if your cat peed in his flower bed.

'Do you know where he went?'

The man stuck his chin out. I could tell he fancied himself the self-appointed guardian of the neighborhood. 'No and I don't think you'll find out by trying to look in his window.'

'Is it all right if I leave him a note?'

'I'm going to watch you while you do.' Obviously he didn't get my sarcasm.

'What do you think I'm trying to do?'

The man sniffed. 'I don't have the vaguest idea.'

He crossed his arms over his chest. I wondered if I looked that disreputable. I'd showered and combed my hair and put on a new pair of jeans and my blue turtleneck sweater. Discounting the black circles underneath my eyes I thought I looked pretty good.

'Well?' he said. 'Are you writing a note or aren't you?'

I changed my mind. When I told him that he gave me an I-told-you-so smile. He'd caught me out. I could just hear him talking to his wife. I caught her just before she broke into John's house, he would say. But when I thought about it I realized that there was no point in leaving a note. I'd already left several messages on John's machine. The problem wasn't that he didn't know I wanted to talk to him; the problem was that he wasn't responding.

'If you see him, tell him Robin Light is looking for him,' I said to the neighbor.

The man nodded and watched me while I got into my vehicle and drove away. As I rounded the corner, I could see him heading for his garage. If I waited a few minutes more he'd be gone and I could go back and have another look at John's house, but that would have to wait till this afternoon. It was getting late and I had to open the store.

I felt a sense of pleasure as I stepped inside Noah's Ark. I always do. That was one of the reasons I'm working a second job to keep the place going. Besides, what would happen to the macaw and the African gray I'd taken in? I couldn't abandon them and I really didn't want them in my house.

Zsa Zsa ran ahead of me, sniffing to make sure that nothing had changed since yesterday. Occasionally she'd let out with a woof when she found a piece of rabbit or gerbil food that Manuel or I had dropped on the ground. I turned on the lights and reconciled the register receipts. We hadn't done too badly yesterday. Not great, but we'd sold two hundred and fifty-seven dollars' worth of merchandise. Enough to keep the metaphorical wolf from the door for a little while longer.

My rent wasn't expensive, but the utilities were killing me, and I'd had to raise prices to compensate. Places like Wal-Mart could absorb the costs but I couldn't. My profit margin was too small. I sighed as I checked on the fish and the reptiles. Everyone seemed to be doing fine.

Next I cleaned the small rodents' cages, and took care of the birds. They cackled and cooed and nibbled on my hair while I cleaned their cages and perches. The UPS man came with my order of dog food and biscuits and I paid him with the cash I had in the drawer, a practice my accountant disapproves of, but it was easier than writing a check. I was just stacking the bags on the shelves when Manuel walked through the door.

I glanced at my watch. 'Can we say the word "late"?'

'Saw you on TV,' he said as he headed into the back-room to hang up his starter jacket.

Just what I needed.

'What did they say?'

'Nothing much. That you were cooperating in the investigation concerning the death of Benny Gibson. Who is he?'

I explained.

'Nice, Robin,' Manuel said. 'Good job.'

He scratched his chin. Recently he'd grown a soul patch under his chin and gotten stretchers in his earlobes. It was not a good look in my estimation, but I hadn't been consulted.

'Want me to do that?' Manuel asked, indicating the dog food I was putting on the shelves.

I nodded, straightened up, went over, and started sorting the leashes. I don't know why people can't put them back where they belong. What is so hard about that?

'So,' I said after about ten minutes had gone by. 'Chad came by Shamus's last night.'

Manuel kept stacking the bags of dog food. But I could tell from the slight quiver in his shoulders that he was very interested in what I was saying.

'Ian threw him out,' I continued.

Manuel kept stacking the dog food.

'He's got a nice lump on his head,' I added.

Manuel slid the last fifty-pound bag into place. 'He probably deserved it,' he said.

'Probably,' I agreed.

Manuel cleared his throat. 'What was Chad doing?'

'Conducting business at the bar.'

Manuel rubbed his nose with one of his fingers. 'That wasn't smart.'

'No, it wasn't, but then I don't think Chad is. Smart,' I clarified, noting the puzzled look on Manuel's face. I waited for a comment. When there wasn't any I went on, 'Did you and Chad have fun on your trip?'

Manuel blinked. 'What trip?'

'The trip to Canada that you took in the van that I lent you.'

Manuel's blinking got more frantic. It reminded me of a ship signaling it was going down.

'We went to Buffalo.'

'For your cousin's wedding.'

'Right.'

'Not according to Chad you didn't.'

Manuel ducked his head down.

'Chad said you and he did some business together.'

'We sold a DVD player to one of his friends,' Manuel told me. 'BFD.' He tried to do outrage. It didn't work very well. 'We were in Buffalo. You can call my cousins if you like.' And he got his cellphone out of his pocket and held it out to me. 'Here.'

'So they can cover for you?'

'They won't,' Manuel said. 'I swear.'

'Coming from you that's funny. You promised me you'd stick to our agreement.'

Our agreement was that he could use the van, but he couldn't give anyone else a ride or let anyone drive it.

'I did.'

'I don't believe you.'

I didn't feel like pointing out to Manuel that he and Chad could have gone to visit his cousins and then gone to Canada.

'Robin, you're so unfair,' Manuel wailed.

'I doubt that,' I said. 'But maybe I am. It doesn't matter. I don't want you using the van anymore. Period.'

And I turned and walked away.

'It wasn't what you think,' Manuel said.

I turned back. 'Then what was it? Coke? Guns? Cigarettes? What were you smuggling?'

'Nothing.'

I stared at Manuel. He began to fidget.

'It was . . .' and his voice drifted off.

'You know,' I said, 'I'm tired. I've had a really bad night. You don't want to tell me, that's fine. All I can tell you is that Chad is bad news and that one of these days he's going to find himself going away on a long vacation and it's not going to be to Aruba.'

Manuel yanked his pants up. He was still into wearing them five sizes too big. 'You're exaggerating.'

'Am I? A big guy was in Shamus's talking to Ian about Jellybean. He was looking for him. Ian said he didn't look real happy.'

Manuel paled. Now I had his attention. 'It wasn't like that.'

I leaned towards him. 'Then tell me what it was like.'

'It wasn't a big deal. We just gave this guy and his daughter a ride from St. Catherines into Buffalo.'

'And?'

'There is no more. That's it.'

'That's it? So you're telling me you and Chad and Jellybean have branched out from smuggling weed to smuggling people? And you used my van to do it?'

'We weren't smuggling, we were helping.'

'Helping? That's an interesting word choice. How much did you get?'

'Two thousand.'

'Each?'

'No. To split.'

'And that's why you borrowed my van?'

'No. I really did go to my cousin's wedding. We just did this before that.'

'Tell me.'

Manuel fingered his chin. 'I told Chad I was going to Buffalo and he wanted to know if he could come along.'

'So you said sure.'

Manuel nodded. 'I figured he could pay for the gas. When I picked up Chad, Jellybean was there too. He told me that this guy would pay us to drive him and his daughter across the border, that he had some sort of problems he had to settle, and he didn't have time to go through security.'

'What kind of problems?'

'I don't know. I didn't ask.'

'Naturally.'

'I figured it wasn't my business.'

'And you used my van for this? Lovely.'

Manuel fidgeted. 'I thought you'd want us to help. They were Americans.'

'Which of course made all the difference. And you knew this how?'

'I just knew.'

'Your ESP kicked in.'

'Exactly.'

'Which makes it OK. After all, as you said, you were just helping out.'

Manuel nodded, but he looked doubtful.

'But,' I prompted.

'Nothing.'

'Then why is this guy looking for Jellybean?'

'I don't know about that. Honestly. We did what we had to do, then I dropped Jellybean and Chad by the bus stop and I went on to the wedding. Maybe they went back over.'

I studied Manuel for a moment. I could tell from the way his eye was twitching he wasn't telling the truth. 'You want to try that again?'

Manuel took a deep breath and let it out. 'We got stopped by the troopers just before we got to the Rez. Somehow they knew we were coming. Anyway, the next thing I know they're searching the car. You've got to believe me, Robin. I didn't know Jellybean had anything on him. I almost died when the trooper found fifty grand.'

'And he let you go, just like that?'

'He took the money and asked for our names and stuff.'

I didn't say anything.

After a moment it dawned on Manuel that they'd been had. He thrust his chin forward. 'So are you saying it was a scam?'

'Yeah. I am.'

'He showed us some ID.'

'You can buy those anywhere.'

'Shit.'

'Exactly. And the guy that's looking for Jellybean? Who is he?'

'It was his money. He wants it back.'

'Naturally. And the thing about the father and the girl. Is that true?'

Manuel bit his lip.

'Well, is it?' I repeated.

'Jellybean does it from time to time.'

'He brings people across the border?'

Manuel shrugged. 'Sometimes.' Then he gave me his best smile. 'Now that I told you, do I get to use the van?'

Manuel's sense of entitlement never fails to amaze me.

'Are you out of your mind? You were going to use it to

smuggle drugs back into this country and you're asking me that.'

He gave me his puppy-dog eyes.

'Cigarettes. We was going to smuggle cigarettes. Marlboros. I'd never do weed.'

I couldn't help it. I burst out laughing.

'So I can have the van?'

'No. You definitely cannot.' I pointed to the aquariums. 'What you can do is feed the fishes.'

'I'm serious.'

'So am I.'

I went back to work. But it was hard to concentrate. I had too many other things on my mind. Like where John was. Like who had killed Benny Gibson. Like whether I was going to need a lawyer and if so how I was going to pay for one.

It was almost four when John called me. He called me on the store line, which is how come I didn't know it was him. I keep meaning to get caller ID and I keep forgetting.

'Robin,' he said.

'John?' His voice was so low I could barely make out what he was saying.

'I am so, so sorry for what's happened,' he said. 'You have to believe that. I never meant for things to turn out like this. I didn't know what else to do.'

'What's going on?' I repeated.

'You won't like me if I tell you.'

'I'm not liking you very much now.' The minute those words left my mouth I wanted to take them back but John was talking again.

'I'm sorry,' he repeated. 'I mean that.'

And before I could say anything else he hung up.

I called back. He didn't answer. I called back again figuring maybe I'd dialed the wrong number by accident. He didn't pick up. I gave it two more tries. Nothing.

Manuel came up behind me and asked what was going on. I explained the situation.

'Doesn't sound good,' he said.

'No, it doesn't, does it,' I agreed.

I had a bad feeling in my gut.

'I'll be back as soon as I can,' I told Manuel.

Zsa Zsa woofed at me as I went into the office to get my jacket. I fed her a dog biscuit and told her to stay. She looked at me with reproachful eyes. I ignored them and headed out.

Maybe Ian was right, I reflected as I closed the office door. Maybe I should just learn to mind my own business.

Seven

It was snowing when I went outside. Big wet flakes swirled around me. The sky was the color of slate. The clouds I'd seen that morning had arrived. I put the collar of my jacket up as I hurried towards my car. I brushed the snow off the side mirror with my arm and wondered when spring was ever going to come. I'd just opened the door when George's SUV pulled up behind me. He got out and came towards me. He was dressed the way he was last night, only this time he was wearing a white wool turtleneck sweater instead of a black one. I don't know why, but he never seems to feel the cold.

'Shouldn't you be teaching right now?' I asked him.

'Today's my day off.'

'Wow,' I said. 'I'm seeing you two times in one day. How did I get so lucky?'

George stopped in front of me and crossed his arms over his chest. 'You were the one that threw me out, remember?'

'With cause,' I reminded him.

He gave me a rueful smile. 'I can't argue that, but that doesn't mean I don't still care about you.'

'So you said last night.'

'And I meant it.' George went to take my hand in one of his but I moved away before he could.

I didn't want to talk about our relationship. It just made me remember what a moron I'd been so I changed the subject. 'What are you doing here?'

'I've just come by to see how you're doing,' he explained. 'If you mind I'll leave.'

'No. You can stay.'

'Good.' George gazed at me intently. 'So how are you doing?'

I shrugged. 'I've done better.'

'I bet you have. Heard from anyone yet?'

'I just heard from John.' And I told George about the telephone conversation I'd had. Even though I wanted to deny it, it felt good to talk to him.

'Really.' George's eyebrows shot up. 'So what do you think it means?'

'I don't know.' I wasn't giving him an entirely truthful answer, but I didn't want to voice my suspicions because when you do that it makes them real and I didn't want to go there yet. 'I'm going there now to check things out.'

'Mind if I ride along?'

'Not at all.' In fact, I was glad. Even though I didn't like admitting it to myself I was happy for the company. More importantly, in situations like this an ex-cop is always handy to have around.

George smiled and got into my vehicle. That surprised me. When we'd lived together he was always the one who had wanted to do the driving.

'Nice ride,' he commented looking around. 'I especially like the duct tape on the seats.'

I turned the ignition key. 'It gives it that homey touch.'

'No doubt. So how long have you known John for?' George asked me as I pulled away from the curb. 'I don't recall hearing his name come up when we were living together.'

'That's because I didn't know him then. We met at the Syracuse International Film Festival last spring.'

George turned to me. 'I didn't know you like movies.' There was real surprise in his voice.

'I love movies. I just got out of the habit of seeing them.'

George grunted and faced forward. He reminded me of a statue carved out of ebony, all hard polished surfaces. The snow was letting up already. It had been one of those brief snow showers we get in upstate New York, winter's way of showing he isn't quite ready to give it up yet.

'Did you read the local paper this morning?' George asked after a few moments.

'I didn't get a chance. Why?'

'They had an article about Benny Gibson.'

'I'm not surprised.' In fact, given the circumstances I would have been surprised if there hadn't been one. 'Did they say anything about me?'

'It's always about me, me, me.'

'Well, did they?'

'Not too much. Just that you were cooperating with the investigation.' George rubbed his chin. I could see a slight stubble on his cheeks. Surprising. George always shaved no matter what. 'Did you know Gibson bought three properties downtown in the last nine months?'

'How would I know that?'

I realized I was snapping. Too little sleep and too much caffeine had not put me in a good mood.

George shrugged. 'I figured since you were following him you might have done a little research on him as well.'

'No. I didn't. I already told you John just wanted to see if Trent's car was in Gibson's driveway. Period. What else did the article say?'

'That Gibson owned several buildings.'

'Did it say how he died?' Since I was being accused of the crime it would be nice to know how it was committed.

'He was shot in the chest.'

'Any signs of a robbery?'

'If there was, the paper didn't mention it.'

'Anything else?'

'Nothing of importance.'

George ran a finger around his turtleneck. I watched him watch the streets out of the corner of my eye. Like Ian, he was always on alert, always weighing and assessing.

George remained silent for the rest of the trip and so did I. It took me ten minutes to get to where John lived on Kensington Place. By the time I got there the snow had stopped completely and the flakes on the street were melting. At this time of year snow was ephemeral.

In the spring the entrance to John's house was almost hidden behind a walkway filled with a profusion of grape arbors overrun with morning glories and rambling roses winding their way around trellises. Russian sage, lemon balm, lily of the valley, and herbs bordered the path to his house. Then the air was heady with the green scent of spring, but now the air smelled of smoke and cold, the trellises were bare, the doorway exposed.

I parked in John's driveway. George and I got out and walked up to his front door and I rang the bell. I could hear it echoing inside the house. No one responded.

'Maybe he didn't call from here,' George suggested.

'He doesn't have a cellphone.'

'Maybe he called and left. Or maybe he's staying at someone else's place.'

There were lots of possibilities. That was the problem.

I peeked in John's mailbox. 'He's been here today already, or someone has, because they've taken in the mail.'

'If he got any.'

I thought of the catalogs neatly stacked in the wicker basket on the counter. 'He gets lots of junk mail.'

George reached over and rang the bell. The result was the same. No one answered.

'What's the matter,' I said as I stepped off the porch, 'you think he'll answer to your ring and not mine?'

'Still touchy, I see.'

'You betcha.'

George laughed but there wasn't any warmth in it. This time no one yelled at me when I tried to look in John's front window. The blinds were down and the curtains were drawn. It was impossible to see anything.

'Let's go around to the side,' George suggested.

We did. I gripped the fish-shaped brass knocker on the side door that John and I had found at a garage sale last summer and hit the door with it. There was no response. I tried again. Nothing. George and I looked at each other. He leaned over, grasped the doorknob and pulled. The door swung open. He raised an eyebrow.

'John might have forgotten to close it,' I told him.

'He might have,' George said but he didn't sound convinced.

Neither was I. George stepped inside.

I called out John's name as I followed. I wasn't expecting to get a response and I didn't get one. I'd been in John's house about a week and a half ago. He, Zsa Zsa, and I had gotten takeout Chinese food and watched *Valley of the Dolls* together. We'd been supposed to go to the movies tomorrow night. I'd been looking forward to it. I shook my head to clear it and glanced around.

The kitchen seemed unchanged from the last time I'd been here. John was a neat-freak. He exemplified the adage 'a place for everything and everything in its place.' I opened cabinets and peered in the fridge. Unlike mine it was full of food. John wasn't planning on going any place soon. George went over and checked the answering machine while I took a look in the pantry.

'Nothing here, except some calls from you,' George told me.

George was behind me as I moved into the dining room. The chairs were still evenly spaced around the gleaming dining-room table, the knick-knacks in the china cabinet looked the way they had the last time I'd been here. I moved on to the living room. Again everything was in place. There was no sign of a struggle. No sign that anything was wrong. It looked as if John had just stepped out for a moment and would be right back. That should have reassured me but somehow it made things worse.

'Does John have an office?' George asked.

I pointed to the hall on the left. 'First door on the right.'

'Why don't I take a quick peek in there while you go up and do the bedrooms.'

I nodded and headed up the stairs. There were three bedrooms and a bathroom. I wandered through all of them. I didn't feel comfortable opening John's drawers or going through his closet, so I didn't. It seemed like an intrusion. I knew that was irrational but I didn't care. I just looked around the rooms instead. If something was out of order I couldn't see it. George was already in the kitchen when I came down.

'Find anything?' I asked him.

George shook his head. 'You?'

'Nope.'

I don't know what it was that I'd been hoping to see but whatever it was, it wasn't here. It was time to go. After a moment's hesitation I left the side door the way George and I had found it.

'Maybe John forgot his key,' I said.

George grunted. There was really nothing to say. There

was one last place to check. The garage. John's house had
been built in the thirties and so had the garage. It tilted towards
the left as if it were tired of standing and wanted nothing
more than to lie down and rest. When I peeked in the window
I could see John's car. I could hear the engine running and
somehow I just knew. My stomach started churning as George
bent down and raised the garage door. A cloud of exhaust
blew out, followed by the smell of gasoline.

'Wait,' George cried as I moved inside. 'Stay here.'

And before I could say anything George ran past me
towards the car. He yanked the door open. Then he turned
towards me.

'Call 911,' he yelled as he dragged John out of his vehicle.

I made the call even though I knew it was too late. I could
tell from the way John's body sagged that he was dead.

The police came fairly quickly. I remember that. I
remember the rest of the day too. It wasn't particularly
pleasant.

All I could think about were my last words to John. How
awful they were.

Later that evening, Ian convinced me that whatever I'd
said to him wouldn't have mattered.

John was going to do what he did anyway. I finally believed
it. More or less.

But it didn't make me sleep any better.

Eight

Trent came over to my house at two thirty the next afternoon. I watched him wander around my living room. He looked like a heron trying to find a comfortable place to perch. He'd been wandering for the last couple of minutes and hadn't found anything that suited him yet. Given the expression on his face I didn't think he was going to, either.

'Why don't you sit down?' I finally said.

Trent looked at me from hooded light blue eyes. 'I think I'd rather stand, if you don't mind.' And he brushed an imaginary speck of dirt off his jacket. I thought about how John used to say Trent was stiff as a board. John had meant it in a metaphorical sense, but it was true in a physical one as well. Trent Goodwell moved stiffly, as if each piece was bolted on to every other piece and the bolts had rusted.

He rubbed his hands together, then raised one and ran it over the top of his buzz cut. 'I still can't believe it,' he said.

'Neither can I.' I got up and poured myself a hefty shot of Scotch and offered one to Trent. He shook his head.

'I only drink vodka. You wouldn't happen to have some of that around, would you?'

'Sorry,' I told him. 'It's Scotch or nothing.'

'Then I'll take some water, bottled if you don't mind.'

I didn't have any bottled water, instead I gave him water from the tap. I figured it would be OK because Syracuse has some of the cleanest drinking water in the country. As I was filling the glass it slipped out of my hand and shattered in the sink. I cursed.

'Everything OK in there?' Trent called.

'Fine. Just a little mishap.'

I cleaned up the shards and then dabbed at the cut I'd managed to get on the palm of my hand. I was so exhausted

I couldn't hold on to things. This was my second day with practically no sleep. I'd spent a long time with the police yesterday afternoon. Too long. They hadn't been pleased to see me at the scene of John's death, even though John had clearly died from carbon-monoxide poisoning.

They hadn't been pleased to the extent that this time they'd taken me downtown and asked me the same questions over and over again. My answers didn't satisfy them, but they'd finally cut me loose and I'd gotten Zsa Zsa from Manuel and gone to Shamus's to talk to Ian.

Two hours later I'd come home. I took a hot shower and went to bed but I couldn't sleep. Finally after an hour of twisting and turning I'd come downstairs and spent the rest of the night watching infomercials on TV and trying to figure out what the hell was going on.

I was no closer to an answer now than when I'd started, so when Trent called me at the shop earlier in the afternoon and asked me if he could drop by my house and talk to me I'd welcomed the opportunity. I was hoping he could shed some light on what had occurred.

I came back into the living room and handed Trent the glass of water. He regarded it suspiciously, took a sip, and set it down on the coffee table.

'John was fine when I left for Toronto,' Trent informed me. 'Just fine. And then my neighbor called me up at the hotel to give me the news.' He clasped his hands together and cracked his knuckles. The noise startled Zsa Zsa and she jumped up and barked. 'I don't understand. I don't understand at all. That's why I'm here. You were his friend and I'm told you sometimes find things out for people.' He cracked his knuckles again. 'I mean it's so odd. We were talking about moving in together. Finally. It was something he really wanted. And then he goes and does something like this. I don't get it. I don't get it at all.'

I looked at Trent. I wanted to make sure I was hearing him correctly. 'What do you mean, you were in Toronto?'

'Exactly what I said. I was at my great-aunt's eighty-fifth-birthday party. I had to change my ticket to come back. It cost me over one hundred dollars.'

'Did John know?'

'That I was going?'

'Yes.'

Trent gave out a brittle little laugh. 'Of course he knew. I invited him, but he couldn't go. He told me he couldn't get the time off from work.'

'You're sure?'

Trent took another sip of water, wrinkled his nose slightly, and put the glass down before replying. 'Absolutely. We had a big fight over it. He was always nagging me to meet my family and when I finally arranged it, he didn't want to come.'

'So you weren't in Syracuse?'

Trent gave me an odd look. 'I just said that.'

'I just wanted to make sure.'

I sat down on the sofa and took a big gulp of my drink. I could feel the Scotch working its way down my throat. Usually it helps take the edge off things, but not this time. I had a feeling I could drink the whole bottle and it wouldn't have mattered. I guess I must have showed what I was feeling because Trent asked me what the matter was.

'Nothing,' I told him. 'Nothing is the matter.'

'Obviously something is.'

I took another sip of my drink and put it down. I looked at Trent's face. It was smooth and sharp-angled and didn't give anything away.

'Well,' he said.

I decided to tell him and see what he said.

'I think John set me up.'

'Set you up?' Trent repeated. 'I don't understand.'

'I'll explain.' I watched a blush of anger bloom on Trent's face as I did.

'So you've been following me for the last two weeks?' he said when I was done.

'On and off.'

Cracked went Trent's knuckles. 'That's an intolerable invasion of my privacy.'

'Maybe it is but John didn't think so. He thought you were seeing Benny Gibson.'

Trent's eyes became an even lighter shade of blue. 'I explained Benny to John. I told him I was helping Benny with one of his projects. He needed advice.'

'What kind of advice?'

'With one of his building projects. I used to be in construction. In Yonkers,' he said when I didn't say anything.
'Goodwell Construction. I retired about five years ago and
was thinking of getting back in the game. Gibson was my
entrée. I told John that. I told him I wasn't even remotely
interested in sleeping with the man. Besides, he was straight.'

'I guess John didn't believe you.'

Trent rubbed his forehead. 'I can't believe he had you
follow me.'

I didn't say anything because there was nothing to say.

'He didn't trust me.'

I shifted my weight. 'Apparently not.'

'Not even a little.'

From what John had told me he'd had ample cause not to
trust Trent. According to John, Trent was a player, but maybe
that wasn't true. Maybe John had made the whole thing up.
Maybe John was pathologically jealous. Maybe Trent was a
quiet homebody who spent most of his evenings refinishing
furniture and playing the violin. Or maybe not. The only
thing I knew for certain was that I didn't know.

'And you say that John called you,' Trent continued. 'That
he asked you to drive over to Benny Gibson's house and see
if I was there.'

I nodded.

'Are you sure it was John?' Trent asked.

'I'm positive.'

'Maybe it was someone pretending to be John.'

'Like who?'

Trent gave me a blank stare. 'I don't know,' he admitted.
'It's just that the other makes no sense. No sense at all.'

'I know. Unless you're lying about the family gathering.'

I thought Trent would say something nasty. Instead he
whipped out his phone and punched in a number. 'This is
my aunt,' he said holding his cell out to me. 'Ask her where
I was for the last three days. Go on and ask her.'

And I did. Somehow her answer didn't make me feel any
better.

Trent took the phone back from me and returned it to its
clip on his belt. 'Maybe I will have a Scotch after all.'

I went into the kitchen and got him a glass. When I came back he was sitting on the sofa petting Zsa Zsa. I poured him a stiff shot and handed the glass to him. He stared at it for a moment and then drank the whole thing down. When he'd stopped spluttering I asked him a question.

'Was John in any trouble?'

Trent shook his head. 'Not that I know of.'

'Are you sure?'

'If he was he didn't confide in me.'

I lit a cigarette and took another sip of my drink. 'Can you think of any reason why he set me up?'

'You don't know he did that,' Trent protested, loyal to the end.

'Then what would you call what he did?'

'I don't know.' Trent cocked his head to the side. 'Maybe it was an honest mistake.'

'How can it be an honest mistake? You just told me he knew you were going to be away.'

Trent put his face in his hands and rested it there for a moment.

I finished off the last of my Scotch and then I asked Trent another question. 'Was his car getting fixed?'

Trent looked up. His face looked fuzzy, as if everything had gone out of him. 'I don't think so. He'd just gotten it inspected a week ago. Everything was fine.'

'He lied about that too.'

'I don't get it,' Trent repeated. 'You were his friend. He liked you. He liked you a lot. Why would he do something like this to you?'

'I don't know,' I told him. 'But I think I'd better find out.'

Trent came over and took my hands in his. His palms felt cool and dry.

'You'll tell me when you do, won't you?' he asked me.

I told him I would. He left five minutes later and I went back to Noah's Ark.

Nine

After I closed the shop for the day and dropped Manuel off at his aunt's house I decided there was no way around it. I had to talk to Janet Gibson, Benny Gibson's daughter. I knew it wasn't a good idea, but with John gone I needed to find out why she'd said what she had to the police. Besides, I had an idea that her actions and John's actions relating to me were linked.

They had to be. I don't believe in coincidence and this whole thing had been as choreographed as a ballet. I didn't understand how and I didn't understand why, but I was damned well going to find out. I was going to find out why my friend had done what he had to me and then gone and killed himself. There had to be a reason and I wanted to know what it was.

I was hoping I could convince Janet Gibson to talk to me, although circumstances being what they were she might just call the cops instead when she saw me at her door. Given that possibility it would have been nice if I could have worked out some clever way of meeting up with her, but nothing was coming to mind so I dropped Zsa Zsa at the house, and fed her and my cat, who'd finally deigned to make an appearance after a two-day absence. Then I drove over to Liverpool. The drive took me a little under twenty minutes. I spent it the way I had the night before: going over scenarios. But I couldn't come up with any that made sense.

I parked a little ways down from Benny Gibson's house. The crime-scene tape was still wound around the house. As I ducked under it I thought that it seemed like forever since the night I'd been here with Ian. It's funny how time expands or contracts depending on events. The lights in the Gibson residence weren't on. It looked as if no one was home. Either that or they were asleep. Then they wouldn't be happy to be woken up, but it was really early for anyone to be in bed so I nixed that idea and lit a cigarette and thought about what I was going to say if someone was there. The rudiments of an idea formed.

I got out of the car, took another puff of my cigarette, and ground the remainder out on the sidewalk. I was trying to cut back because I'd been smoking enough to get smoker's cough in the morning. Not a good thing. I was thinking about that as I walked to the door and rang the bell.

No one answered. I seemed to be getting a fair amount of that lately. And I'd stopped eating raw onions too. I tried again. There was no movement in the house that I could discern. Another time I might have tried entering the house to have a quick look around and see what I could find out, but I wasn't going to do that now. That would be my last resort. Instead I went over and rang the neighbor's bell. An older woman in a leisure suit that was two sizes too small for her and hair that was two sizes too large answered the door.

'Yes,' she said.

I smiled at her. She gave me a wary smile in return.

'I'm trying to return something to Janet Gibson,' I explained. 'I tried her house and no one seems to be there. I was wondering if you knew when she'll be coming home.'

'She's gone,' the woman answered.

'Gone?' I was surprised. Given the situation this was not what I was expecting to hear.

The woman screwed up her face and peered at me. 'You look familiar.'

'I have that kind of face,' I told her.

Her tower of hair wobbled as she moved her head from side to side while she studied me. 'I'm sure I've seen you before.'

'Everyone says that to me.' Over the years I've noticed that people have trouble identifying people when they're out of context. 'So,' I said, bringing the conversation back to the subject at hand, 'do you know where Janet is? It would be mighty handy if you did. That way I wouldn't have to come out here again.'

The woman scowled. 'She took off for Vegas.'

'Vegas?' I echoed. 'Are you sure?'

'That's what she told my husband. Can't blame her neither. Living in that house after what happened.' The woman clasped her hands to her bosom as if to ward off evil.

'Did her mother go with her?'

The woman snickered. 'Janet's mom has what you might call a condition.' And she pantomimed drinking before I could ask her what condition she was talking about. 'Has for a while. Now she's in one of those fancy places somewhere in Connecticut or Vermont. One of those states, anyway. Not that that's going to help after this. It'll send her right back to the bottle – I tell you it cost Benny lots of money to keep her there.'

'That's generous of him,' I said to see what the woman would say.

She leaned forward. 'Maybe that's because he was the one who put her there.' She put a hand up and steadied her hair, which was threatening to come undone. 'And in case you think I'm speaking out of turn, I ain't. Ask any of the neighbors. They'll tell you the same thing.'

'Really?'

'Absolutely. I would have told the cops if they'd bothered to ask me. It's really a pity what he put her through, him with all that money. He's supposed to be so high class. Him with all his deals, but I told my husband when I saw Benny Gibson that he was no good. No good at all.'

The woman's eyes gleamed. I figured the murder was probably the most exciting thing that had ever happened to her.

She went on, 'Who would have thought something like that would occur here? Do you know what these houses cost? And then to be near something like . . . like . . . that.'

'It's terrible,' I said. 'Simply terrible.'

She bobbed her head in agreement. 'I applied for my pistol permit today, that's what I went out and did. First thing in the morning. My daughter called me up all the way from California and begged me to.' The woman tugged her bra straps up. 'All that blood. And who is going to clean it up? That's what I want to know.'

'They have specialists,' I interjected, but it didn't staunch her flow.

'I mean something like that,' she continued, 'it can't be good for resale value. It drags the value of the rest of our houses down.'

'I'm sure that management will paint and repaper and do whatever they have to,' I said in my most soothing voice. 'It'll look just the way it did before.'

The woman looked mollified for the moment.

'You don't happen to know how I can get in touch with Janet, do you?' I asked.

Her eyes narrowed. I had the feeling she was starting to remember where she'd seen my face and if she did that she would be only too happy to call the authorities. Then she'd be a celebrity. Maybe she'd even be quoted in the paper.

'I would just like to give her this package,' I explained.

The woman's hair was bobbing back and forth like a boat on the stormy sea. 'What package? I don't see any package.' She'd sprung a self-righteous whine in her voice.

'I left it in the car.'

'You can leave me a note if you want and I'll give it to her.' The neighbor's tone was growing frostier by the second.

'No. No. It's fine. I'll come back another time.'

And I left. For once in my life I was going to get out while the going was good. I could always come back if I needed to. When I got home I took Zsa Zsa out for her walk, poured myself a Scotch, and sat down in front of my computer.

In ten minutes I had Janet Gibson's cellphone number and it only cost me nineteen dollars and ninety-nine cents. Sometimes the Internet is a wonderful thing. I sat back in my chair and punched it into my phone. Now maybe I'd get some answers. A moment later a canned voice came on telling me that the number had been disconnected. No other information was given. I tried to come up with a new address. This time the computer gave me nothing.

Zsa Zsa came over and rubbed her head on my calf. I reached down and scratched behind her ears.

'This is not good,' I told her. 'This is not good at all.'

She woofed in agreement.

The two people who could support my story were both unavailable for comment. The only good thing that I could see was that all the evidence against me was circumstantial. But that still didn't answer the question of who had set me up and why. I tapped my fingers on my desk while I thought about what I was going to do. I decided I was going to talk to John's friends and then I was going to find out what I could about Benny Gibson and his daughter. I was convinced that somewhere along the way those two men's lives had intersected and it was up to me to find out when. I started by Googling Benny Gibson.

Ten

The next night I was bartending at Shamus's again. It was a little before nine o'clock and business was slow. My guess was that people would start coming in around eleven if they were going to come in at all. The dim lights, the hum of the cooler, the drumming of the rain on the window were all conspiring to put me to sleep. Not that I needed much encouragement.

Ian was leaning against the bar watching CNN while he rolled cigarettes with machine-like precision. When he had a pile he'd carefully put them in his Marlboro box. World news was not good, but then what else was new. Electra, our only customer, was slumped over the bar sleeping.

She had her head on the counter and every once in a while she would let out a gentle snore. Watching her reminded me of how little sleep I'd had in the past two days. I got a glass of water and filled Ian in on what Trent had said about his whereabouts.

'And he was telling the truth?'

'Unless his cousin was lying, yeah he was.'

'So John lied from beginning to end.'

'Apparently.'

'Let me ask you this. Do you think that Trent was actually seeing this Benny Gibson at all?'

'You mean as in playing around with?'

'Exactly.'

I thought that over for a moment. 'No. I don't,' I finally said.

'Why couldn't he be lying?'

'I guess he could. But what would be the point?'

'He makes himself the injured party. It supplies a motive for him killing Gibson.'

'But he was in Toronto,' I protested.

'He could have hired someone.'

'For what reason?'

Ian took a sip from his mug of hot chocolate. 'A lovers' spat. Gibson could have been blackmailing him.'

'I don't think so.'

'Why?'

'It just doesn't feel right.'

'Is that your feminine intuition talking?'

'Yes, it is.'

Ian took another sip of his hot chocolate and put the mug down on the counter. 'Suit yourself.' For a moment he didn't say anything else. Then he asked if I'd heard from George.

'No. Not since we went to John's house.'

Ian cleared the last shreds of tobacco off the counter into his cupped hand and threw them in the trash. Then he lit a cigarette and took a pull.

Finally he said, 'And George just happened to be around.'

'He came by to see how I was doing. What's so strange about that?'

'I didn't say it was strange.'

'You implied it.'

'Did I?'

Ian remained silent. I studied his face. He had a grim expression.

'You just don't like him.'

Ian uncoiled himself. It was like watching a burst of energy that exploded and then vanished. But you always knew it was there.

'Why?' he asked me. 'Because he's a worthless piece of shit.' Then before I could say anything Ian held up his hand. 'I know. I know. I just don't understand him. He had a hard childhood or some such crap like that.'

'Having a bad day?'

'This has nothing to do with me. George helped you out because he wants something from you.'

'How do you know that?'

'Because that's what men like that are like.'

'Unlike you.'

'Yes. Unlike me.'

'What could he possibly want?'

Ian raised an eyebrow. 'You mean you really don't know?'

'Know what?'

'His blonde walked out on him.'

I did a double take as I remembered what George had said to me.

'How do you know she walked out?'

'Her cousin used to work for me at Twenty-Two's as a stripper. I met her at the gas station the other day.'

'You never told me that.'

Ian tapped the ash from his cigarette into a paper cup half filled with water. 'You never asked. Benny Gibson's brother used to go in there too. He was a regular.'

'Brother? The article in the paper didn't say anything about him having a brother.'

'The article didn't say lots of things. I don't think he was real happy with him.'

'Who? Benny?'

'Joe. Joe wasn't real happy with Benny. You should go talk to him. He and Benny were partners. They had a big fight a while ago. Benny said he caught him stealing. He said he was doing a lot of coke. Joe says it was the opposite. He says Benny was going down to the hood to score some crack. Lots of shady stuff going on there.'

'The articles I Googled about Benny made him sound like a model citizen,' I countered. 'Friend of the mayor. On the committee to improve downtown. Buying buildings so he can improve them and rent them out at reasonable rates. Give something back to the community. Building Syracuse up. Et cetera.'

'Right. Talk to Plastic Man. He'll tell you something different.'

'Plastic Man?'

'Yeah. Joe.'

'And you call him that because . . .'

'Everyone calls him that. He's had lots and I do mean *lots* of plastic surgery. Got his nose straightened and his chin built out. I think he did something with his eyes and I know he got those hair plugs put in.' Ian gave a snort of contempt. 'I wouldn't be surprised if he got his dick made bigger while he was at it. He looks like some sort of doll. I don't know why anybody would do that to themselves.' Ian shook his head at the strangeness of it all.

'So where does Plastic Man live?'

Ian picked a piece of tobacco from his tongue. 'Don't have a clue. Look it up in the phonebook.'

I did. Joe Gibson wasn't in it.

'I'll get the address for you,' Ian told me. 'I know the person that manages the club Joe Gibson hangs around in now.'

'Thanks.' I reached over and lit one of my cigarettes. 'One more thing. I went to talk to Benny's daughter. She's taken off for Vegas. And her cell is disconnected. And the wife is in some sort of rehab facility.'

Ian leaned forward and studied my face. 'And you know this how?'

'I talked to one of the neighbors. She told me.'

Ian made a minute adjustment to one of the glasses on the rack. 'Maybe you shouldn't be talking to Benny Gibson's neighbors. Maybe the police wouldn't like it.'

'But don't you think it's odd her taking off like that?' I persisted.

'Maybe she had a family emergency. Maybe she hasn't paid her cell bill and they cut her off.'

'Maybe,' I said. But I didn't believe it.

'You could always ask the police.'

'Ha. Ha. Like they're going to tell me.'

'Maybe your buddy George will find out – if you ask him nicely.'

'He's not my buddy.'

'Right.' Ian gave the word a derisive twist.

'Why are you being like this?'

'I'm not being like anything.'

'You're . . .'

Ian held his hand up. 'Stop. Don't worry about me. Worry about yourself. If I were you the question I'd be asking myself right now is: Who did I piss off?'

'I haven't pissed anyone off.'

Ian smirked. 'You always piss people off.'

'I don't. OK. Maybe it's true,' I admitted. 'But that wouldn't make someone want to set me up. There has to be another reason.' Unfortunately, I couldn't think of one.

'Was John mad at you?'

'Not in the slightest. Why should he be?'

'I don't know. That's why I'm asking you.'

'He wasn't.'

'Are you sure?'

I thought for a moment. 'I'm positive. He was my friend.'

Ian chuckled. 'Get real. Friends kill each other. Friends lie to each other. Friends cheat on each other. It happens all the time.'

'Maybe with your friends, but not with mine.'

Ian made a dismissive noise.

I pushed a lock of hair out of my eyes. 'Hey, we used to have dinner together, go to the movies, and talk. Period.'

'The next possibility is that someone was making John do it, someone who is really mad at you, someone who is orchestrating this whole thing.'

It was an unsettling idea.

'Think about it,' Ian said to me. 'And you should also think about the fact that John might have been killed.'

'I know.' That had already occurred to me. I didn't know which would be worse, John committing suicide or John murdered.

Ian flicked a shred of tobacco off the counter. 'It's easy enough to make a murder look like a suicide.'

I got myself another glass of water. 'I guess we'll have to wait for the autopsy to find out.'

'I guess so, and while we're on unpleasant subjects the guy I was telling you about dropped in here earlier this afternoon looking for Chad. He seems to have vanished as well. He wanted to know if I'd seen him.'

'First Jellybean and now him.'

'Suggestive, isn't it?' Ian said.

'And what did you tell them?'

'That I haven't seen him since I threw him out.' Ian brushed ash off the counter. 'About an hour after he left I got a call from Chad's grandmother asking me if I knew where Chad was. I told her he didn't confide in me.'

'And what did she say?

'Nothing. She hung up.'

'So where do you think he is?'

Ian shrugged. 'My guess is that he's hiding out with his relatives in Canada, but it's only a guess.'

'So Manuel is the only one of that group left.'

Ian nodded. 'He's the last of the three little pigs.'

'Nice.'

And I told him what Manuel had told me.

Ian just shook his head. 'Bunch of idiots.'

'For sure,' I agreed. 'How much trouble do you think Manuel is in?'

'Could be a lot. Unless he can come up with fifty grand.'

'He says he wasn't part of this thing. He says he didn't know anything about it.'

Ian tapped his fingers on the counter. 'Maybe he's telling the truth. After all, no one is looking for him. Yet.'

'I hope it stays that way.'

Ian didn't say anything.

'I'd like to kill him.'

'Someone might.'

God I hoped not. What a mess. I'd known Manuel for a long time now. He was always teetering on the edge of disaster. I hated to think of him going over.

Ian gestured to Electra with his chin. 'Go wake her up. It's bad for customers to have to deal with her taking a nap at the bar. If she wants to do that she can go home.'

I pointed out that there were no other customers here at the moment.

'And there won't be either if you don't get her up,' Ian replied.

'Fine,' I told him. 'I'm going.'

I went over and shook Electra awake. She looked around wildly, but before she could say or do anything I put a can of PBR in her hand and she began to drink. Ordinarily I'd feel guilty doing something like that, but Electra is so far gone – I don't know if it's the drinking or Alzheimer's – that whatever I do really doesn't matter.

Half an hour later three guys drifted in. They were in their early twenties and they were all wearing baseball hats, starter jackets, and baggy pants – the gangsta uniform of the day.

They shook themselves at the door like dogs coming in from the rain.

'You seen Chad around?' the wider one with the two pierced ears asked me.

This was just getting better and better.

'Nope.'

'You sure?'

'She's sure,' Ian said from the back of the bar.

Pierced ears and Ian locked glances. Pierced ears looked away first.

'Hey, big guy,' he said. 'Ain't no harm in asking.'

Ian nodded, got up, and made himself a cup of hot chocolate. 'You moved?'

'We've been traveling. You know how it is.'

Ian took a sip of his hot chocolate. The three guys sat down at the bar and ordered PBRs and a couple of bags of chips. Our big sale for the evening. The wide one paid with a fifty. When I brought him his change he put a twenty in my hand.

'Thanks,' I said.

'No problem. Listen,' he said, 'Chad comes by tell him, Dylan is looking for him.'

'Will do.'

Dylan leaned forward. 'You seen Jellybean?'

'Sorry.'

Dylan shrugged and finished his beer. His friends did the same. Three minutes later they were out the door.

I went over to Ian. 'Who were they?'

'Dealers. I'd say Chad's in trouble with a lot of people.'

'I'd say so too.'

'At least they didn't ask for Manuel,' I said. 'That's something.'

Ian snorted and shook his head. 'You excel at small consolations.'

'What the hell is that supposed to mean?'

'Look it up.'

No one else came in. At one thirty Ian called Electra's son to come and get her, which he did. I was mopping down the floor when Ian came over and handed me a slip of paper.

'Joe Gibson's address,' he explained.

I unfolded the paper and looked. It was another Liverpool address. His development was right next to the one his brother had occupied. I'd been over there to deliver a monitor lizard. Maybe Benny and Joe didn't get along but they definitely shared the same taste in houses, because the developments were mirror images of each other.

'Although you might do better talking to him at Wonder Women,' Ian told me. 'He might be a little less constrained away from the wife and kiddies.'

'He has them?' I asked.

'Well, he did when I knew him. Or,' Ian continued, 'you might try Gibson's business address. After all, his brother Benny just died. Joe might be over there trying to make sense of things. I don't know. It's your call.'

I thanked him, folded up the paper, put it in my jeans, and continued mopping. Nothing like a good rain to make the floor a holy mess. When I was done I got Zsa Zsa from the back and went home.

This time when I got into bed I slept.

Eleven

When I woke up the next morning it had stopped raining. A faint ray of sunshine was tap dancing on my alarm clock. The weatherman was calling for temperatures in the forties and assuring everyone that the worst was behind us and we were moving towards spring. The robins would be here soon. Personally I could hardly wait.

Next the news came on. First the announcer told about the latest shooting on the West Side – it was right near Shamus's too. Anyone with any information was asked to contact the police. Then he talked about the new commission that was being formed to revitalize downtown Syracuse. They were going to do another study. Bring in more experts.

Wow. I was really excited. This had to be the sixth commission in ten years. They always came back with the same recommendations and nothing ever happened. Ever. I could never figure out whether the reason was stupidity, corruption, or a combination of both. But in the end it didn't matter because the result was the same: the city was dying and when all the talk was done no one seemed to give a damn. Things just got worse and worse while our elected officials stood in front of TV cameras and jabbered on about what a great job they were doing.

Take my store, for example. You'd think that the city would want to help small businesses. But despite what they say they just keep on coming up with more and more rules and regs, all of which take money to comply with. Oh well. No point in thinking about that now and getting aggravated when I could get aggravated about so many other things. I fed the cat and walked Zsa Zsa. She and I had our usual breakfast at Dunkin' Donuts – an extra-large coffee and two maple-glazed donuts for me, a strawberry-glazed donut for her – after which we opened the store.

By eleven o'clock I'd sold two ten-foot Burmese pythons, a three-foot gecko, and two rose tarantulas. Not bad for a morning's work. Maybe the store was getting over its winter blahs. That would be nice. Around eleven thirty Manuel sauntered in. I told him about Chad.

'Yeah, I know. Jellybean told me.'

'You spoke to him?'

'For about thirty seconds. He wanted to know if anyone had been asking for him.'

'A guy called Dylan stopped by Shamus's last night looking for Chad.'

'Kind of fat?'

'Yes.'

'He had two other guys with him?'

I nodded.

'He's bad news,' Manuel said.

'In what way?'

'He said he fucked some guys up real bad.' Manuel shrugged. 'I don't know, maybe he was talking trash.'

I looked at Manuel.

'What?' he said.

'I was just thinking about what a nice group of friends you have.'

Manuel yanked up his pants. 'Like the ones you hang out with are so great.'

'What's that supposed to mean?'

'Ian's not exactly on the up and up.'

'He's not like Chad and Jellybean.'

'I wouldn't be so sure. And at least they never hurt anyone for a living.'

'He doesn't do that kind of thing anymore.'

'But he did,' Manuel told me. 'So I don't think you should be lecturing me about my friends.'

Manuel yanked up his pants again and went off to sweep the floor. I thought about what he had said as I went into the backroom. There was a part of me that knew it was true, but for some reason I was willing to grant Ian latitude I wasn't willing to give to anyone else.

I sighed and started on my paperwork. I did that till twelve thirty when I asked Manuel to hold the fort while I went off to the offices of J & B Real Estate to talk to Joe Gibson and see what I could find out from him. If I could get him to speak to me, that is.

'I have to leave by two thirty,' Manuel informed me as I started out the door.

I came back towards the counter. 'Why? You're supposed to be here until six o'clock.'

'I have an appointment.'

'What kind?'

'The important kind.'

'Seriously.'

'I have to babysit my cousin's new baby so she can go to work.' Manuel raised his hand. 'I swear. They changed her shift today. She has to fill in for someone who's sick.'

'OK. I'll be back by then.'

I zipped up my jacket. It was nippy outside. 'Hey, call me on my cell if one of your gangsta friends comes and drags you away before I get back. I don't want to leave the store open. Someone could come in and steal the livestock.'

'Cute, Robin,' Manuel said.

'I think so,' I replied as I finally headed out the door.

I got in my car and drove over to Armory Square. By now the clouds had cleared out and the sun was shining. It illuminated the old cans, paper bags, bottles, chairs, and sofas that had resurfaced once the snow had melted. In Syracuse, early April really is the ugliest time of the year.

Gibson's office was located on West Fayette Street, which is the backside of the Armory. The parking was brutal – it always is down there. The meter maids come around every twenty minutes – and after spending way too much time trying to find a spot I caved and put my car in a lot and walked a couple of blocks to the three-story brick building that housed the office of J & B Real Estate.

The place was narrow and flat-roofed and looked as if it might have been a storage place in its former life. According to the brass plaque on the door, J & B was on the second floor, while a lawyer had the first, and an advertising firm had the third. As I walked up the steep set of carpeted stairs, I couldn't help notice the small holes and snags in the fabric. At the landing I found myself at J & B Real Estate. If I hadn't known that the company had been there for a while, I would have sworn they'd just moved in. But maybe I had it ass-backwards. Maybe they were moving out.

A desk that looked as if it had been bought on sale from one of the big-box stores sat on a sea of bare, refinished wood. The desk was piled high with papers. A telephone teetered on top of them. A dried-out stag-horn fern hung from the ceiling while two frayed-around-the-edges Degas posters were stuck to the brick walls with duct tape. If any thought had been put into a decorating scheme I couldn't see it. I also couldn't see the secretary that was supposed to inhabit the desk. Maybe she'd been let go.

I stepped inside and took a second look around. There was dust on the blinds that covered the two front windows. There were dust bunnies under the desk and a couple of old coffee cups on the arm of one of the chairs that leaned against the far wall. The other two chairs, presumably for clients, were filled with stacks of magazines and files. It wasn't what I'd call your client-friendly environment.

'Can I help you?' a voice behind me asked.

I turned. Ian's description of Joe Gibson was spot on. His skin was stretched so tightly over his face it looked as if it had no pores. What Ian hadn't said was that Joe Gibson's head was enormous. It seemed to balance precariously on his slight shoulders, making him look like one of those bobble-headed dolls they sell in gift stores. The fact that his hair was slicked straight back didn't help either.

'Possibly,' I replied.

Gibson pursed his lips. They were too small for his face. In fact, now that I was taking a closer look, I realized that none of his features seemed to go together.

'We have nothing to rent right now,' he told me.

'That's not why I'm here.'

Joe Gibson took another look at me. I could see the expression on his face changing as recognition settled in.

'I know who you are,' he exclaimed. 'They had your picture

in the paper. You're Robin Light. You're the person the police
are saying killed my brother.'

'No,' I corrected. 'They're saying they suspect I might
have had something to do with his death. That's different.'

'Sounds the same to me.'

'Well, it's not. I didn't shoot your brother. I don't even
know your brother.'

Joe bounced up and down on his toes. He wasn't listening
to me.

'All I can say is that you have a hell of a nerve coming
in here.'

His voice was almost a falsetto. As he moved towards me
I noted that his fists were balled into knots. I guess that even
someone who doesn't like his brother feels bad when he
dies.

'I realize that, but there's something you should know.'

'What's that?'

'Your niece is gone,' I told him.

'What the fuck are you talking about?' he said, coming
closer.

'Your niece, the one who accused me of murdering your
brother.'

'Get on with it,' Gibson ordered.

'According to your brother's next-door neighbor she's
skipped town and gone to Vegas.'

It was obvious this was a surprise. 'So?' he blustered.
'Given what happened she probably needed a change of
scene.'

'Also her cellphone's not working. It's been disconnected.'

'Meaning?'

'Meaning you can't get hold of her.'

'So what?'

'So I'm guessing she's taken off because she doesn't want
to be questioned about the testimony she gave to the police
about me. What she did was a criminal offense.'

'She didn't do anything.'

'She lied about me. She could be prosecuted for it. And
probably will be. The DA doesn't like looking like a fool. I
could even sue her in civil court.' I wasn't sure if that was
true, but it sounded good.

Joe stopped advancing. 'The police know that she's left town. I'm sure they have a number where she can be reached.' But his certainty had been shaken.

'Do they?' I asked him. 'I have a feeling they don't.'

'Of course they know.'

'Call Keene and find out.' Keene was the detective in charge of the case. I took out the card he'd given me and handed it to Joe. 'Here's the number, in case you don't have it.'

'Why should I even listen to you?' he demanded.

I remembered what Ian had said and went with that. 'Because I have a feeling you know everything with your brother isn't kosher and you know I'm not a part of whatever it is that's going on.'

Joe hesitated for a moment. Then he took his cellphone out of his pocket and walked into the other room. I heard him say, 'May I please speak to Detective Keene,' and then he must have closed the door because I couldn't hear anything else.

A moment later he came out. I could tell from his face the way the conversation had gone.

'Keene didn't know, did he?' I said. I smiled, thinking of Keene's reaction. He was going to catch flak for this from his superior, who in turn was going to catch it from the DA's office. Not that I was a petty person or anything, but sometimes you have to take your pleasures where you find them.

Joe didn't say anything.

'Did he?' I insisted.

A moment went by. 'No, he didn't,' Joe admitted. He ran his hand over the top of his hair. 'I'm sure she'll get in touch with the police when she's settled.'

'Maybe. Maybe not. Does she know anyone in Vegas?'

Joe shook his head. 'I don't think so. But even if she did I wouldn't know. She never confided in me.'

'Who would she confide in?'

Joe spread his hands wide. 'I have no idea.'

He seemed to be telling the truth.

I decided to try a long shot. 'Would her mother know anything?'

'She's been out of the picture for some time,' Joe replied. 'Even when she was there she wasn't, if you get my drift.

Basically,' he continued, 'my niece ran around and did whatever she wanted to.'

'Which in this case is something that's gotten me in a hell of a lot of trouble. Can you think of any reason she did what she did?'

Joe thought for a moment. 'Not really.' He turned his gaze back to me. 'How do I know that you're telling the truth? I mean, you didn't just happen to be in the neighborhood. And I read you'd been at my brother's house a couple of times before.'

'This is true.' Now came the tricky part. The newspaper hadn't explained why I'd been there, so I was going to have to. I couldn't see any way around it. I took a deep breath and began.

'What?' Joe yelped when I was done talking. To his credit he'd let me finish. 'Are you out of your mind? My brother was married. He had a child.'

'Lots of married men do this kind of thing. One thing doesn't obviate the other.'

'Maybe in your world, lady, but not in mine.' Joe pointed to the door. 'Get out of here. Get out of here now.'

I put my hands up. 'I'm not saying he did do it. I'm saying that my friend John thought he had.'

'And that's supposed to make me feel better?'

'No. But this might. Evidently, John made the whole thing up. His friend Trent was helping Benny with some sort of project and John got very jealous.' Which may or may not have been true, but it would make our conversation easier.

I had the feeling Joe's eyebrows would have shot up if they could but the most they could manage was a feeble quarter of an inch.

'Trent Goodwell is a fag?'

I didn't say anything. I felt bad. I'd unintentionally outed Trent. I guess that's what the military calls collateral damage.

'He doesn't look like a fag.' Joe went behind the desk and sat down in the receptionist's chair. 'Who would have thought? Who would have friggin' thought?'

'Anyway,' I said, trying to steer the conversation around to where I wanted to go, 'I wondered, what project were they working on?'

Joe opened the desk drawer and closed it again. Hard. As if to say he didn't want to think about what I'd just told him.

'Don't know. Benny and I weren't on good terms recently so I can't really tell you. Why don't you ask Trent?' he said derisively.

'I'm going to. I just wanted to get some information from you.'

'To see if we both said the same thing?'

'Something like that,' I allowed.

Joe shook his head. 'All I know is that it had something to do with the city. Maybe one of the municipal garages, maybe the Hotel Eastern, maybe none of those things. I really don't know.'

I tried a different tack. 'Did your brother have any enemies?'

Joe shrugged. 'Developers usually aren't the best-liked people. And this town can be a hard sell. Especially if you're not plugged into the right network.'

'Could one of your brother's business associates dislike him enough to shoot him?'

'Unlikely. Those kind of people sue your ass off, they don't go looking for you with a nine millimeter.'

Which was probably a fairly accurate assessment.

'I understand your brother was running with a group of people you didn't approve of.'

Joe gave me a hard look. 'Who told you that?'

'It doesn't matter.'

'It matters to me.'

'Look, don't you care about who killed your brother? That's the thing that's important here.'

'No. What I care about is that my sister and my mother don't read about his name in the papers. This has been upsetting enough for them. My mother is over eighty. Imagine how she feels. There have been enough accusations—'

'Accusations? What kind of accusations?'

'What I want is a decent burial for my brother. What I want is my family not to be dragged through the papers. Now I want you to go.'

'Give me a name.'

'Didn't you hear what I said?'

'Yes I did and if you don't give me a name I'll call your mother and sister and ask them questions. Give me a name and I'll leave them alone.'

'You wouldn't.'

'Normally no, but in this case yes.'

I watched Joe think. Or tried to. It was hard to read his face. He'd had so much plastic surgery he didn't seem to have many expressions left.

'Fine,' he said. 'Melody Mannes.'

Then he turned around and walked down the hallway, leaving me to show myself out. Which I did. As I went down the stairs I thought about how odd Joe's answer was to my question about finding his brother's killer. Even if he didn't care, most people would have pretended that they did. Then I wondered what kind of accusations Joe was talking about.

When I hit the street I called my friend Calli, who works on the local paper. Actually, I was surprised I hadn't heard from her already given what had happened.

She answered on the second ring. 'Hello,' she said. 'It's my own little criminal.'

'What? No call? No concern?'

'I just got back in town.'

'And you don't check the local news?'

'Not when I'm staying on the beach in Aruba.' I guess things with Calli's new boyfriend were going well. 'So you've had an exciting couple of days.'

'I like boring better.'

'Don't we all. So what can I do for you?'

'I was wondering if you could check your files and see what you come up with for B&J Enterprises and Janet Gibson, and if you have the time could you look up Melody Mannes as well?'

'Do you think I'm your own personal reference service?'

'Something like that.'

'And naturally you want this immediately,' Calli said. I could hear voices in the background.

'Naturally,' I said. 'I mean I would do it if I had access to your resources.'

'And I should do this because I have nothing better to do?'

I repositioned the phone. 'How about because you love me.'

'Not good enough.'

'That's cold,' I told her. In the time I'd been talking to Joe Gibson the sun had vanished and a light drizzle was falling. I hurried along the street. My jacket didn't have a hood and my umbrella was at home. 'OK. I'll pay you. How's that?'

'And you'll pay me how? I'm not taking something like a hissing cockroach.'

'Heaven forfend. I was thinking of a tarantula.'

'Ugh.'

'Fine. How about I buy you dinner.'

'At a nice place.'

'I did that last time.'

'McDonald's is not a nice place.'

'It's all in the definition.'

'Well, my definition is upscale French or Italian. With wine.'

'You got a deal.'

'Fine. Call me late tomorrow morning.'

'Tomorrow morning,' I yelped.

'At the earliest. And I've changed my mind. Don't call me. I'll call you.'

We said goodbye. By now I was at my car. I checked my watch. It was one thirty. I had plenty of time to get back to the store before Manuel left. I decided to stop and get some takeout pasta. Zsa Zsa was particularly fond of fettuccine Alfredo.

Twelve

I closed up the shop at seven o'clock and walked out the door with Zsa Zsa trailing behind me. I was going to go straight home, but at the last moment I decided to drive by Trent's house instead and see if he was in. I had some questions I wanted to ask him about the project he was working on with Benny Gibson and I figured that for something like this face-to-face is always better than the phone.

Trent's house was a tidy colonial about a quarter-mile away from John's house. But whereas John's neighborhood was nine-tenths residential, Trent's was half residential and half student. You could tell the student houses by the number of cars around them, the rental signs, and their general messy appearances. Recently, homeowners had been trying to restrict rental properties but they were having little success. I remember that John told me Trent was one of those homeowners as I parked in front of his house.

I sat in the car for a moment and smoked a cigarette and tried to focus on what I was going to ask Trent, but it was hard because suddenly I was thinking about John and realizing how much I was going to miss him. We'd been friends. Despite what Ian had said about friends we'd been good ones.

And I wanted to know what had driven him to do what he had to me. It must have been something very compelling. Some sort of blackmail? That seemed the most likely. So what was he so afraid of people finding out?

Was he dealing in child porn? Embezzling money? Had he killed someone? It had to be something that could send him to jail or hold him up to public humiliation or both. But what? I didn't have a clue. So maybe Ian was right. Maybe I didn't know John at all. I wondered if Trent knew and if he would tell me if he did. And then I wondered if Trent was telling the truth about him and Benny Gibson. John had seemed so sure.

I turned towards Zsa Zsa. 'Do you have any ideas?' She woofed and licked my hand. I laughed and fed her a doggie treat. 'I don't know what I'd do without you,' I told her. And I meant it. She was my comfort in a way that few other things are. I could always depend on Zsa Zsa. She was always there for me. She gave me another lick. I promised we'd get dinner after this and told her to stay. Then I got out of the car and started up the walkway to Trent's house.

He'd painted it light green, with slate-blue shutters. Dark-red window boxes hung from the first and second stories. Somehow the color combination worked. A neat laurel hedge encircled the property. The driveway was black brick. The shrubbery close to the house was wrapped in burlap to protect it from winter's ravages. A weeping peach tree stood to the left side of the house while a rose of Sharon stood a little ways away. Even the mailbox was in good taste. It was one of those expensive metal ones from Home Restoration. Everything about the house exclaimed that care had been taken with it.

I rang the bell and waited. A moment later the door opened and Trent was looking out at me. He was wearing a pair of tan corduroy pants and an expensive black turtleneck sweater. He'd gotten a hair cut since I'd seen him last and his scalp was pink and shiny.

Somehow that made him look even taller and skinnier than he was.

'Can I come in?' I asked.

He hesitated for a minute while he thought.

'Please,' I said.

'Oh all right.' And he jerked his head to indicate I could enter.

It was probably the please that had done it.

'Most people call first,' he scolded.

'So I guess you're not a drop-by kinda guy.'

He looked at me as if I'd suggested getting it on with him on the dining-room table. 'Most definitely not.'

'I'll bear that in mind for the future, but I was driving by and I thought I'd stop and chat.'

He grunted and walked into the living room. I followed. A large flat-panel TV dominated the living room. It was tuned to the sports channel. Trent made no attempt to turn it off. I glanced around. The walls were cherry red. The furniture was expensive. There was a chocolate-brown leather sofa. Two big matching comfy leather armchairs sat on either side of it, while a Stickley coffee table was positioned in the middle. A couple of tribal oriental rugs lay on the floor, and a series of black-and-white photos decorated the walls. The window treatment consisted of tan Roman shades. In front of the window was a table on which was arranged three blooming orchids.

'Nice,' I said appreciatively.

'I'm glad you approve,' Trent said.

I ignored the sarcastic tone. I also ignored the fact that he kept casting glances at the television set and the fact that he hadn't asked me to sit down. Instead I removed my jacket and plunked myself in one of the armchairs.

Trent looked down at me. This time I was reminded of a stork. 'They've released John's body,' he said.

'How do you know?'

He shrugged. 'The obit ran in today's paper.'

I hadn't read the paper. 'So where's the funeral?'

'At that place on East Genesee Street.'

'Hoffman's?'

'Yes. I'll get the paper for you.' And he walked out of the room. A moment later he was back. 'Here,' he said, handing it to me.

The newspaper was carefully folded. The obit was outlined in red. There was a picture of John at the top of it. I recognized it as the one that had sat on his fireplace mantel. It had been taken by a tourist when he was in Sedona, on his way around the country.

I scanned the piece. Basically it said that John was forty-one years old, that he had gone to school at Howe High School, and graduated from LeMoyne College with a bachelor's in history. He had worked for the county, as well as US Air, and several department stores.

He was an avid film-goer and dance buff and was survived by his father, brother, and nieces and nephews. Calling hours for the public were from two to seven tomorrow at the Hoffman Funeral Home. The funeral was private. People were asked not to send flowers. Charitable contributions could be made to the church of St Paul the Apostle. No mention was made of the cause of death.

I handed the paper back to Trent. 'Are you going?'

He swallowed. I could see his Adam's apple bobbing up and down. 'Probably not.'

'How come?'

His gaze flitted around the room looking for an object to land on. He finally chose my face.

'I called up John's dad to ask him if he needed anything. When he heard who I was he hung up on me.'

'I'm sorry,' I replied. And I was.

'They want to pretend John wasn't gay.'

The words deflated Trent and I watched as he folded in on himself and half fell, half sat on the sofa. Then he leaned forward, rested his arms on his thighs, and clasped his hands. His right eye had developed a microscopic twitch since I'd seen him last. He gave me a small deprecating smile.

'The truth is I miss him.'

'So do I. I still can't believe it.'

'Me either.' Trent leaned back. After a moment he said, 'I'm not mad at you anymore.'

'I'm glad.'

'I was. I was glad the police are giving you a hard time. I figured it served you right for invading my privacy. But now I'm not. Now I want to help.'

'Why?'

'Because you were John's friend and you were helping him. That's got to mean something.' Trent unkinked his spine and straightened up. 'OK. What do you want to know?'

'I want to know what you think John was involved in.'

'He wasn't involved in anything.'

'He had to be.'

Trent scratched his chin. 'I can't imagine what. You know . . . knew him. He liked to go to the movies, he liked to read, he liked to watch television. He didn't like to party. He didn't like to drink. He didn't like to go to bars. He was . . . boring. I hate to say it, but it's the truth. He was Miss

Goody-Two-Shoes. I always wanted to get him out some-where and he never wanted to go. His idea of a good time was eating takeout food and watching movies. He didn't like being with lots of people.'

'He was shy.'

'Yes, he was,' Trent agreed.

'He didn't do drugs,' I added. 'At least as far as I know.'

'He didn't do them at all.'

'Maybe he was stealing money.'

Trent gave me an incredulous look. 'Well, if he was he sure wasn't spending it. He was still shopping at the sales tables. Spending twenty dollars on a T-shirt was a big deal for him. And whom would he be stealing money from?'

'I don't know.'

'His Dad doesn't have any.'

'Work?'

'Get serious. He worked at Seven Seasons. That's a book-store. They're going broke. How much could he be stealing from them? One hundred bucks? Two hundred bucks?'

'I suppose you're right.'

'I know I'm right,' Trent said.

The truth was: the John I knew was a dear, quiet soul who I was willing to wager had never harmed anyone in his entire life. But there had to be another John, a John I didn't know, a John who did things I couldn't image him doing. The problem was going to be finding out what those things were.

'What about John's other friends?' I asked Trent.

Trent shook his head. 'He doesn't have too many left. AIDS. One of the ones left is in California, while the other one is in New York. He really doesn't – didn't – have anyone here. Except for me, that is.'

'Maybe he got into something on the Internet,' I mused.

But I couldn't check that out. I wondered if the police had impounded his computer or if it was still in his house. If it were I wondered if I could figure out the password. It would sure be interesting to look. It might be possible. I needed to ponder that for a while so I decided to change the subject.

'What were you and Benny Gibson working on?' I asked Trent.

'We weren't really working on anything.'

'I thought you said you were.'

Trent hunched forward. 'I was.'

'But?' I prodded.

'This really doesn't have anything to do with what happened.'

'Maybe not,' I told Trent. 'But I'm interested anyway.'

'Actually it's a pretty sad story.'

I waited.

Trent ran his hand over his scalp. 'Long story short, I've been out of work for a while. I'm not going to go into the reasons why. But anyway, John kept nagging me to get back into the trade. I tried to explain that I'd only done big stuff – for big stuff you need lots of contacts and I've been kind of reclusive lately – and then I was at a cocktail party and someone introduced me to Benny Gibson. We got to talking and he told me he had a big deal going with the city.

'He had this building that he was going to rehab. Very fancy. Stores – just high-quality ones – on the first floor. Condos on the next three. He'd got the funding, got the permits, he was almost set to go. And this one was the first of five buildings. And best of all from my point of view, he wanted me onboard. I've got the experience, he's got the contacts. Life is good all around.

'I'm ecstatic. And I decide I'm going to keep this from John. It's going to be my present to him. But I want everything in place first. I want everything perfect.'

I clarified. 'Which is why he got the idea he did about you and Benny Gibson.'

Trent nodded. 'Exactly. So we meet once or twice and start going over plans and then it turns out there's a hitch – he's a little cash poor. Can he borrow some money?'

'How much?'

'Half a mil.' Trent's words came faster. He began tapping his foot in time with them. 'Like I said when I was working I did well for myself and I came into a little family money of my own. Not a big deal. He'll put one of the buildings up for collateral. Well, I get a little curious and I start investigating. And guess what I find?'

I shook my head.

'The building is in really bad shape. Much worse than

Gibson says. Leaks from the top floor that are going to the first. Wiring totally out of code. Things that would be very expensive to fix. And then I find out this guy owes lots of taxes. Which for some reason the city has let go. Which the city should have known because he pulled this deal in Omaha five years ago. Bought up stuff and let it sit.' Trent shrugged his shoulders. 'I don't know. Maybe what you do in Omaha doesn't count. And on top of everything else I find out some of the tenants in these buildings have contracts for the next four years. Which means he's going to have to get them out of there. I spoke to a couple in one building. They don't want to go and he's trying to muscle them out, so they're getting ready to sue. This is the kind of thing I really don't need to get involved in.

'Naturally, I tell him I'm not lending him the money now. At least not until he answers some of my questions, which he doesn't want to do. The more I look at the situation the less I understand. That Benny Gibson was crooked I have no doubt. That that might have led to his being shot is a distinct possibility. But how any of this ties in with John, I don't have a clue.'

'Me either,' I admitted.

Trent and I sat in silence for the moment. Then Trent stood up. I did too.

'I'm tired,' he explained as he walked me to the door. 'Sorry I couldn't be more help,' he told me once we got there. 'If I think of anything else I'll call you.'

I nodded and walked outside. When I got back in my car Zsa Zsa was sitting in my seat with her paws on the dashboard. I gently pushed her out of the way and started my car up. Then we headed off to the Chinese restaurant. It was egg-roll time.

Thirteen

It was a little after nine at night and Zsa Zsa was sacked out on the sofa watching a Lassie movie on television and digesting her dinner, which had consisted of one and a half egg rolls and some moo shu chicken. I, on the other hand, couldn't seem to settle down. Even though I'd tried I kept pacing around the house. Instead of getting calmer about what had happened to me I was getting more and more jazzed.

I needed help. For a moment I thought about calling George. He could phone his buddies in the police department and find out what was going on. It was an attractive idea and I almost dialed the number, but stopped myself. If I did that, things would become more complicated than they already were, meaning that I didn't want to give George another opportunity to drop by.

But I did need someone to talk to about what was going on. I needed someone to help me sort everything out. To bounce ideas off of. Normally, that would have been John, but Ian might do. Sometimes he was really good to talk to, sometimes not. It depended on his mood. If he were in a bad mood he'd just make sarcastic comments. Although he might answer the question I wanted to ask him. He enjoyed doing that.

The question was a simple one. I just wanted to know how I could get hold of Melody Mannes. I'd looked in the phonebook and hadn't found anyone by that name listed. Not that I was surprised. I was about one hundred percent certain that Melody Mannes was her stage name. Ian might know her real name, though. In any event, it was worth a ride over to Shamus's to find out. At least it was something to do. I located my keys, told Zsa Zsa to guard the house, and left.

On the way I called Calli. She didn't pick up. Probably out with her new sweetie. I didn't bother leaving a message on her answering machine. Especially since she'd already said she'd call me tomorrow morning. Ten minutes later I was at Shamus's. I found a parking spot out front and went inside.

Ian looked up when I walked in. When he saw who it was he brought his cigarette out from under the counter where he'd been hiding it and took a puff.

'Another busy night,' I said when I reached him. He was sitting on a stool near the gate that cordoned the bar off.

The clientele consisted of three kids in the far corner. They were busy watching television and taking sips out of their cans of PBR. I didn't know their names, but they'd come in with Chad a couple of times. According to Ian they spent most of their time drinking and when they weren't doing that they were selling weed.

'Yup,' said Ian. 'Business is booming. Positively booming.'

'Maybe you should advertise.'

Ian snorted and took another drag off his cigarette. 'What would be the point? Any person that reads about us in the newspaper won't come here because the neighborhood is so bad, and the people that come here can't read.'

'You may be right.'

'I may be right?' Ian spaced the words out for emphasis. His tone was incredulous. 'Of course I'm right. I'm always right. You should know that by now.'

I laughed. 'Forgive me. Occasionally I forget.' I pointed to the bottle of Black Label sitting on the shelf behind him. 'I'll take a shot of that.'

'Black Label?'

'Yeah. On the rocks.'

Ian put his hand over his heart. 'My heavens, this is a first. A virgin bottle. I don't know whether I can bring myself to open it or not.'

'The trauma would be overwhelming.'

'For the bottle, definitely.'

'But you'll be kind and gentle.'

Ian grinned. 'Exactly. Because that's the kind of guy I am.'

'Tell me. If no one drinks this then why stock it?'

'It classes up the joint a little.' And Ian moved off to pour my Scotch. 'On the house,' he said as he gently set my glass in front of me. 'Couldn't stay away from here, could you?'

I indicated the interior of Shamus's. 'The ambience. The clientele. The decorations. How could I resist?'

'I don't know. A lot of people evidently can.'

I took a sip of my drink and put it down. 'I want to ask you something.'

Ian feigned enthusiasm. 'Oh goody.'

'Having a bad day?'

'Peachy keen,' Ian shot back.

'Meaning?'

'Meaning I don't want to talk about it.'

I waited. Because that meant that he did.

'Someone might want to buy this building.'

'Why?'

'To put a drug store here.'

'Interesting. They don't have anything like that here.'

'It's only a rumor.'

'But disturbing none the less. A poor thing but mine own.'

Ian nodded his head vigorously. 'Exactly.'

Without thinking I reached over for Ian's lighter and picked it up.

'What are you doing?' he cried.

'Lighting my cigarette, obviously.'

'Don't you have a lighter?'

'Yes.'

'Then why don't you use it?'

'Because I'm too lazy to get it out of my backpack,' I confessed.

Ian leaned over and grabbed the lighter back. 'Well, don't be so lazy.'

'You are so weird.'

'I'm not weird. I just don't like people taking my things without asking first. What's weird about that?'

'You carry it to extremes.'

'No. You just have to be politer.'

'Fine. May I use your lighter?'

'No. Use your own. Just kidding,' Ian said when I turned and started digging in my pack.

'Thank you.'

'Now, what can I do for you?'

'Do you know where I can find someone called Melody Mannes?'

Ian took a last drag of his cigarette and threw the butt in a half cup of water. 'Why do you want to talk to her?'

'According to Joe Gibson she was seeing his brother, Benny.'

'Sounds as if Benny was a busy boy,' Ian reflected. 'Between Melody, Trent, and his wife it's amazing he had time to do anything else.'

'The wife's in rehab and I already told you Trent says the thing between him and Benny isn't true.'

'So he says.'

'That's right.' And I explained what he'd told me.

'I think he's lying.'

'How do you know?' I demanded.

'I just do. It's a talent. But, hey, believe what you want.' Ian waved his hand in a gesture of dismissal. 'What do you think Melody can tell you?' he asked, changing the subject.

I shrugged. 'I'm hoping she can shed some light on what was going on with Benny.'

'That would be nice.' Ian reached for the phone. He picked it up and walked down to the other side of the bar so I couldn't hear what he was saying. He was back a few minutes later.

'Melody will be here at one thirty.'

I looked at my watch. It was a little before ten. I had a ways to go.

'Not any earlier?'

'She's got a couple more shows to do. And by the way I told her you'd pay her for her time. A thousand bucks.'

'What?' I squawked.

Ian grinned. 'Just kidding. I told her you'd throw a couple of hundred her way.'

I peeked in my wallet. 'How about one hundred?'

'That'll probably do.'

'What's Melody's real name?'

Ian shrugged. 'She can tell you if she wants.' He gave me his most charming smile. 'Hey, since you've got some time why don't you come around here and work the bar. Give me a little time to run home, let my dogs out, and put my feet up. I've been on them since eleven o'clock this morning.'

I said yes. Of course. When it came down to it Ian knew the right buttons to push. I spent the next hour and a half watching CNN and supplying Bud Lights to the crew down at the end of the bar. They all looked like the kid that was looking for Chad only they were a little bit older and they didn't tip nearly as well. Then they shot a couple of games of pool and left. When Ian came back an hour and a half later the place was as empty as a doll's coffin.

Ian glanced around. 'What did you do?' he demanded. 'Everyone's gone.'

'Guess I must have forgotten to use Listerine.'

'You must have pretty powerful breath to clean out a whole bar.'

'I ate raw onions and Limburger cheese right after you left.'

'Nice.' Ian folded his jacket up and put it on one of the shelves underneath the bar. Then he sat on his stool, took his cigarettes out of his pocket, put them on the counter, removed one, and lit it. 'Everyone will be coming in tomorrow. I remain optimistic.'

'Why tomorrow?'

'Because tomorrow is when our clientele get their social-security checks.'

'True. True.'

We spent the time until Melody showed up talking about the implications of what I'd found out and also about how the city was condemning buildings in his neighborhood and knocking them down instead of rehabbing them because it cost less. Melody arrived fifteen minutes early.

She came in wearing tight hip-huggers, a white T-shirt with Bitch written across her chest in big red letters, a purple leather jacket, and cowboy boots. Her hair was long, blonde, and wavy. She was sporting a cheap tattoo of a rearing cobra on her cheek and heavy black liner around her green eyes. She moved slowly across the floor, like she was waiting for everyone to admire her. She seemed disappointed that no one was here to do it. I figured her for a serious bitch.

'Benny Gibson, huh?' she said once she was seated next to me.

Ian put a can of Coors down next to her and she got a pack of Camels out of her jacket pocket and lit up. She inhaled the smoke and blew it out through her nose. Miss Sophistication.

'Yeah, I knew him,' she said.

I waited. When she didn't say anything else I said, 'As in how?'

'He used to come by Wonder Women.'

'He was your customer?'

Melody took another drag off her cigarette. 'From what I remember he wasn't anyone's customer. He used to just sit there, and sip his OJ, and watch the show.'

'And,' I prompted. I could see that this was going to be slow going.

'Ian said you'd pay me.'

'After I hear what you say.'

Melody exhaled more smoke out her nostrils. 'OK. Occasionally, he'd meet other guys there. It was like the place was his office or something.'

'What kind of guys?'

'The usual type. Two arms, two legs, a dick.'

'Do they have names?'

'Everyone has a name.'

'So what are theirs?'

Melody shook her head. 'I don't remember them.'

'I find that difficult to believe.'

She shrugged. 'I've got a learning disability.'

I snorted.

'Really. I have problems remembering names and stuff like that.'

I wanted to wipe her smirk off her face, but I didn't. She was saving the names. They were like money in the bank to her. If I badgered her for them now she'd probably just up the price.

'Anything else?' I asked.

'Like what?'

'I don't know, but I don't think what you've told me is worth one hundred dollars.'

Melody shot a look at Ian. 'I thought you told me it was going to be two hundred bucks.'

'He lied,' I said before Ian could open his mouth. 'And you won't even be getting one hundred if you don't come up with a little more usable information.'

Melody gazed at me with soulful eyes. 'There is no more, honest.'

'I'm not one of the guys, so save the act.'

She looked at Ian. 'She's a real bitch, isn't she?'

'Just like you,' I replied sweetly.

Melody's lips narrowed, then they curved up into a smile. 'Fair enough.' She took a gulp of her beer. 'There's something. But I can't really explain it.'

I gave her an encouraging nod.

'It's just a feeling.' She leaned forward. 'I don't think Benny was interested in any of the girls. Not really. I think he just came so he could meet up with the guys he was seeing there.'

I described John. 'Did he ever turn up?'

Melody shook her head.

'What did the guys look like?' I asked, deciding to try that line of questioning again.

Melody shrugged. 'They were all suits. Business types.'

'What? They all look alike to you?'

Melody laughed. 'Yeah. They do.'

'And they didn't have names attached to them?'

'Not that I heard.'

I was about to say something to the effect that that wasn't possible when Ian caught my eye. He was shaking his head ever so slightly. I backed off and changed direction.

'That's not what Benny's brother says about you and Benny.'

'You're talking about Joe?' Melody asked.

I nodded. 'He's the one that gave me your name.'

'He and Benny used to come in together a lot.'

That was interesting. 'A lot? What's a lot?'

'Enough. Now Joe was a piece of work.'

'How so?'

'Well, he used to sit at the bar and ask me or one of the girls to kick him in the balls with her high heels. Wham.

Then he'd kind of gasp and double over. A minute later he'd give you a fifty and he was ready to start all over again.'

The idea made me cringe.

Evidently it didn't bother Melody because she said, 'Hey, the money was good. If that's what he liked then that was fine with me.'

'I heard that Benny and Joe weren't getting along.'

Melody thought for a moment. Then she said, 'They never seemed real tight to me. Well, they did have some sort of thing going on in the club three or four weeks ago. I couldn't hear what they were saying, but Benny shoved Joe and Joe shoved back and then Monster—'

I cocked an eyebrow.

'One of the bouncers broke it up and escorted both of them outside. I haven't seen either of them since.'

Now we were getting somewhere. I took five twenties out of my wallet.

'Anything else you can tell me about Benny Gibson? Did he get into a fight at the place with anyone else? Piss someone off?'

Melody shook her head. 'Not when I was around.'

'So why do you think Joe gave me your name?'

Melody took another sip of her beer. 'Don't know. Maybe he just wanted to get rid of you and I was the easiest way he could think of to do it.'

I slipped the five twenties towards her. 'You could be right.'

'I know I am.' Melody drained her beer and stood up. 'If you want any information next time, I expect two hundred, not one fifty, not one ninety-nine. Two hundred.'

'How much would it cost to get the names of the men Benny used to hang with?'

Melody ignored me and strolled out the door. I looked at Ian.

'So what do you make of what she said?' I asked when she'd left.

Ian shrugged. 'Maybe it's time to talk to Joe again. See what he has to say.'

I nodded. I'd been thinking that too.

As I left Shamus's I realized that I still didn't know Melody

Mannes' real name. I turned around and walked back to where Ian was standing.

'What's her real name?'

'Melody.'

'Seriously.'

'I am serious.'

'No. You're not.'

Ian grinned. 'Betty Heath. Doesn't have the same ring, does it?'

'Not at all. Is she in the phonebook?'

Ian shook his head. 'I could give you her cell, but she only picks up for people she knows.'

As I walked out the door I reflected that technology was supposed to bring us closer together, but it seemed to me that it was doing the opposite. That it was getting harder to talk to people, not easier.

Fourteen

Waking up next morning was a bitch. I'd gotten back from Shamus's around two and fallen asleep around three in the morning. I could have slept for another four hours at least, but that wasn't an option. When you have a store it has to open on time. People expect it. If they come by and you're not open, they're liable not to come back. And anyway I was expecting a new UPS shipment and the UPS man usually came around ten to ten thirty in the morning.

When the alarm went off it woke me out of a dream. My heart was beating fast and my breathing was ragged. The only thing I could remember was a little boy standing in the road. He had his arms out to me and he was saying something I couldn't understand, something important, something that terrified me.

I stayed in bed for fifteen minutes trying to calm myself down while I watched the branches of the spruce tree across the street dance in the wind. My cat James and Zsa Zsa were curled up by my side. I don't think they wanted to start the day either. When I finally dragged myself out of bed, they took over my pillow. I staggered into the shower and stood there for a good ten minutes letting the warm water sluice over my body. I only got out when the water started going cold on me. Kind of like my relationship with George, I reflected.

I hadn't done laundry in about three weeks so I put on what I had left, which was my newest Marshall's purchase, a light green cashmere turtleneck sweater, my semi-good blue jeans, and my black boots. Inspired by the result, I pulled my hair back and braided it and then I put on a little blush and some mascara. I certainly needed something to help counteract the dark circles under my eyes and my winter pallor. I looked at myself in the mirror and added a little lip-gloss for good measure. I decided that today I could use all the help I could get.

As I was leaving Dunkin' Donuts I got my call from Calli.

'Hey, girlfriend,' I said. 'You're early . . .'

'I'm turning over a new leaf and hitting the gym at five thirty in the morning.'

'I'm impressed.'

'Don't be. It's more like panic. I need to lose the ten pounds I gained when I was in the middle of that thing with Sean. I have a wedding to go to and I want to fit into my black sheath and anyway you know I always give preference to paying customers. Meaning you,' she said when I didn't respond.

'I get it.'

'I sound like a hooker,' she reflected. 'Of course,' she went on, 'some people don't see much of a difference between journalists and hookers.'

'I do. Hookers get paid more.'

Calli laughed. 'True. True.'

I got into my car and took a sip of my coffee. 'Tell me what you got,' I said as I took a maple-glazed donut out of the bag and fed it to Zsa Zsa.

'I got some stuff on Benny Gibson.' And Calli pretty much told me everything that Joe Gibson had told me, plus a few other tidbits that he hadn't. 'My sources down at City Hall tell me Bad Boy Benny was about to get served for back taxes and code violations.'

'So how come this hasn't been in the papers?'

'It was going to be. The article was assigned and then it was killed when he was, and now it's back on the boards again.'

'Anything I might be interested in?'

'Off the record, there was talk that Gibson was about to leave town. Evidently the state's AG office was about to open up an investigation into some of Benny's projects. Now that he's dead, though, that's gone by the wayside.'

'Well, that's a good motive,' I said.

'Isn't it, though. Kill the guy and close the investigation.'

I brushed donut crumbs off my lap. 'But they're not investigating his brother?'

'Nope.'

'So they were about to investigate Benny Gibson, not his business?'

'They were going to investigate his building – each building is held by a different limited-liability corporation and Benny held the ones that were being investigated.'

'Interesting. So Joe benefits from his brother being dead?'

'That's a stretch, but yes, I suppose you could say that. The big rumor is that Benny Gibson was involved with the Russian Mob.'

'And the substantiating data for that is?'

'Zippo. However, there's another rumor that he was talking to some Native American guys about a casino they were thinking of building around here and I'm thinking that's where the rumor about the Russians came from.'

I told Calli about the meetings Benny had had at Wonder Women.

'Probably just some kind of boys' night out thing,' she observed.

'What ever happened to bowling?'

I heard Calli laugh as I pushed Zsa Zsa away from the empty donut bag. She would eat the paper if I let her, which was not good for her digestive tract.

'Have you heard any more about the murder?' I asked. 'Do the police have any more leads? Suspects? Anything?'

'Aside from you, you mean?'

'Yes. Aside from me.'

'No.'

'That's encouraging. They're probably not even looking for someone else,' I reflected gloomily.

'Well, I know they haven't been able to locate Gibson's daughter.'

'Are they looking hard?'

'I'm not really sure. No one is really talking.'

'Is the DA taking this to the grand jury?'

'I think they're waiting to see what else shows up.'

'Great.'

'But there is one piece of good news.'

'I'll take anything. Anything you've got.'

Calli laughed. 'You're going to like this. In fact, this is easily worth a bottle of good wine, and I'm emphasizing the word good here.'

'In addition to dinner?'

'Absolutely.'

'Wow. You're getting more expensive all the time. Don't forget I'm just a poor shop owner.'

'That's why I'm not asking you to buy me a bottle of the widow.'

'You're too kind.'

'I think so. You know how small this city is. It's not six degrees of separation here, it's more like three. Anyway, I have a friend who knows the Gibsons. Her daughter went to school with the Gibson girl.'

'Do I know her?'

'Carrie Walmouth.'

'Why does the name sound so familiar?'

'Her husband, Richard Walmouth, is trying to get one of those big-box stores in Eastwood.'

'Right.'

If I remembered correctly the project was very controversial, eliciting all sorts of protests. It was the typical fuss: people liked the prices but no one wanted shops like that on their block, with all the attendant traffic and other problems. Which suited me just fine since I estimated I'd lost half of my business to Wal-Mart and places like that.

Calli continued. 'From what Carrie said, Janet Gibson was quite a handful. Bad grades. Running around. Stole her father's car and wrecked it. That kind of thing.'

I took another sip of my coffee. 'Is there any chance that I could meet her?'

'Carrie's daughter? I already set up an appointment for you. She's going to meet you in the lounge of the Beauregard at eight fifteen. Her name is Wendy.'

'Wendy Walmouth. Very alliterative.'

'Isn't it, though? And by the way, what's up with George?'

I stonewalled. 'What do you mean?'

'You know exactly what I mean,' Calli snapped. 'Like

I just said, Syracuse isn't really a small city, it's a big town.'

'Nothing is up with George. He just helped me out with the cops.'

'And you're going to leave it there.'

'Absolutely.'

'I'm serious. His blonde walked out on him.'

'So I heard.'

'Did you also hear she's claiming mental abuse?'

'She's extremely manipulative.'

There was a short pause then Calli said, 'Given the circumstances, I can't believe you said that.'

'Well, she is. That's how she got him in the first place.'

'No. She got him in the first place because he's an inveterate womanizer who can't keep his dick in his pants, as well as a liar. And did I mention that he's not very nice when he's crossed? That's why you threw him out, remember? Or have you forgotten?'

'No. I haven't forgotten,' I said quietly. 'I just didn't like remembering.'

'You have to promise me you won't go back with him.'

'I have no intention of doing that.'

But Calli knew me too well not to hear the slight hesitation in my voice.

'You have to swear. He is nothing but bad news and you know it.'

'I . . .'

'Swear,' Calli insisted.

'I swear.' I knew she was right. I just didn't like to admit it.

'Good. If you need anything call me.'

'Anything?'

Calli laughed. 'Almost anything.'

Wendy Walmouth was a little late showing up for our appointment and I had time to settle myself down in the hotel lounge and order myself a Scotch on the rocks. The Beauregard is a hotel that mainly caters to business travelers, people visiting Syracuse University, and the occasional tourists, who expect amenities and can afford to pay for them.

Once an eyesore, the hotel was taken over and rehabbed five years or so ago by a company out of Florida and it hasn't looked back since. People point to it as a symbol of Syracuse's coming regeneration and maybe they're right. Anyway, I'd like to think so.

The lobby is marble floors, recessed lighting, and cherry wood. The staff is professional. The dining is good if expensive, and the lounge is furnished with sofas and big comfy armchairs. Books line the walls and there are magazines and newspapers on the tables for those who care to catch up on the latest news.

The plants are large and well cared for. There's no dust on their leaves. Someone comes and wipes them off every day. I felt a pang of guilt when I thought about the condition of mine.

I was sipping my Scotch, reading yesterday's *New York Times*, and keeping an eye on the door when a woman walked through it. She stopped and looked around. From the description Calli had given me I was betting it was Wendy Walmouth. I waved. She waved back. I was right. It was.

Wendy looked like someone who skied in Davos and shopped in New York City. I put her in her mid-twenties. She was thin and gym-fit. She had on a funky plaid coat which must have cost at least a thousand dollars and brown suede high-heel boots. She was carrying a Louis Vuitton bag. Her haircut was casual, the kind of casual that takes an expensive stylist to achieve. Her makeup was letter-perfect.

Obviously, this was a woman who was doing well for herself. As she wended her way through the chairs to me I caught a flash of her diamond engagement ring. It had to be two, two and a half carats. At least. She came from money and she was marrying money. The American Dream. It made me wonder why she was talking to me. People like her usually don't. Not if they don't have to.

She stopped in front of the chair I was sitting in and extended her hand as if she was tendering something of inestimable value. I shook it and she sat down. I watched while she carefully put her purse by her side and her coat around her. She had all the time in the world. She knew that people would wait for her. The waiter came over and she ordered a vodka martini.

'Jim, with Gray Goose if you don't mind.'

The waiter nodded and hurried off. She turned to me.

'I come here a fair amount,' she informed me.

'It's a nice place. Thanks for agreeing to see me.'

She waved away what I said. 'No problem. I'm meeting my fiancé here in about thirty minutes.'

Meaning we had half an hour to talk. I got right to it. I figured if she didn't have something she wanted me to hear we wouldn't be sitting here. I leaned forward slightly. 'So,' I said, 'tell me about Janet.'

Wendy crossed then uncrossed her ankles and smoothed down her brown tweed skirt. 'She's a loser. Always has been.'

'Could you be a little more specific?'

The waiter came and handed Wendy her drink. She took a careful sip. Then she started talking again.

'Janet is a real piece of work.'

'Even in high school?'

'Even in high school. She started going off the deep end after her mother went psycho. After a while my mom didn't want her hanging around with me. None of the other moms did either.'

I couldn't help but think that that hadn't helped things any for Janet.

'What happened when Janet went off to college?'

Wendy shrugged. 'I lost track of her.'

'So you can't tell me about her recently?'

'I can tell you she's still a loser.'

'As in how?'

Wendy smoothed her skirt with a manicured hand. 'I saw her at the Christmas party at the country club. She was so drunk she could hardly talk. Even her dad was embarrassed. He kept on trying to get her to leave, but she wouldn't. She came over and showed me her new tattoo.' Wendy's lips curled as she remembered.

'What was it?'

Wendy shrugged. 'A spider on a spider web. It was ugly. At least if you're going to do something like that make it attractive.'

I had an idea with Wendy everything was about aesthetics, and maybe she was right.

'But then,' she went on, 'given the way Janet looks what can you expect.'

'What do you mean?'

'She's gotten fat.'

I didn't think she'd looked that fat when I'd seen her the night her dad had been murdered, but judging by Wendy's tone of voice she didn't agree. In her eyes Janet had committed the cardinal sin. Wendy took another sip of her drink. 'Her dad even offered to send her to a fat farm and she refused. Then he offered to send her to Milan to do her shopping if she lost thirty pounds.'

'And did she?' I asked even though I knew the answer.

Wendy snorted. 'According to my mom, she gained another five.'

'Were she and her dad close?'

Wendy shook her head. 'They were always fighting.'

I leaned forward in my chair. 'Would Janet shoot him?'

Wendy looked at me as if I had lost my mind. 'Why would she do something like that?'

'Well, someone shot him and you just told me they didn't get along.'

'That doesn't mean Janet would shoot her own father.'

'Maybe she was drunk and they got into an argument. It happens.'

'Don't be ridiculous,' Wendy snapped. 'If Janet was going to shoot anyone it would be herself. As it is she's busy eating herself to death.'

I tried another tack. 'Does Janet have any friends in Vegas?'

'I don't know.'

I thought I detected a moment's hesitation but I wasn't certain. 'Are you sure?'

'Positive. Why would I lie?'

'I don't know. Would you?'

She waved her hand in the air. 'I don't care enough about her to lie. She's not worth the trouble.'

'Is there anyone here she's kept in touch with that I could talk to?'

Wendy ran a finger around the rim of her martini glass and took a sip.

'You could try Andrea Thompson,' she told me. 'I hear they're still tight.'

'Do you happen to know where she lives?'

Wendy shook her head again. 'I don't even know if Andrea's in town right now. She might have moved away.'

'Do you know anyone who would know?'

'She was another loser.'

'And you don't associate with losers?'

Wendy's jaw tightened. 'What's that supposed to mean?'

'Nothing. It was just an observation.'

Wendy raised a well-waxed eyebrow. 'The only reason I agreed to speak to you was because my mother insisted.'

Well, that answered one of my questions.

'I told her I didn't know anything,' Wendy continued, 'but she said I should talk to you anyway. She said it was the right thing to do. Personally, I don't care.'

'Care about what?' I asked. 'About Benny Gibson being shot? About Janet Gibson? About her fingering me for something I didn't do?'

Wendy looked at me as if I were an insect on the end of a pin. Then she looked at her watch. I glanced at mine. Twenty minutes had elapsed. Time goes by fast when you're having fun.

'Maybe you should go,' she said. 'My fiancé will be here in ten minutes.'

'And you don't want him to meet me?' I asked.

'Look,' she said, 'he's from a very private family. He'd kill me if he knew I had anything to do with this. Anything at all.'

'Even talking?'

'Even talking,' she said firmly.

'Then how come you agreed to meet me?'

'I already told you. My mom. Once she gets an idea in her head, she never gives up. She's taking one of these courses on chanting or something ... I don't know ... It has to do with this lady. From India. I guess she's pretty famous over there. The whole thing is weird. Anyway my mom insisted I talk to you – something about some karmic debt – and I have.'

And that as they like to say was that.

I stopped at the lobby on my way out and asked for their phonebook. Andrea Thompson wasn't in it. Somehow I wasn't surprised. These days what with cellphones and all lots of people aren't.

Fifteen

I walked out of the warm hotel lobby into a raw early April evening. The wind had kicked up since I'd left the store. The air smelled like a storm was coming in from the west. I zipped up my jacket, buried my hands in my jeans pockets, and headed for my vehicle. I'd parked a little ways down the block. By the time I got there my eyes were tearing up from the wind.

Zsa Zsa lifted her head from the old rabbit-skin coat she was curled up in and then put it back down when I opened my car door.

'Are you going to say hello?' I asked her.

She grunted, got up, came over, gave me a cursory lick on the chin, and went back to the coat. She was pissed at me for leaving her in the car.

'We'll get KFC,' I told her to make it up to her.

Suddenly her tail was wagging. The way to Zsa Zsa's heart was through her stomach, no doubt about that. On the way over to KFC, we passed a utilities crew fixing a blown transformer. On the corners small groups of boys in oversized white T-shirts and baggy jeans milled around waiting to do business. The parking lot at KFC was deserted. I parked right by the front door and hurried inside, got six pieces of extra-crispy chicken, two biscuits, and a small side of coleslaw, and hurried out again. The coleslaw was for Zsa Zsa. I don't touch it. Then I made Zsa Zsa wait until we got home to eat, which meant I was driving with the bag of food wedged between my legs while I fended her off.

I could see my cat crouched by my front door as I pulled into the driveway. His green eyes glowed in the darkness. I let James in and fed everyone dinner. Afterwards, I did household chores. Even I couldn't stand the way the place looked anymore and anyway sometimes restoring order helped me think.

First I cleaned up the kitchen. Then I gathered up my laundry and started doing that. I always vow I'll do it every week, but somehow I never do. Next I changed my bedding, vacuumed the rug, and sat down to do my bills. When I was done with those I poured myself a shot of Glenlivet single malt, got myself a yellow pad and a pen, and turned on the TV for background noise. It was time to try and make some sense of what I'd learned from Trent, Joe, Calli, and Wendy.

I sat on the sofa and stared at the yellow pad. It didn't tell me much. I printed Benny Gibson's name in the center of the page and circled it. Very good, Robin, I told myself. Now you're getting somewhere.

Next I wrote down John's and Janet's names and drew arrows from them to Benny Gibson's. Then I printed my name on the other side and drew an arrow from me to John. I wrote in Joe Gibson's name and Wendy Walmouth's on the other side of the pad. Then I stopped and examined my handiwork.

It didn't tell me a damned thing. Absolutely nada.

I knew John. Janet knew her dad. John knew Benny, or at least knew who he was, but Benny and Janet didn't know me. Or at least I didn't think they did. Only Janet had known me. She had to have, otherwise she wouldn't have been able to finger me for her dad's murder. At least that was the assumption I was working on. So the question was: How did she know who I was? Had she seen me outside her house? I couldn't believe that she had. If she had, where? Or hadn't she seen me at all?

Was my assumption wrong?

Had she just gotten a call from someone telling her I was coming out to her dad's house? But that would have meant that the person making the call knew that Benny Gibson was already dead. His murderer?

It also implied that someone knew what I was up to. That they knew that John had asked me to do him a favor.

Who?

I didn't know.

Another question: Who knew John and Janet and me?

No one that I could think of.

OK. Maybe the trick was to approach it from John's angle. Did John know what he was doing? Did he already know that Benny Gibson was dead? How did he know? Who told him?

Trent knew John and me. He could have called John and set this up. But to what purpose? None that I could see. From what he said Benny Gibson had tried to scam him, but that didn't strike me as grounds for shooting someone, nor did Trent strike me as the kind of person who would take that route.

Back to John. Did he know Janet Gibson? If so how? What was the common link between the two?

Janet was a screw-up. She drank too much. John didn't drink at all. He was into movies and TV. Was Janet? Who knew? Had they both worked in the same place at some point?

Possibly.

I drew three stars on the page. John had temped a lot. Maybe Janet had too. Maybe they met in an office somewhere. But even if they had, that still didn't solve my original question. Why was I involved in all of this? Was it just bad luck on my part?

The whole thing made no sense. There was a string here I wasn't seeing. The lynchpin that was holding everything together. But what?

I felt like screaming.

Instead I took another sip of my drink and stared at the yellow pad until my eyes felt as if they were burning.

There had to be a common link. Had to be. Given the circumstances, coincidence was out of the question. But what was it? I didn't know and I didn't think I had the resources to find out. That was something the police department should be doing. And might be doing if they didn't already have a suspect. Why should they go out and look for someone else, when they had a perfectly good suspect right here?

Me.

Now that was a depressing thought. It was better not to go there.

I sighed and turned back to my pad. Maybe the trick was

to work backward. Maybe I should start with Benny Gibson's murder and go from there.

What did I know about his murder? Not much. According to Calli, Gibson had been shot twice with a Tech nine millimeter, which was the most common murder weapon used in America today. You could buy the bullets for it in any sporting-goods store because they were used in rifles as well. So nothing there.

Gibson had been lying in the hallway when his daughter had come home. The door had been locked. She'd used her key to let herself in, found him sprawled on the floor and called 911.

The obvious inference was that Benny Gibson had opened the door and someone had shot him. As he staggered towards the phone someone had shot him again, one shot to the chest and another to the back, then left, closing the door behind him. So it was a good bet that Gibson knew whoever had shot him well enough to open the door to him.

According to what the police had told Calli, nothing had been taken from the Gibson house and nothing had been gone through.

This wasn't a robbery.

This was some sort of payback. Or a warning? To Joe.

The cops had found a bag of Doritos on the coffee table, along with a Diet Coke. The television was on. Benny Gibson had been enjoying a relaxing evening at home when he was killed.

None of the neighbors had seen anything. None of the neighbors had heard anything. No one knew anything.

The investigation was continuing. Not reassuring.

What did I know about Benny Gibson? Not much, really.

His wife was in rehab somewhere, his daughter was screwed up, he ran a real-estate company that was about to come under scrutiny for some of the stuff he was doing. He was dirty. But how dirty? Was that what got him killed? Or was it drugs? Or women? Or something else entirely?

Were the men he met at Wonder Women involved in the killing? Were they locals? People he was doing business with? Friends?

And how about Benny's brother Joe? Where did he fit in

to this? Did he stand to inherit the business now that his brother was gone? Probably.

How much coke were the two brothers doing?

Could Benny have been stealing money from the business to support his drug habit? That would be a motive. Joe was certainly protective of his sister and his mother. Maybe he was equally protective of the business. Maybe he felt a sense of outrage that something he'd worked hard to build up was about to be sullied by his brother's behavior.

I got up, topped off my drink, and sat back down. Zsa Zsa came over and put her head on my thigh. I sat there and scratched behind her ears for a while. The problem was that all I had were suppositions. But I guess in this case that was what I was going to have to start with.

I tore out a piece of paper and wrote down my 'to find out' list.

Who were the people Benny Gibson was meeting at Wonder Women?

Where had Janet worked? Had she and John met someplace?

I had to talk to Trent and find out. I had to talk to John's acquaintances.

I had to locate Janet's friend Andrea Thompson, and try and talk to her.

I had to find out what Wendy's story was from Calli.

I had to find out more about Benny Gibson's business dealings, if that was possible.

It was a lot of finding-outs. Too many.

I put my pen down. I didn't know if finding any of this stuff out would help.

But I'd be doing something. And movement in any direction was movement in every direction.

At least that's what I told myself as I put the pad and paper on the coffee table. I looked at my watch. It was almost eleven. Time to go to bed. I was finishing off the Scotch in my glass when Zsa Zsa jumped off the sofa and started barking.

Sixteen

Zsa Zsa barked at anything that moved, be it man, beast, or insect. She had this high, little-dog yap that drove me crazy. It was the only thing about her I didn't like. I told her to shush. She kept on going. I was certain she was barking at her arch enemy, the neighbor's cat, a ginger tom that liked to sit on our kitchen windowsill and torment her. I told her to be quiet again. She gave me a reproachful look, moved to the hallway, and went back to barking. This time she was looking straight at the door. By now she was hitting a truly irritating pitch and from past experience I knew she wouldn't stop until I showed her there was nothing there.

'Sometimes you are such a pain in the butt,' I told her as I pushed myself up from the sofa.

Zsa Zsa wagged her tail in agreement and kept on yapping.

'Seriously.'

Zsa Zsa barked some more.

As I walked towards the hallway I happened to glance out the living-room window. Someone was running down the path from my house towards a car parked out front. He was moving at a pretty good clip because a few seconds later he was in the vehicle. A few seconds after that, he was pulling out. By the time I got outside all I could see were tail lights disappearing around the corner.

I tried to think about what he had looked like. It had definitely been a guy. Around six feet tall. Chunky build. Or maybe that was the hoodie he was wearing. It hid his face so I didn't see that. As to the car he was driving, it was some kind of SUV. Dark color. On the smaller side. Maybe a foreign make? And that was it. The whole thing had happened so fast I didn't have time to register anything else. I glanced down. Zsa Zsa was dancing on my feet.

'OK,' I said to her. 'When you're right, you're right.'

I looked around my front steps. There was nothing amiss. I checked the van. I'd locked it when I'd left this morning. It was still locked. I moved on to my car. From the outside everything seemed to be all right. I opened the door and slid inside. Zsa Zsa jumped in after me. She lay down. A good sign that no one had been inside. I looked anyway. Everything seemed the same. I checked the glove compartment. Nothing had been taken. I sat for a moment and thought.

It had probably been nothing. Someone had stopped and walked up to the doorway before reading the number and realizing they were in the wrong place. The only trouble with that was that you could read my house number from the street.

Perhaps someone had something to say to me and chickened out? I tapped my fingers against the steering wheel. Who? And what were they planning to do? Hopefully not what someone did to Benny Gibson. Which meant that someone knew I was snooping around. Which meant this had originated with someone I had talked to. Unless one of those people had talked to someone else and they had done this.

There was no way to find out. This was like a big jigsaw puzzle. You started with the corners and the edges and eventually you filled in the rest of the pieces. If you were lucky.

After a few minutes I realized this was getting nowhere and I was getting cold. Time to go inside and smoke the last cigarette of the day.

I scanned the path on the way in. I don't know what I was hoping to see. A dropped note? A footprint? But there was nothing new. The cracks in the concrete that had been there this morning were there now.

I climbed my front step and took a last look. I couldn't see anything. And yet. And yet. There was something different. A small thing. But something. I stopped for a moment and thought. It was hovering at the back of my mind, but I couldn't grasp it. I closed my eyes and tried to focus.

The driveway was the same. There was nothing different about the steps. I thought about the pieces of intertwined metal that held up the porch roof. Nothing there. Then what? All of a sudden it came to me.

The mailbox flap.

It was up. I had left it down after I'd gotten my mail on my way in.

I went over and glanced in. I don't know what I expected but it wasn't what I saw.

A matchbook.

I took it out. The matchbook was one of those kinds you get in a gas station when you buy a pack of cigarettes. I opened it up. The tips of five matches were burnt off the first row. Someone had scribbled two letters. I had to squint to make out them out because they were written in pencil in a shaky scrawl. TG? TB? I couldn't decide which. It really didn't matter though because neither struck a chord.

I went inside and closed my front door. I stared at the matchbook some more. I studied the letters again. Absolutely nothing came to mind. I turned the matchbook over and examined the printing. It had an ad for a tractor-driving school on the back cover. Could we get any more generic? Doubtful. I held it up to the light. It looked like an ordinary matchbook to me. I weighed it in my hand. Then I called Ian. Maybe he could tell me something. He always did well with weird stuff.

'I've got twenty people in here right now,' he told me before I could ask my question. Then he hung up. Super.

I called Calli. She wasn't home. I left a message on her machine.

I thought about it for a moment and called George's cell. His voicemail came on. I left a message and called his house. The blonde answered. I was so surprised I hung up before I knew what I was doing. I guess everyone was wrong. George and the blonde were back together again. I didn't know whether I was relieved or disappointed. Probably a little bit of both.

I lit a cigarette. Then I went back to looking at the matchbook. I showed it to Zsa Zsa.

'What do you think this means?'

She continued licking her paw.

'Not interested, huh?'

She gave me a cursory wag. I poured myself another shot of Glenlivet, lit a cigarette, and went upstairs to the room I was using as an office and sat down in front of my computer. I Googled TB. I got lots of sites about tuberculosis, but not much else. I tried TG and got a site for a company that made hydraulic cylinders. Then for the hell of it I tried to find a phone number for Janet Gibson. Nothing. I read all the newspaper articles about Benny Gibson. Again. They didn't tell me anything new.

I tried to find Betty Heath's address. I struck out on that one too. I read about Carrie Walmouth and her husband. The articles didn't tell me anything that had any bearing on Benny Gibson's murder. The couple were involved in charitable activities and had a showcase garden that featured a large collection of day lilies, as well as a greenhouse devoted to orchids.

I sat back and stared at the matchbook again. That's when I decided the hell with it. I shoved it in my backpack and went to bed. I had a headache and the beginnings of a sore throat and a major case of frustration.

I slept badly. I kept seeing dragons. Their claws were out and I kept trying to keep Zsa Zsa inside but she wouldn't listen to me. Somehow she'd gotten outside and I ran out trying to find her but she was gone. Then Murphy was there, shaking his head, telling me the dead should stay dead.

I woke up in a cold sweat. Murphy. My dead husband. I'd been blamed for his death. I'd been cleared, but with something like that the stigma was always there. Maybe that's why the police were so interested in me for Benny Gibson's death. Maybe they figured I'd walked on one crime and they were going to nail me for another.

I told myself I was just being paranoid. Or was I? Is that why I'd been set up? Because I was a likely victim? No. That was nuts. It was true my case had made the papers, but it was a small item. Plus it was a long time ago. Aside from Calli and Manuel, I don't think anyone who knew me knew about that.

I got up and stared out the window and looked at the branches tossing in the wind just the way they did when I was in camp. They twisted themselves into different shapes.

I made out a pig's snout, a table, and George Washington without his teeth. Finally I went downstairs and turned on the TV and lay down on the sofa. Zsa Zsa joined me and I put a comforter over us. For a while she and I watched a program about dredging for gold in Nome, Alaska. Then I watched a program about crab fishermen in the Bering Sea. According to the program it was the most dangerous job in the world. Who knew? Eventually I closed my eyes and fell asleep.

When I woke up daylight was coming in the window. I checked my watch. It was eight o'clock. I got up and showered. Then I put on the only skirt I owned and my black turtleneck sweater and black tights. I put on my boots downstairs, donned my jacket, and left the house with Zsa Zsa in tow. It was time to go to work.

I had one of the big boas out of her cage when Manuel walked through the door. I glanced at the clock. It was a little after eleven. Manuel followed my glance.

He smirked. 'I was busy,' he said.

I unwound Patricia from my arm and held her in both my hands. She has a tendency to constrict when startled, which was why I'd locked Zsa Zsa in the office.

'Partying?'

Manuel's smirk got bigger. 'The girls can't get enough of me.'

'What? You finally found one that would talk to you?'

'Talk? Who wants to talk?'

No twenty-something male that I know. That's for sure.

'You got lucky?'

'Luck has nothing to do with it. No one can resist my charm.' Manuel grinned and threw his jacket over some bags of rabbit pellets.

'Come to daddy,' he crooned as he took Patricia from me, and put her on the counter. She's twelve feet long and solid muscle.

'Be careful. She's shedding,' I warned.

Snakes that are shedding can't see, which makes them more prone to strike out. Not a good thing because they leave a nasty bite.

While Manuel watched Patricia I cleaned out her cage. It was easier to do when she wasn't in it.

'I think one of my friends might buy her,' Manuel said.

'Someone responsible?'

I always worry about the big boas. Lots of times drug dealers want them to protect their stash, but in my experience they rarely take very good care of them. Almost all reptiles are delicate creatures that need lots of tending to. Even a slight chill can weaken their immune system and make them vulnerable to a host of diseases.

Manuel looked offended. 'Of course.'

'Who?'

'You think I don't have responsible friends.'

'I'm just wondering who it is.'

Manuel recaptured Patricia as she was about to slither off the counter top. 'One of my brother's friends. He teaches in the city. Suddenly he's gotten interested in reptiles. He's got a baby red-tailed Haitian boa, a corn snake, a milk snake, and an egg eater.'

'An egg eater?' I repeated.

Manuel grinned. 'They're pretty cool.'

'Yes, they are.' You put an egg in one end and an empty shell comes out the other.

'He's going to change Patricia's name, though.'

'I don't think Patricia will mind.'

'Why did you name her that, anyway?'

'I didn't. That's the way she came.'

'It's a stupid name for a snake.'

'The guy who brought her in named her after his wife.'

'What did the wife say?'

'I gather she wasn't very happy. That's how come Patricia is here.'

'I heard from Chad,' Manuel told me as I put fresh ripped-up newspaper in Patricia's cage.

I straightened up and waited to hear what Manuel had to say.

'He's in Canada, on the—'

I held up my hand. 'Don't tell me. I don't want to know.'

'But—'

'Seriously. That way if someone asks me I can honestly tell them I don't know.'

Manuel nodded. 'I get it.'

'Good.' I emptied out Patricia's water dish and put in fresh water.

'Jellybean is with him. I guess they're not coming back for a while.'

'Given the circumstances, I wouldn't if I were them, would you?'

'Nope.'

I went over and picked Patricia off Manuel's shoulder. She tried to slither around my arm. I quickly carried her back, put her in her cage, and fastened the top before she could get out. She was an escape artist. The last time she'd gotten out it had taken me a week to locate her.

'Chad wants me to go with him. He says we could make some serious cash.'

'Because he's done so well so far.'

Manuel grinned at me. 'Don't worry. I'm not going. Then who would run the shop?'

I smiled back. 'Exactly.'

Manuel looked me over for a minute. 'You're all dressed up today. Are you going someplace?'

'To John Gabriellas' calling hours.'

'He's the dead guy, right?'

'One of them,' I replied.

I was going for two reasons. The first was because I wanted to say goodbye to John. The second was that I wanted to talk to his friends and family and see if anything turned up.

'I have a question for you,' I said to Manuel.

'About Chad?'

'No. About this.' And I went and got the matchbook out of my backpack and showed it to Manuel.

He took it in his hand and turned it over. Then he opened it up.

'What about it?' he finally said.

'I don't know. Someone put it in my mailbox last night.'

Manuel shrugged. 'It doesn't mean anything to me.'

'Do the initials TB or TG?'

'Aren't they STDs?'

'With you everything is sex.'

'At my age I'd be weird if it weren't.'

'True.' I took the matchbook back. The initials didn't mean anything to me either.

But they had to mean something.

It was just a question of finding out what.

Seventeen

The Hoffman Funeral Home was located off of East Genesee Street in a long, low white-and-gray building. It shared space with an ophthalmologist, a travel agency, and a daycare center. Their entrances faced front, while the funeral home's entrance was discreetly placed in the back away from everyone, as if it was apologizing to everyone for its existence.

We don't see the dead in America. When people die they're quietly whisked away with a minimum of fanfare so they don't disturb people. As I followed the road up to the back I realized I was surprised that his family had chosen this particular funeral home. With a name like Gabriellas I thought they would have chosen something on the North Side, something a little more Italian.

I got to Hoffman's at five forty-five, which was when I figured most of the callers would be coming, but then I thought maybe I was too early because there weren't many cars in the lot. I parked my vehicle close to the doorway, took a last puff of my cigarette, and flicked it out the window. Then I locked up and went inside.

The door was heavy wood and I had to push hard to get it to open. The hallway radiated good taste with a capital T. The walls were decorated with a muted gray-and-white-striped wallpaper. The carpet was dove gray. The lighting was subdued. Two dried floral arrangements in waist-high white vases sat on either side of the door. It was so quiet inside I could hear the traffic on East Genesee Street. I felt as if I'd stepped into a cocoon.

A row of wooden chairs with padded backs and seats stood flush with the far wall. No one was sitting in them. In fact, no one was in the hallway. When I'd come to my neighbor's calling hours last August the place had been packed. I walked over to the register and glanced at it.

So far a total of ten people had come to pay their respects. I remembered that Trent had told me John hadn't had many friends. Apparently he was correct. Or maybe John's father had told John's gay friends not to show up, the way he had with Trent. Still, I expected to see neighbors and family friends.

I wondered why they weren't here. Maybe the family was estranged from everyone. It was sad, but it certainly made my job easier. I checked to see that no one was watching me, and quickly jotted down the visitors' names on the back of my checkbook. Then I slipped it into my backpack and walked inside.

The receiving room was longer than it was wide. It was a large room and its dimensions served to emphasize the lack of people. John's family was sitting in a row of chairs off to the right-hand side. They had that shell-shocked look that people in times of sudden disaster wear.

I immediately identified John's father and brother. All three of them shared the slightly hooked nose, the brownish hair, and the mouth. I figured that the women sitting next to John's brother must be the cousins that John talked about from time to time. Two of the women had swollen eyes, evidence that they'd been crying.

I nodded at them and they nodded back at me. Then I went over and looked at John in his coffin. The undertaker had dressed him in the suit John and I had bought at a high-end shop down at the Armory. It had been expensive, the most John had ever paid, and he'd joked that he'd be buried in it. Guess he'd been right. I wondered if his good-luck piece of apple jade was still in his inner jacket pocket.

As I stood over him, I felt no sense of connection. Neither anger nor grief, nothing. Maybe it was because I was numb or maybe it was because anything that had marked John as John was gone. He looked like someone I'd never ate and laughed with, someone I'd never gone to the movies with, someone I'd never shopped with. Hopefully he'd do better in his next life. Come to think of it, hopefully I would too.

After what I judged was the appropriate amount of time I walked up to John's father to express my condolences.

'Mr Gabriellas,' I began but before I could say anything else he raised his hand and waved me away.

'Dad,' John's brother, Theodore, chided as he put his hand on his father's forearm.

Mr Gabriellas flinched at his son's touch. He pushed his son's hand off and quickly moved his arm away. As if he couldn't stand being near him. I noticed Mr Gabriellas' bottom lip was trembling.

Theodore colored slightly. He clenched his hands, realized what he was doing, and unclenched them.

'He's very upset,' he explained. 'You'll have to forgive him.'

'Of course,' I murmured.

I remembered John saying something about his father and brother not getting along since his brother had moved back up here from New York City.

I glanced back at John's father. He was staring straight ahead. He looked old and frail, rubbed to the vanishing point by the years, and it wouldn't surprise me to read his obit in the local paper this year.

'It was nice of you to come,' Theodore said to me. 'John talked about you all the time.'

'That's good to know.'

'He considered you one of his best friends.'

The woman sitting next to Theodore dabbed at her eyes. I judged she was in her early thirties but she'd already settled down into middle age.

'You're Robin Light, aren't you?' she asked me.

I nodded.

'You were helping John?'

'I was trying to.'

At which John's father turned his face towards me. I could see him thinking.

'Robin Light?' he asked. His voice was hoarse, as if he'd spent the last fifty years of his life smoking two packs a day.

'That's right.' I realized that I hadn't had a chance to introduce myself before. 'I'm—'

'I know who you are.' There was a pause while he gathered his breath. Then he cried, 'Get out. I don't want any murderers in here.' He started to rise, got halfway off the chair, then fell back into it. A thin line of saliva ran down to his chin. He didn't wipe it away.

I could feel my face go beet red. Maybe I should have tried to explain, but I didn't. Instead I turned and walked out the door. The cold outside felt good. I headed straight for my car. I was just opening my door when I felt a tap on my shoulder. I spun around. The woman I'd been talking to before was standing behind me.

'You have to understand,' she said, 'John's father is a devout Catholic. And this . . . the way John died . . .' Her voice trailed off. 'It's a mortal sin.'

I made a noncommittal noise.

'And his lifestyle . . .'

'I take it you mean John being gay?'

'Yes.' She rubbed her arms. She'd run out without her coat and it was thirty-eight degrees out. She had to be freezing. 'Angelo could never get used to that. Ever. But he loved John. He really did. You have to believe that.'

'He has a funny way of showing it.'

'He's a hard man. Thickheaded. But that doesn't mean he doesn't care.'

I sensed that she hadn't followed me outside to stand in the cold and apologize for John's father. There was something else she wanted to tell me about. So I nodded and waited. I've found that people usually fill silences with words. A moment later she handed me a card.

Do It Right Construction Company. We do it right the first time. Underneath was an East Syracuse address. Underneath that was a phone number. An email and fax number were printed on the lower left-hand side. On the lower right-hand side was the name Carmella Gabriellas.

'That's me,' she said pointing to her name.

'I figured,' I told her.

She rubbed her arms again and stamped her feet. She was wearing a thin black shirt, a black skirt made out of some sort of knit material, nylons, and dress boots. She wasn't dressed for standing outside. Even in the dim light thrown off by the parking-lot lights I could see her face was beginning to look pinched with the cold.

'I'm the administrative assistant for the office. It's a good place. We do high-quality stuff.'

'Somehow I don't think you followed me outside to tell me that.'

'True.'

She touched her shirt buttons one after the other. As if they were going to give her permission to speak. I waited. I could hear tires squealing on East Genesee Street as someone stopped short. Then the blare of a horn. Two short bursts. Then someone yelling. Then nothing. A near miss.

'I need to show you something,' Carmella said.

I dug my cigarettes out of my backpack. 'So show me.'

She took a deep breath and let it out. Then she did it again.

'I can't. It's not here.'

I zipped up my jacket. 'Where is it?'

'At my house.'

'I take it this has to do with John?'

Carmella nodded.

'I figured as much.'

She pressed her hands to her face. All I could see were her eyes. 'I don't know what to do. I'm hoping you can advise me.'

'I'm not sure I can help, but I'd be willing to look.'

'Nine thirty? I should be done with this,' she nodded towards the funeral home, 'by then.'

'That works.'

She took back the card she'd given me and wrote down her home address on the back of it.

'I have a pit bull,' she told me as she returned her card.

'As long as it doesn't try and bite me that's fine with me.'

'She's a sweetie,' Carmella said. 'In fact that's her name.'

Then she hurried inside without a backward glance. I lit a cigarette and looked at my watch. It was six fifteen. Plenty of time to do what I had to do before I had to show up at Carmella Gabriellas' house. As I got into my car I decided to try to not think about what Carmella wanted to show me. I'd find out whatever it was soon enough. In the meantime it was silly to waste time trying to figure it out. Not that that would stop me from making the attempt.

Eighteen

Carmella Gabriellas lived in a house on the North Side of Syracuse. The North Side had taken a precipitous decline in the past two decades. Once a bastion of middle-class Italian families, it was now rampant with gang-bangers and the violence they bring. However, certain areas were experiencing a resurgence and Carmella Gabriellas lived in one of them.

I had to circle Carmella's block three times before I found a parking spot near her house. Although it was dark, from what I could see the houses I'd passed were all two-story well-maintained wood-and-brick colonials. They didn't have boarded-up windows and piles of refuse in the yard. Clusters of boys in white shirts weren't hanging out in front of them waiting to make a sale. I didn't see a convenience store selling Lotto tickets and bottles of Colt 45. These were all good signs.

I found Carmella's house without any trouble. She lived in the bottom apartment of a tidy two-story brick house. The moment I pushed open the wrought-iron gate and started up the path her dog started barking. It was a deep bark and if I was a burglar I'd have turned around and found someplace else to rob.

As I got nearer to the door, I could hear Carmella talking to her dog. It was still barking. I heard her tell the dog that I was a nice person. The dog didn't seem to be convinced. I wondered if Carmella could hold the dog if she decided to go for me.

I thought she probably couldn't. Carmella was a big lady, but it was mostly fat and pit bulls are very strong, very muscular dogs. After all, they were bred to fight.

I looked around for something to defend myself with if

it came down to that. My eyes lit on a snow shovel leaning against the railing. I went over and picked it up. It wasn't great, not nearly heavy enough, the dog could probably break the wood with one bite, but it would have to do. I love dogs, but I've seen what pits can do and I wasn't taking any chances.

'Carmella,' I called through the door.

'It's fine,' she said. 'Sweetie is just taking a little time to settle down.'

'Sweetie doesn't sound fine to me.'

'She has transition issues.'

'Transition issues?' I think I squeaked when I said that.

'You know, she has trouble with people coming through the door. After that she's fine.'

Great. Sweetie was still growling.

'I'm going to open the door now,' Carmella said. 'Just stay absolutely still for a moment and everything will be fine.'

Then before I could say anything I saw the door swing open. Carmella was holding on to an all-white pit bull that didn't seem particularly glad to see me. Maybe I got that impression because her fangs were showing.

I was aware that Carmella was telling her to be a nice doggie, but I wasn't concentrating on what Carmella was saying, I was concentrating on my aim. I figured I had one chance to give Sweetie a good whack on the nose. After that, I was lunch. Then Sweetie gave another growl and sat down and wagged her tail.

'You can come in now,' Carmella said.

I put the shovel down. I could feel my heart rate slowing.

Carmella frowned. 'You weren't going to hit her, were you?' she asked.

'If she came for me I was,' I replied as I stepped over the threshold.

'I thought you liked dogs.'

'I do,' I countered. 'But there are limits.'

Carmella clucked at her. 'Poor thing. She was abused.'

Sweetie came over and sniffed my boots and worked her way up to my skirt. I extended my hand. She sniffed it. I slowly patted her head. Her hair was bristly. She gave me another lick.

'I told you, she's fine once you're inside,' Carmella said. 'It's just the getting inside that's the problem.'

'It's a big problem.'

'I know.' Carmella took my jacket and hung it up in the hall closet. 'We're seeing a trainer.' And she motioned me to follow her down the hallway.

Which I did. Sweetie padded along by my side. Carmella had changed since I'd seen her at the funeral home. She was wearing a sweatshirt and a pair of jeans. Her hair was stuck back in a clip.

'I'm cleaning,' she explained as I followed her into her kitchen. Which probably explained the faint odor of bleach I'd smelled since I'd entered the house. 'It's what I do when I'm upset.'

'I can see that.'

All the counters were full of cans and jars and bags that had once filled the kitchen cabinets.

Carmella gestured to three rolls of paper she had on the kitchen table. 'I've decided I need to reline all the cabinets.'

'Reline?' I didn't know you were supposed to line. I put my cans and jars on the bare wood.

Carmella cleared a seat and indicated I should sit down in it. Then she cleared another chair, moved it next to me, and sat down.

'I'm not sure if I'm doing the right thing showing this to you,' she told me.

I knew she wanted to do it, otherwise I wouldn't be here, but she wanted me to convince her.

'Why don't you tell me what this is about?'

Carmella took one of the rolls of paper and started picking at the plastic covering it. 'I don't know. I'm thinking that maybe I made a mistake.'

'Having me come here?'

Carmella picked some more. 'Yes.'

The pile of plastic pieces on the table was growing.

I thought for a minute. Finally I said, 'Obviously you're disturbed by this – whatever it is. Otherwise you wouldn't have asked for my help.'

'That's true,' Carmella admitted.

'So why don't you let me help. I was a good friend of

John's. He trusted me. You should do the same. If you don't want to tell me what this is about that's fine too, but I'm betting that somewhere down the road you're going to regret that decision. Your choice.' I looked at my watch. 'You have to make up your mind, though. I've had a long day and I want to go home.'

Carmella wavered for a moment. I started to get up.

'Wait,' Carmella cried. And she rose from her chair and went out of the room.

I sat back down. Sweetie kept me company. She was a heavy breather. Probably sinus problems. I could hear a drawer open and close in the next room. A moment later Carmella was back with a manila envelope.

'I found these under John's mattress,' she said as she pushed them towards me.

I opened the envelope's clasp.

'I don't understand,' Carmella was saying as I took the pictures out. 'This doesn't make any sense to me.'

'It doesn't to me either,' I agreed as I gazed at the pictures of what looked like six-, seven-, and eight-year-old girls.

There were ten photographs in all. They were printed in sepia tones like old-fashioned photographs. The girls were dressed in either underwear, bathing suits, or over-sized shirts. They were wearing lipstick and eyeliner. Some of the girls were blonde, while others were brunette. All of them had their hair arranged in elaborate styles.

A few were wearing large straw hats with wide brims. One had a veil over her face. They were suggestively posed in front of a pedestal or reclining on a divan. A lot of thought had obviously gone into the photos. Maybe that's what made the results disturbing.

'They could be for a book,' Carmella said.

'They could be,' I agreed.

'They could be pictures for a beauty pageant.'

'That's also a possibility.' But I could tell from the expression on her face that she didn't believe that, and neither did I.

Carmella frowned. She rubbed her arms the way she had

when she was standing outside the funeral home. 'I can't believe it's the other.'

'The other' meaning kiddie porn. Carmella couldn't bring herself to even say the words.

They weren't that, but they weren't photos of kids playing Little League either.

They were suggestive.

They were posed.

The poses were intentional.

I guess the best word for them would be soft-core.

'John is gay,' Carmella continued. 'So what would he be doing with something like this?' And she tapped the top picture with a stubby finger.

'I don't know. Would Theodore?'

Carmella gave a vehement shake of her head. 'Absolutely not. Those two weren't close. They never have been.'

'So John wouldn't confide in his brother?'

'I don't think so. You know how it is. John liked to paint and Theo liked to play baseball. John was a good student and Theo barely made it through high school.'

'I see.'

A new thought struck Carmella. 'You can't talk to John's father about this. You know that, don't you? You just can't. It would kill him. Promise me that you won't.'

'I wasn't going to.'

There was no point. I was certain John and his father had existed in separate worlds for a long, long time. I still might talk to Theodore, though. I wasn't ready to promise anything on that. And I wondered what Trent would say about the photos. That would be interesting.

Sweetie nudged my hand with her paw. I patted her then turned one of the pictures over hoping to find the name of the person who had taken them. Naturally, it wasn't there. I really hadn't expected it would be.

Carmella rubbed her arms again. We sat there in silence for a few minutes. The only sounds were the refrigerator turning itself on and off, the sound of a car passing, and Sweetie yawning.

Finally Carmella said, 'And you can't give these to the police.'

'That's where they really belong. They can answer any questions that you have better than I can. They have access to databanks. They can give them to the Feds . . .'

'No.' Carmella banged the table with her fist. The rolls of paper jumped. Sweetie looked alarmed. 'Our family has been through enough. I don't need to read about this in the newspaper.'

'It wouldn't get in the newspaper.'

'Can you swear that won't happen?'

'I . . .'

Carmella brought her face close to mine. I could smell her scent, a mixture of baby powder, sweat, and a perfume that was mostly composed of attar of roses.

'Can you swear?'

'No,' I admitted. 'I can't.'

She sat back, satisfied with my answer.

'Where did you find them?' I asked.

Carmella flushed. 'Under John's mattress.'

I raised an eyebrow. Carmella's flush turned redder.

'He owed me three hundred dollars, well actually two hundred ninety-eight dollars and fifteen cents, for some tickets I bought him.'

'And you thought he kept money under the bed?' That didn't fit in with the John I knew, but then neither did the photos.

Carmella shrugged. 'He used to keep his money in a box of blintzes in the freezer.'

'Blintzes?'

'Blueberry blintzes,' Carmella said firmly. 'He always hid his money there, because that way he wouldn't forget where he put it. He called it his "get out of town stash". But it wasn't there, so I started looking around. I didn't find the money, I found these instead.' She tapped the photos again with her finger. 'I wish to hell I hadn't.'

'Karma,' I murmured.

'It's true,' Carmella said. 'I should have just let the money go.' She gathered up the photos and pushed them towards me. 'It's what I get for being greedy. Take them, please. Having them around gives me the creeps.'

I looked at the photos again. 'I really don't think they're John's.'

'I don't think so either. But then whose are they?'

'That's the question, isn't it?' I got up to go, then something else occurred to me. 'How did you get into John's house?' I asked Carmella.

'I have a spare key.'

'Does anyone else?'

Carmella thought for a moment. 'I'm pretty sure they don't. I just have it because John went away a couple of years ago and I volunteered to water his plants.'

'And you still have it?'

'The key?' Carmella gave me a puzzled look. 'Why shouldn't I?'

'No reason. Did you look anyplace else in the house?'

'The closet. The bathroom. Then I found the pictures and I didn't want to look around anymore. Why?'

'I'd like to look around, if you don't mind. See if there's anything else.'

Carmella shuddered. 'I hope not.'

'Me too.'

'Do you really think there is something else there?'

'No,' I said. 'But I want to make sure.'

I'd looked around once and hadn't found anything, but I hadn't really searched the place.

Sweetie butted her head against Carmella's leg. She gave her an absentminded rub. 'I don't think so either. And I need the key back. I've got people coming in to clean the day after tomorrow.'

'I'll have it back to you by tomorrow,' I promised.

Carmella hesitated for a second. Then she went over to the pegboard near the telephone and took down one of the keys dangling there.

'Here you go,' she said handing it to me. 'When you're through, you can put it in my mailbox.'

I thanked her and slipped the key in my jacket pocket. Carmella nodded. She started spreading a roll of the lining paper out on the table.

'You can let yourself out, can't you?' she asked me as

she reached for the scissors sitting on a stack of cookbooks.

She looked relieved I was going. Now the problem was mine.

'Of course,' I told her.

Sweetie walked me to the door and stood there until I closed it.

Nineteen

I glanced at my watch. I'd been in Carmella's house twenty minutes. It felt like an hour and twenty minutes. My head was still spinning from what I'd found out. I hadn't known what to expect when I got here but it certainly wasn't this, that was for sure. As I walked to my car, I thought about my game plan. Originally, I was going to go home, have a bowl of cereal for dinner, watch a little TV, and go to bed.

But not now. No way. Now I was going to pick up something to eat and then go on to John's house. I wanted to see if there was anything else in there I needed to know about. After that I'd drop by Shamus's and show Ian the pictures Carmella had found. I was interested to hear what he had to say about them.

But as Murphy always used to say, first things first. Which meant food. I stopped at the McDonald's on Erie Boulevard and ordered a Big Mac, a large fries, and a Coke. When my order was ready I took it outside and ate in my car. I just didn't feel like being with people at the moment. I needed to quiet myself down so I sat in the parking lot, listened to the radio, and made some calls while I ate. I was still hungry after I'd finished my meal so I went back in and got an apple pie and a cup of coffee.

I took a sip of coffee and spat it out. It tasted like lukewarm dish water. Why was it so hard to make a decent cup of coffee? It wasn't. It's just that people didn't care. Why should they? It was the same with the building I'd nicknamed the Mansion. The reporter on the news was talking about how lots of people in the community thought tearing the Mansion down and building a Target was a good idea. How could they believe that? It beat me. But then I didn't understand lots of things. Like John. Like the photographs. I checked my watch. It was time to get moving.

I threw the coffee out and drove over to John's house, parked my car on the street, took my flashlight out of my glove compartment, and went up the path to his house. I could hear the thin layer of ice crunching beneath my feet as I walked. Frozen tendrils of last summer's plants brushed my cheeks. They felt like cobwebs and I shuddered as I put my hand up to brush them away. As I put the key in the lock I expected the neighbor to come running out and demand to know what I was doing there. But he didn't. No one did.

The odor of wood smoke hung in the air. The street was quiet. I heard snatches of music intermixed with snippets of television shows. Then I spotted someone pulling up to the curb halfway down the street. But that was it. I guess everyone was winding down and getting ready for the next day. Which was what I should be doing too.

The key turned easily and a moment later I was in John's house. It felt strange standing in the hallway. I'd been here so many times before, but now it felt different. As I moved towards the living room I realized that while I'd come to look around and see if I could find anything else, I'd also come to say goodbye, to untie the strings of friendship.

The atmosphere in the house felt close. It had always smelled fresh when John was alive. Now I detected old garbage and dirty laundry. The house needed to be aired out. I turned on the lights in the hallway, took off my jacket, and draped it over the radiator.

Then I thought about how I wanted to do this. The fact that I didn't know what I was looking for was a complicating factor. Carmella had found the photographs under John's mattress. Where else would he hide something? The best thing to do was to be methodical and start at the bottom and work my way up to the top.

I remember John saying he never stored anything down in the basement because it leaked, but I figured I should check it out anyway. I could feel the dampness as I descended the stairs. The basement consisted of three rooms and an old furnace in the center. The first room held the washer and drier and a rack for folding clothes, while the other two rooms were empty.

The floors of all three were cement as were the walls. Which meant I could eliminate floors and walls as hiding places. I looked in the washing machine and drier and under them and found two missing socks and mouse droppings. I walked over to the furnace. It was old and dirty and full of dials and I couldn't imagine John ever coming near it, much less hiding something in it, because he hated machinery. I played my flashlight over it and gave it a quick inspection just to make sure. Then I went back upstairs and started on the first floor.

Usually people hide things where they're the most comfortable, which in John's case meant the kitchen and the bedroom. I started in the kitchen. I didn't bother with the fridge, assuming Carmella had gone through it. Instead I pulled out the appliances and looked behind them. I went through the kitchen cabinets and looked into the canisters of flour and sugar. I took out the paper bags and cleaning supplies under the sink. I got out the stepladder and checked the top of the kitchen cabinets. There was nothing but dust and a golf ball that had somehow found its way up there.

I moved on to the living and dining rooms. I picked up the sofa cushions and put my hands down in the crack where the seat and the back meet. I did the same with the chairs. I looked under the rugs. I shook out the magazines on the coffee table. When I got to the dining room I checked the hutch, after which I turned the chairs upside down to make sure nothing was taped under them. Then I got down on my hands and knees and checked under the table.

I walked into the office next. I noticed that the computer was gone. I assumed it had been taken by the police. John's calendar and address book were gone as well. Since this would have been the room the police would have looked through, they had probably found anything worth finding. However, to be on the safe side I took out the desk drawers and looked underneath them to make sure nothing was taped there. Then I looked under the rug and behind the drapes, after which I sat down and went through John's file cabinet.

He'd been a neat man and everything had been filed

according to subject and date. It was full of tax and insurance
stuff, warranties, duplicates of medical bills. I put everything
back and looked through his garbage can. It was black wire
mesh. I took out two pieces of crumpled-up pieces of white
printer paper and smoothed them out with the flat of my
hand.

The first one was filled with doodles of cubes and tri-
angles. John had printed *should I ask, or shouldn't I ask* on
the second piece. I recognized his handwriting. He'd drawn
a big question mark below it. And below that he'd written
'for' on one side of the paper and 'against' on the other.

Then he'd drawn a line down the middle, but that was as
far as he'd gotten with his list. Below that he'd printed
T Rex in block letters and underlined it several times after
which he'd drawn a crude dinosaur, with the word *dino*
above it. I thought about it for a couple of minutes but for
the life of me I couldn't figure out what it meant other than
the obvious. After another minute of fruitless thinking I
moved on.

I tackled the cellphone number John had scribbled at the
bottom of the page. When I dialed it I got the message that
it had been disconnected. Just like Benny Gibson's daughter
Janet's had been. So far I was batting zero for zero. I carefully folded the papers up, put them in my backpack, and
went upstairs.

The carpet on the stairs swallowed my steps. By now I
was tired and discouraged but I had to finish this. I told
myself I owed it to John. I started in John's bedroom because
I judged that was the most likely place he would have hidden
something. I didn't bother with his bed, but I did check all
the dresser drawers and the two nightstands. Nothing. I moved
the furniture. Still nothing. I checked behind the radiator. I
moved the air-conditioning unit that John and I were supposed
to have pulled out of his window at the end of September.

Then I went through the closet. Going through mine would
be a nightmare. But all of John's clothes were on hangers.
His shoes were all in plastic shoeboxes on the closet floor.
His sweaters were neatly folded in plastic bags on the top
shelf. I took them out, opened them up, then refolded them,
and put them back in their bags. After that I got the stepstool

from downstairs and inspected the shelf. Aside from a few dust bunnies there was nothing there.

I looked at my watch. By now I'd been at this for an hour and a half and I didn't hold out any hope of getting any more results. I went on to the bathroom, and the guest bedrooms. Half an hour later I was done. I was hot and tired, but I'd done what I'd set out to do, and that felt good. I walked down the stairs and turned off all the lights.

'Goodbye, house,' I said.

I tried the garage next. It was empty. Someone had carted everything away. As I was closing the door I felt as if someone was looking at me. I turned and checked the street. There was nothing there. I shook my head to clear it and told myself to get a grip. Then I got in my car and drove over to Shamus's. I wanted to talk to Ian. Come to think of it, a beer wouldn't hurt either.

The man watched Robin come out of John Gabriellas' house. He watched her lock the door. He watched her turn and scan the street. He shrank down in his seat a little even though he was positive she couldn't see him. But it didn't do to take chances. Especially unnecessary ones. He hadn't gotten where he was by doing that. He watched her narrow her eyes. She just stood there for a moment looking up and down the street with her hands jammed in her jacket pockets. It seemed as if she sensed something.

For a moment he thought she might walk down the street. There was a slim chance of that, but he was betting on the fact that she was tired and cold and ready to get out of there. As she walked towards her car, he congratulated himself on being right. He usually, no make that always, was. Right. The truth was, she thought of herself as being unpredictable, but she was very predictable.

He really didn't even have to be here. He just wanted to make sure that everything was OK, that everything went according to plan. He always believed in making sure all the loose ends got tied up. That was the sign of a professional. To not do that would have made him sloppy and he was anything but that.

He'd arrived just after she'd pulled into John's driveway.

He'd watched her standing on the sidewalk. She'd seen him pull up to the curb, but fortunately she hadn't given the matter any consideration, which he would certainly have done. Instead she'd turned around and gone into the house. When she'd come out, the light in his car had been out, and he'd been slouched behind the wheel. Because he'd parked out of the range of the streetlight it was difficult to see him. In fact, Robin would have had to walk down the block and there was no reason for her to do that.

There was no reason for her to be in the house, either. But that was Robin. Always poking her nose in where she wasn't wanted. Or needed. She never listened. Ever. He'd already been through it and knew that she wasn't going to find anything. He was confident of that. This was his show and he controlled it all. He quickly did another mental scan of the house, though. Just to make sure. No. He was fine. He was more than fine. He was golden.

He watched Robin get into her car. She started it up and drove down the street. When she got to the corner she took a left. So predictable. He put his car in gear and took off after her. It was fun following Robin. Fun watching her run around in circles. Kind of like watching a dog chasing its tail. Especially since she had no idea of what was going on. Absolutely none.

Which was gratifying.

OK, it was more than gratifying.

He loved it.

If she did know what was going on she wouldn't be wasting her time in John's house. He wondered if the DA would present her case to the grand jury. He might. And then they might move to indict. Grand juries really were nothing more than the yes men for the DA. In general. Sometimes it didn't work that way but mostly it did.

They didn't have quite enough evidence yet, but he could take care of that if he felt like it. He probably wouldn't, but the knowledge that he could gave him a warm feeling inside. He always felt best when he was in control. But then, who doesn't?

Twenty

I took a two-block detour on the way to Shamus's and drove by the Mansion. I wanted to see it before they tore it down. The house had withstood over one hundred years of history. It had been a rich man's house. John Basterville's, to be precise. Then it had been a museum for his collection of china. It had been a rooming house and a shop. Now it was going to be the site of large big-box store.

Just stupid. We had enough big-box stores. We didn't have enough houses like these. George always said I was overly sentimental about things like this and maybe he was right. But it just seemed wrong to take what was unique in Syracuse and get rid of it and make the city look like every other city. But then given enough money most people will do anything and rationalize it away. I headed off to Shamus's.

I was driving down West Fayette when I got that feeling again, the feeling that someone was watching me. I told myself it was crazy. But when I got to Richardson I made a hard left. I looked in the rear-view mirror. The SUV that was in back of me went cruising on by. I was getting spooked and there was nothing to get spooked by. Nothing at all. Must be the accumulated stress was frying my nerve endings. I probably needed a drink.

I made a U-turn, got back on West Fayette, drove down to South Geddes, made another left, and headed for the bar. I checked my rear-view mirror. There was no one behind me. There was no one in front of me either. There was no one on the side of me. I was alone on the road.

In the unlikely event that someone had been following me, they were now gone. I decided I was really going nuts. Then I thought about what had happened with John and revised my opinion. Maybe it wasn't so unlikely after all. Maybe I was being watched. Maybe I was being followed. Maybe the person that was following me was the person who had set me up.

When put like that, the idea wasn't so farfetched.

But who was doing it?

Why were they doing it?

I guess if I knew the answer to one question, I'd know the answer to the other.

But one thing was clear: whoever had set me up had gone to a lot of trouble to do it. And they had to have known both John and Janet Gibson and me. I was back to that again. I was still thinking about it when I parked in front of the bar.

Ian was making himself a hot chocolate when I walked in. He briefly looked up, and then went back to spooning out the chocolate mixture into a glass filled with water. He stirred it, put the glass in the microwave, and pressed the button. It occurred to me that in all the time I'd known Ian, I'd never seen a drop of liquor pass his lips.

None of the regulars were in and I didn't recognize the three men and one woman sitting at the bar. If they'd been in before, it hadn't been on my shift. Which was just as well. They had sour mouths and cold eyes. They looked like the kind of people that would give you trouble just for the fun of it.

The four of them were nursing their drinks and staring at the television. All of them looked up when I entered. Flickers of interest lit up their faces until they realized they didn't know me. Then the interest died. Their faces went slack and they picked up their beers again. Seeing them was like seeing extras from *Dawn of the Dead*.

As I went by the jukebox I pressed the button for the credits. Then I punched in the number for the Eagles. 'Desperado' came on.

'Hey,' one of the guys yelled at me, 'I don't like that song.'

'Tough,' I told him.

I think the guy muttered 'bitch' but I wasn't sure.

Ian looked up. 'Thanks for running off my customers,' he told me when I got closer to him.

'They don't look very nice.'

'They're not, but that's not the point.'

'Who are they?'

Ian shrugged. 'People who are passing through.'

'You told me we don't get people who are passing through around here.'

'Sometimes we do.'

'So you're not going to tell me?'

Ian grinned. 'Very good. It takes you a while but eventually you get it.'

I shrugged. 'Fine.'

I'd learned that the people Ian didn't want to introduce me to were probably people I didn't want to meet.

'By the way,' Ian said as I sat down across the way from him, 'you look like shit.'

I took my jacket off and handed it to him. He put it behind the counter.

'You're always so sweet,' I told him. 'Not to mention tactful.'

'That's what I'm known for.'

'That's why I come here.'

'I know. Manuel been arrested yet?'

'Funny. Despite what you've been telling me, no one's even turned up to talk to him.'

'I guess they haven't caught Chad and Jellybean yet. They will.'

'Not only are you sweet, you're optimistic.'

'No. I'm realistic.'

'No. You just like making me crazy.'

'That too.' Ian took a sip of his hot chocolate. 'Chad called me last night. He wanted to know if he could borrow a couple hundred bucks.'

'What did you tell him?'

'What do you think I told him?'

'That he couldn't.'

'That's right. If I had an extra couple of hundred I'd be paying my utility bill.'

I fiddled with my keys for a moment. 'Guess they're not doing too well.'

'They're not going to do well either. They've screwed up and everyone's mad at them. Witness the other evening.' Ian sipped his drink. 'Seriously. What have you been doing? Besides not sleeping, that is.'

I fished my cigarettes out of my backpack. 'If you give me a beer, I'll tell you. Better yet, make that a Scotch.'

'You got it.'

I watched Ian take the bottle off the shelf and pour a generous shot into a glass. Then he put it down in front of me. I smelled it. Then I took a sip. A moment later I could feel its warmth spreading through my body. I took Ian's lighter and lit my cigarette.

'Why don't you get your own?' he grumbled.

'Because I always lose them.'

'Which gives you the right to use mine?'

'Yes.'

'And you figure this how?'

I didn't have an answer to that so I changed the subject. 'I have something to show you.'

Ian waited.

'John's cousin found them.' And I took the manila envelope out of my backpack, opened the clasp, and took the pictures out.

Ian reached his hand out and I put the photographs in it. He thumbed through them quickly. Then he went back to the beginning and gave his full attention to each one. He studied them and then, when he was through, put them face down on the bar.

'What do you think?' I asked.

He made a shushing sound. One of the men at the other end of the bar called for a beer. Ian put down the picture he was holding and went and got it for him. He was back a moment later. He went back to looking at the photographs.

When he had gotten done he made a neat pile and turned them face up. Then he leaned over and began his critique.

'These are high-end soft-core kiddie porn. Good photos. Good printing job. Expensive paper. These could even be promos from one of those kiddie beauty pageants. Except for the poses. And the underwear.' He stopped talking and surveyed the bar. Everyone was good. 'There are some really sick people out there,' he continued. 'Really sick.'

I didn't say anything.

Ian lit a cigarette. 'Now tell me again how you got these.'

'John's cousin found them underneath his mattress.'

'What was he—'

'She.'

'All right, she, doing lifting up his mattress?'

'Looking for money that he owed her.'

'And you believe her story?'

I thought about how upset Carmella had been. 'Yes, I do.'

'Why?'

'Because of the way she behaved.'

'She could have been acting.'

'She could have been, but what would have been the point?'

Ian nodded. 'And she didn't find money.'

'No. She found the photos instead.'

'How did she get in?'

'She had a key.'

Ian coughed and took another puff of his cigarette. 'Why did she come to you with the photos?'

'I don't think she knew what else to do.'

'She could have just thrown them out. That's what I would have done.'

'I think she wanted someone to talk to about them and I was the logical choice.'

'Being his friend and all.'

'Exactly.'

Ian snorted. 'And John is the one that wanted you to follow his boyfriend.'

I nodded. 'You know he is.'

'And he's also the one that set you up and then committed suicide.'

I lifted up my glass and swirled the amber liquid around, then put the glass to my lips, and took a gulp. My eyes teared up. When I got my breath back I said, 'That's correct. As you are aware.'

Ian tapped the photographs with his middle finger. 'These pictures have nothing to do with John. They're someone else's.'

'That's what I think too.'

Ian leaned towards me. 'Why do you think that?' he demanded. Like he didn't believe I'd come up with the right answer.

'It doesn't fit the picture. He was gay and I don't think pictures of young girls in seductive poses would turn him on.'

Ian took a puff of his cigarette. He picked a strand of tobacco off his tongue.

I started thinking aloud. It was a question I'd been mulling over in my mind since I'd left the house.

'So then the question becomes: Who put them there and why? I don't know who, but I'm guessing whoever put them there might have been blackmailing John.'

Ian shook his head. 'If that was the case why would he have kept them? Why wouldn't he have thrown them out?'

'Because he didn't know they were there. Because someone planted them?'

'Why?'

'They were going to call the police on him. No,' I said before Ian could say it for me, 'that doesn't make sense.'

'Reverse the scenario.'

'You mean what if they were someone else's?' I asked.

'Exactly,' Ian said.

'And John was hiding the photos for them. Except why would you hide something like that?'

Ian dunked his cigarette in the cup of water sitting by the wash sink.

I finished my drink, thought about having another one, and decided against it for the moment. 'Maybe they were a sample of other stuff. Worse stuff.'

'Could be,' Ian said. 'Of course, there is another scenario.'

'What's that?'

'Obviously, John could be the one doing the blackmailing.'

'Not possible,' I said firmly.

'How do you know that?'

'Because I know John.'

'So you keep saying,' Ian cracked.

Before I could answer the front door opened and Stuttering Sam and his new girlfriend, I think her name was Rita, stumbled in.

'I want a b-b-beer,' he called to Ian.

'Coming right up,' Ian told him.

A minute later he'd set their PBRs in front of them and

taken care of the other four customers, then he walked back in my direction.

'I've been thinking,' I said when Ian settled back on his stool.

'Unusual.'

I ignored him. 'This whole thing doesn't make any sense. Except . . .'

'Except,' Ian nudged.

'You're going to think I'm crazy.'

Ian smiled. 'I know you're crazy.'

'Thanks.' I went on, 'And I'd be inclined to ignore the whole thing . . .'

'Maybe you should . . .'

'Maybe I would except when I came out of John's house I had the feeling that someone was watching me. And I got that feeling again when I drove over here.'

Ian grew serious. 'Could you see anyone?'

I shook my head. 'I was probably imaging it.'

'Probably,' Ian agreed.

'Given what's happened, I guess I'm inclined to be a little paranoid.'

'Well, it wouldn't hurt to be cautious,' Ian allowed.

'Maybe I should go get a gun permit,' I mused.

Ian stood up. 'I'm going to make myself some hot chocolate,' he announced.

'You don't think that's a good idea?' I asked him.

'I didn't say that.'

'You don't have to say that. I can see it on your face. I can shoot.'

'More or less,' Ian said.

'More than less,' I snapped back.

He frowned. 'You're not going to get emotional on me, are you?'

I realized my voice was louder than I intended. 'Heaven forfend.'

'Do you see me with a gun?'

'No.'

'And why do you think that is?'

'You can't get a permit?'

'Ha. Ha. If I thought a gun was a good idea I wouldn't worry about getting a permit. I'd just carry one.'

'And why don't you think they're a good idea?'

'Because they're dangerous.'

'Obviously.'

'Not in that way. They're a crutch. Having one makes people careless and complacent. They think because they have something like that they don't have to watch out.' Ian held up his hands and wiggled his fingers. 'And anyway, I have these.'

I'd seen what Ian could do to someone with his hands. I'd watched him break someone's fingers. I'd watched him make someone vomit from pain. It was impressive but I didn't have that particular skill set.

'Yeah. But I don't.'

'Maybe you should think about acquiring a knife.'

'A knife?' Just what I needed.

'On second thoughts, maybe you should just be careful.' Ian turned to go, then turned back. 'Didn't you want to ask me something?'

For a moment I drew a blank, then I recalled what it was. Actually I couldn't believe I'd forgotten about the matchbook. I guess that was a sign of how chaotic the day had become.

I reached in my backpack and took it out.

'Here. Someone left this in my mailbox.'

'You dropped it on the ground and they were being a good Samaritan?'

'Not quite. I saw him hurrying away. I thought he'd come up to my door for directions and changed his mind. But what he was really doing was putting the matchbook in my mailbox.'

'You certainly lead an interesting life, don't you?' Ian said as he turned the matchbook over in his hands. He opened it up and grinned.

'Bobby Bays,' he said.

'And who is Bobby Bays?'

'The person that used this matchbook.'

'And how do you know that?'

Ian threw the matchbook down on the counter. 'The broken matches. He used to work for me at the Isle of Dolls.'

'Do you know where he works now?'

'I heard Wonder Women.'

'What about the initials?'

Ian shrugged. 'I don't know. When we see him you can ask him.'

Twenty-One

It turned out that Bobbie Bays wasn't working at Wonder Women that night. According to the manager, he was at the ER getting stitched up. It seems he'd had a disagreement with a customer about being too drunk to enter the establishment a couple of hours before. The disagreement had turned into a fight and Bays had gotten cut on his arm.

'When you see him, tell him I'm not paying him for not being here,' the manager told us as we left the place.

'Nice guy,' I said when we got outside.

Ian snorted. 'He's right. Bays screwed up. He should have never let things get that far out of hand. He should have put the guy out of commission first. That's his job.'

We missed Bays at the hospital as well. The nurse at the reception desk told us he'd already been released.

'Now what?' I said as we walked to Ian's car. An ambulance came tear-assing around the corner.

'Now we try his house,' Ian replied as I jumped out of the way. 'You should be more careful,' he told me.

Like I'd almost gotten run over on purpose.

'No,' I replied. 'The ambulance driver should be paying more attention.'

Ian snorted again. I ignored it.

'So you know where Bays lives?' Talk about making the obvious comment.

'I know where he used to live. I picked him up for work once in a while. Of course, he could have moved. He tends to move around a lot.'

But he hadn't. Bays still lived over on Spring and Butternut Streets in a house that you could tell had once been someone's pride and now looked as if it should be condemned.

'He lives in the bottom apartment,' Ian said as he parked

the car. 'And be careful on the stairs. A couple of them are rotted through.'

Ian was out of the car and banging on the door by the time I was halfway up the steps. I'd stopped to get my foot out of the hole I hadn't seen on the fourth step.

'Hey, Bays,' he was yelling.

Two minutes later the lights in the house were turned on. Then the porch light went on. Thirty seconds after that the door swung open. A big bald-headed guy, wearing sweat-pants and a sweatshirt, stood there. He had sleep in his eyes and an ugly expression on his face.

'Hey, asshole, what's the matter with you? I'm trying to sleep here.'

Ian grinned. 'Nice to see you too, Carl. Me and my friend are looking for Bays.'

'He ain't here.'

'He just got out of the ER. I figured he'd be recuperating at home.'

'Well, you guessed wrong.'

'So where is he?'

I could see Carl thinking about whether he was going to answer. Then he shrugged.

'Sure. Why the hell not. He's recuperating at Turning Stone. Figured it was his lucky night.'

'Doesn't sound lucky to me,' I commented.

'Who's she?' Carl asked.

'The person that wants to find him,' Ian replied.

'Too bad for her,' Carl said.

He shut the door in our faces and went inside. A moment later the porch light clicked off, leaving us standing in the dark.

'That wasn't very polite,' I noted. But then we'd woken him up and I wouldn't be nice at one thirty in the morning either.

'Neither is Bobby Bays,' Ian commented as we walked back to his car.

For once the night was clear and I could see a sliver of the new moon and two stars. I could see my breath in the air.

'We could call him on his cell,' I suggested as I got in Ian's car.

'He doesn't have a cell,' Ian replied. I must have given him a look because he said, 'He likes to keep on the low-by. He uses a calling card or sometimes he buys one of those prepaid phones.' He turned the car on and lit a cigarette. I lit one too. 'If you want to speak to him we're going to have to go out there.'

'I could talk to him tomorrow.' I really didn't want to go another night without sleep if I could help it. I was past my limit as it was.

'He might not be back.'

'What? He's getting on a plane to Japan in the a.m.?' Although the way things were going that wouldn't surprise me.

Ian explained. 'Bays gets on a roll, he keeps going. He wins, he gets drunk, does some coke to celebrate. He loses, he gets drunk, does some coke to forget. Whichever way it goes he's usually out of commission for three, four, five days. That's why I fired him. The guy can't hold a job.'

I nodded. I was familiar with people like that. Too familiar.

'So what do you want to do?' Ian asked. 'Turning Stone or home?'

I wanted to say 'home', but I said 'Turning Stone' instead. The sooner I got this cleared up the better.

I mean what the hell? Let's get real. I probably wouldn't be able to sleep anyway.

The ride out to Turning Stone took about forty-five minutes from Spring and Butternut. We got on the Thruway in Liverpool and headed east. The Thruway was empty except for the big semis rolling along at eighty miles an hour, hell-bent on getting where they had to go, and the occasional passenger car.

About ten minutes into the trip Ian produced a joint and asked me if I wanted to share it. It had been a while. I'd liked it back in the day and I figured my feeling wouldn't change, so I said yes. It was just like I remembered it. Even a little bit nicer. A little more relaxing. I spent the rest of the time staring out the window, watching the signs flash by, and thinking about nothing much at all.

We got off at exit thirty-three and made a left. I could see the new hotel in the distance. Turning Stone had started out with bingo in a trailer after the Oneida Indians decided not to wait for New York State to settle its land claims.

Those still aren't settled, but in the meanwhile, Turning Stone has grown and grown and grown. It's now an enormous resort complex with gambling, a stage, restaurants, and a golf course. It has two hotels, one of which is the tallest structure in the area. I read recently that Turning Stone makes over a billion dollars a year profit. I don't know if that's true, but I'm sure it's pretty close.

People come there from all over the area. I'm not one of them. I have many vices but I'm not a gambler. At least, not in this way. If I had plenty of money, maybe. But I never do. What money I have I like to keep hold of. In fact, this was only the third time I'd been there.

The parking lots were crowded even at that time of night and I wondered how we were going to find Bays.

'This is when the serious gamblers play,' Ian commented as he parked his car. 'That way they won't get distracted by someone who doesn't know what they're doing.'

'Why does that matter?'

He pocketed the keys. 'It's distracting. It affects your concentration.'

I shot him a look. 'You play a lot?'

Ian looked back at me. 'Not more than I can afford, if that's what you're asking.'

I put up my hands. 'Not my business.'

'You're right. It isn't, but I'm telling you anyway.'

And he pulled the door open and we went inside. We walked down a corridor of restaurants and shops, all of which were closed at this time of night. The biggest of the shops sold tax-free cigarettes.

The Oneidas did a big business with that. They did mail-order too. You could order cartons over the Internet. Right now New York State was trying to close that down, but the case was still in the courts and probably would remain so for a long time. Each side appealed and appealed and appealed again.

Ian and I kept going. I felt as if I was walking on a golf course: the carpet was as thick and springy as sod. The walls

were hung with unmemorable pictures. The corridor ended
in the game room. There was a blaze of color and motion.
There were rows of slot machines, and roulette and blackjack tables. The low hum of people talking pervaded the air.

'I guess we should start looking,' I said.

'Don't bother.' Ian nodded towards the third blackjack
table. 'See the guy with the pierced ear? The one with the
bandage on his arm? The one wearing the black hoodie and
the sagging pants?'

I nodded. I didn't recognize him as the person who'd put
the matchbook in my mailbox, but like I said, it had been
late and I'd only gotten a quick glimpse before he'd got in
his car and sped away.

'That's him.'

Ian started walking towards him and I followed. There
were three other people at the table; one guy was white and
the other two were Chinese, but I kept my eyes on Bays. He
was concentrating on the cards on the table. His eyes never
left them. He gestured to the dealer once in a while and the
dealer would put another card down. He had a pile of chips
in front of him. Just as we got there the dealer pushed some
chips toward him, swept the old cards away and started
dealing out a new hand.

Ian didn't say anything when he got to where Bays was.
Just stood there and waited for Bays to turn around. After
another deal, Bays did.

Ian smiled. 'Long time no see.'

'What do you want?' Bays asked him.

Ian's grin grew. 'That's downright rude.'

'I repeat. What do you want?'

Ian pointed at me. 'I believe she got a message from you.'

Bays glanced at me and then glanced away. He didn't look
surprised, but he didn't look unsurprised either.

'I don't even know her. How can I send her a message?'

Ian turned to me. 'Show him, Robin.'

I dug the matchbook out of my jacket pocket. 'You left
this in my mailbox.'

'What are you, nuts?' Bays asked me. 'I don't even know
who you are, much less where you live. Why the hell would
I put that in your mailbox?'

'Someone did,' Ian told him.

'It's just a crummy matchbook. It was probably in there all along and she just never noticed it before. Maybe the postman put it there, maybe the delivery guy did.'

'No. I don't think so,' Ian told him. He took the matchbook out of my hand and opened the cover. 'No one lights cigarettes like that except you.'

'Don't be ridiculous,' Bays scoffed. 'Lots of people do that.'

'I've never seen anyone,' Ian said.

'Well, I'm sorry, but I'm playing here.'

'You can play after we talk.'

'I don't think so,' Bays said.

'Well, I do,' Ian replied. 'And while you're at it you can pay me the money you owe me.'

'What money?' Bays snarled.

'The money I advanced you so you could get your car fixed. Three hundred and eighty-five dollars.'

'I don't remember no three hundred dollars.'

'Three hundred and eighty-five dollars and ninety-two cents to be exact,' Ian corrected.

Bays turned back to the blackjack table.

'Last chance,' Ian warned.

'Forget it,' Bays said.

Then he made a mewling noise. It took me a minute to realize Ian was digging his thumb into Bays' funny bone. Bays was turning white.

'My friend has a question to ask you,' Ian told him, 'and she'd really appreciate an answer. Especially since we drove all this way to see you. And I, of course, would like my money back. Now.'

I could see beads of sweat forming on Bays' forehead. I could hear Ian telling me, it's all about pressure points.

'It seems to me you've done very well here,' Ian observed. 'But you're looking very tired. Maybe you should take a break. Unless, of course, you'd like me to unstitch your stitches for you.'

Bays shook his head.

'Good.' Ian released his grip. But he still stayed near enough so he could grab Bays again if he changed his mind. The whole thing was over in a second.

'That wasn't necessary,' Bays gasped.

Ian shrugged. 'Obviously I thought it was. Let's walk, shall we. And take four hundred dollars' worth of chips with you.'

'Everything fine?' the dealer asked Bays. His face was expressionless.

'Now or later?' Ian said sotto voce in Bays' ear. 'Your choice.'

Bays bobbed his head up and down. 'Everything's okey dokey,' he said to the dealer. 'Reserve a spot for me, will you?'

The dealer nodded. Bays quickly counted his chips, kept four hundred dollars' worth, and pushed the rest of them towards the dealer, who put them off to the side of the table. Then Bays followed Ian back out to the corridor. He was rubbing his elbow as he went.

'I was on a roll,' he whined.

'Like I care,' Ian said. 'Your money is all going to go up your nose anyway. Just be happy I'm not charging you interest on what you owe me.'

He held out his hand.

'That was money you owed me for working overtime,' Bays griped.

Ian didn't say anything. He just kept staring at Bays. Finally Bays put the chips in Ian's hand. Ian counted them and put them in his pocket.

'Thank you. Now tell Robin what you have to say and I'll let you get back to your game.'

Bays started pulling at his hair. 'I don't know what you're talking about.'

He looked to me as if he was telling the truth.

Ian turned to me. 'He works at Wonder Women. He's one of the bartenders, right, Bays?'

'Right,' Bays said.

I was beginning to see where this was going.

'You ever wait on Benny Gibson?' I asked.

'Once in a while,' Bays said. 'I was usually off when he was on.'

'He ever get into a fight with anyone?'

Bays shook his head. 'Not that I heard. When I was there

he never did anything. He just sat there and drank his fruit juice.'

'Did he have a special girl?'

'If he did I didn't know about it.'

'What about his brother?'

'His brother's a nut job.'

'Did they get along OK?'

'I got the strong impression they didn't like each other much.'

'What about the guys that Benny hung out with?'

'What about them?'

'I'm curious who they are.'

Bays shrugged. 'Can't tell you.'

Ian looked at him. 'Can't or won't?'

'I told you I'm not on much when they come in.'

I pointed to the initials on the inside cover of the matchbook. 'What about these?'

'What about them?'

'What do they stand for?'

'You got me,' Bays said.

'So you didn't write them?'

'Why should I?'

I changed the subject. 'Did Benny do any drugs?'

'Everyone does drugs.'

'What kind did he like?'

'Mostly pills, some coke.'

'Do you know who would want him killed?' I asked.

'Well,' Bays said, 'he owed money to a lot of people. He was about to be investigated. Maybe someone was afraid he'd shoot his mouth off.'

'Like who?' Ian asked him.

Bays shrugged. 'Don't know.'

'Can you tell me anything? Anything at all?'

'From what I heard his daughter wasn't real fond of him. Thought he drove her mom to drink.'

'Maybe he did,' I said.

Bays folded his arms over his chest.

'Anything else about her?'

'I heard she was selling E to some of her father's business associates.'

'I guess she was really pissed at him,' Ian said.

'I guess so,' Bays agreed. 'Now can I get back to my game?'

'Just answer one question for me,' Ian said.

'What's that?' Bays asked.

'Who put the matchbook in Robin's mailbox?'

'We already went through that.' Bays chewed on the inside of his cheek for a moment while he thought. Finally he said, 'Maybe Melody.'

'Not unless Melody has metamorphosed,' I said.

Bays smiled. 'Weird shit happens all the time.'

Ian stepped closer to Bays. 'Tell me something. Have you ever told the truth in your life?'

'I don't know what you mean.'

'Robin didn't see Melody, she saw you putting the matchbook in her mailbox.'

'She's wrong.'

'I don't think so. Was anything you told us true?'

Bays nodded. 'All of it.'

He sounded very convincing to me.

Ian studied his face for a moment. Bays began to fidget. 'I could find out, you know,' Ian told him.

'Go ahead,' Bays sneered.

'And then when I find out you're lying I could make it so you never use your right arm or hand again. Would you like that?'

Bays shook his head.

'Of course you wouldn't,' Ian continued. 'Who would? But I'm not going to do that because it's bad karma. I would have twenty years ago. Twenty years ago I liked to hurt people, but not now. Now I don't like it. And I don't do it. Unless it's absolutely necessary.'

Bays stared at Ian for a moment. Then he sidled around him with a curious crablike motion. Ian watched him go. He looked as if he had enjoyed himself.

'Come on,' Ian said when Bays was out of sight. 'I'm going to cash in these chips and then we're going home.'

'How did you know Bays was lying?' I asked Ian as we walked back in the Casino.

'I didn't.'

'Then why did you say that?'

'To see what he would say.'

'Because I thought he was telling the truth.'

'Maybe he is. Or maybe he's just a very good liar.'

'You know him. Is he?'

'Sometimes.'

'But why would he bother with something like this? It's so elaborate.'

Ian shrugged. 'Don't know. Maybe Melody showed him the money you gave her and he figured he could get some too. Maybe he did it because he wanted to make himself important. Hard to say. And as for the elaborate part – not really. He knows you know me and he figured that you'd show me the matchbook.'

'That's a lot of ifs.'

'Not really.'

'So that stuff about Janet was a lie?'

We were now at the cashier's window. Ian took Bays' chips out of his pocket and pushed them towards the woman on the other side of the counter with the tips of his fingers. 'Large, please,' he said to her.

She counted out four crisp hundred-dollar bills and handed them to him.

'I like fifties and hundreds,' Ian explained as he folded them up and put them in his pants pocket. 'They're neater.'

He started for the exit.

'You haven't answered my question,' I reminded him as I hurried along beside him.

Ian turned to me. 'With Bays you never know. The stuff about Janet might be true. Or it might not.'

'I don't get it,' I told him. And I didn't.

'Get what?'

By now we were near the exit.

'If you knew Bays was like that, why did we even bother coming out here?'

Ian looked at me as if I was crazy. 'Obviously so I could get my money back. I've been looking for that little creep for a long time, but every time he sees me he runs out the back door.'

I wanted to kill him. Not Bays. Ian.

'So this was all a scam so you could get your money back?' I asked Ian.

Ian grinned and put his hands up. 'Now don't be harsh. You had a nice ride out. You're going to have a nice ride back. You got a little stoned. Found an answer to one of your questions.' He put out his hand.

'What's that for?' I asked.

'Money for gas.'

I stared at him in amazement. 'You've got to be kidding.'

'Not at all. I helped you solve a mystery. It seems only fair that you should pay for the gas out here and back.'

'Do the words "unmitigated gall" mean anything to you?'

Ian smiled cheerfully. 'You're not the first person to say that to me.'

'And I bet I won't be the last.'

'Probably not.'

'You think he could have been the one that was following me?'

Ian lit a cigarette while he considered the idea.

'It's a possibility,' he said.

'But not a strong one.'

'No,' he conceded. 'Not a strong one.'

Twenty-Two

I slept badly that night. I spent the four hours I was asleep dreaming I was swimming in a pond filled with viscous green scum. It stuck to my goggles so I couldn't see where I was going and clogged my nose, making it hard to breathe. Which pretty much described the way I felt things were going in the real world. Then the alarm went off and I awoke with a crushing feeling in my chest only to realize that I had twenty pounds of cat sleeping on me. When I tried to push James off, he turned around and hissed.

'Sorry, bud,' I said as I sat up.

James shot me a dirty look and stalked off to the bottom of the bed and lay down next to Zsa Zsa.

I hit the snooze button and went back to sleep. Ten minutes later I hit it again. I did it one last time, then forced myself to get out of bed. As I got dressed I thought about last night. It seemed to me I'd reached a dead end. I didn't know any more now than I did then. I just had more questions. One of my high-school teachers had said that education was a process of finding more questions to ask. That was fine in theory, but it wasn't fine in this case.

The only lead I thought I had concerning John's photos had dried up. I still didn't know anything about Janet Gibson, and I was beginning to develop a sore throat, which always happened when I didn't get enough sleep for two or three days running. I gargled with salt water, which while disgusting is effective, and thought about the list I had made the other night.

Among other things I'd listed was going to speak to Joe Gibson again and talking to Carrie Walmouth about Janet Gibson. I'd heard what her daughter had said, now I was interested in getting her perspective. And I also needed to speak to Trent and find out if he knew what jobs John had held in the past.

I made my calls as I drove to the shop. Neither Joe Gibson nor Trent were answering their phones. I left messages on their voicemail, and dialed Carrie Walmouth's number. She picked up on the first ring. I explained who I was and asked if she could manage to see me.

She told me she had a yoga class at ten and a facial at eleven, but she would be happy to meet me for lunch at a place on East Genesee Street called the Moon at one thirty. I told her I'd be there and hung up. Then I looked down at what I was wearing. Old jeans. A flannel shirt over a white T-shirt. Scuffed-up black boots. My old, stained leather jacket. Oh well. They would just have to do. I didn't have time to turn around and change.

I parked in front of the shop and let Zsa Zsa out of the car. She ran around for a little while, checking things out, and then we went in the shop together. I spent the morning waiting on customers, stocking shelves, and doing paperwork.

I left Noah's Ark about one fifteen. One of the advantages of living in a place like Syracuse is that everything is pretty close by, but I got snarled up in a detour around a water-main break and by the time I found a place to park I was almost ten minutes late.

The Moon was a pretty little spot that judging by its appearance and clientele catered to ladies who lunch. The walls were painted in pale peach and pale green, while the tables were a deep burnished orange, and the floor was a black-and-white checkerboard. Ceramic vases with daisies on them sat on the tables.

I spotted Carrie the moment I walked in. Her daughter looked just like her. She was a pretty, well-cared-for woman in her late forties to early fifties. Her blonde hair was swept back in a ponytail, her skin glowed with health, her smile was white, and her body well toned. She was wearing yoga pants, a zip-up jacket, and lavender Uggs. Her sheepskin coat was slung over the extra chair. Her Louis Vuitton bag was snuggled next to it. Everything about her said money and plenty of it. God, how I wished I'd gone home and changed my clothes.

'Robin Light?' she asked in a cordial voice as I approached the table.

I nodded and she put out her hand. We shook. Her skin felt dry and cool.

'Why don't you order?' she suggested. As I studied the menu she said, 'I like the greens and beans soup.'

'I guess I'll go with that,' I told her.

She smiled again and I went up and placed my order. The woman behind the counter said she'd serve it to me. I nodded and sat back down.

'So,' Carrie said. She smiled again.

I decided she smiled a lot as I smiled back.

'You've already talked to my daughter.'

'And I want to thank you for that.'

Carrie nodded absentmindedly. The lady behind the counter brought my soup. As I looked down at it I realized two things: one, this soup was the first healthy thing I'd eaten in at least a month and two, I really didn't like it. I took a spoonful anyway and managed to choke it down.

'Good, isn't it?' Carrie asked.

'Wonderful,' I agreed.

Carrie took another spoonful and swallowed. 'So I'm just wondering why you want to speak to me since you've already spoken to Wendy.'

'I thought maybe you could provide a different perspective.'

'What did my daughter say?'

'Not much really. She called Janet a loser.'

'And?'

'She said she had problems with food and alcohol.'

'Anything else?'

'She said that a girl called Andrea Thompson might know where Janet was, but she didn't know where Andrea Thompson was.'

'Hmm,' Carrie Walmouth said. She conveyed another spoonful of soup to her mouth, swallowed, and dabbed at her lips with her napkin. 'It's funny how people turn out,' she mused.

I waited. While I waited I ate a piece of the slice of bread that had come with the soup. At least that was good.

'I could have sworn Janet was going to grow up and run the family business. I know her dad wanted her to.'

Carrie picked off a small crumb of bread and nibbled at it.

'So what happened?' I asked.

'I think Janet's parents happened to her.'

'So was she using drugs?'

'That was the rumor I heard,' Carrie said.

'Do you think it's true?'

'Let's just say it wouldn't surprise me if it were.'

'One of the neighbors told me Janet said she was going off to Vegas. Do you know if she has any family or friends there?'

Carrie shook her head. 'Not that I know of. I think most of her family is on the east coast.'

'How about Andrea Thompson?'

Carrie tapped her front tooth with her fingernail. 'If I remember correctly her mother lives over in East Syracuse.'

'I don't suppose you have an address?'

'No. But her name is Sylvia Stiles. That's Stiles with an "I". She should be in the phonebook.'

I was about to thank her but her attention was suddenly focused on what she was seeing out the window. I followed her gaze.

'My husband,' she murmured.

He was getting out of a shiny Cadillac Escalade. He was a tall, good-looking guy with perfectly regular features, the kind of guy you'd see in golf ads. I looked at Carrie's face. She didn't look happy to see him. Then I looked at her hands. She was compulsively picking at her pinkie with her forefinger. She looked even unhappier when it was clear he was coming in. She turned and gave me a bright, insincere smile.

'What an unexpected treat.'

There was a bitter undertone to her words.

'I'll leave you to it, then,' I told her.

She nodded and went back to eating her soup. I could tell she was relieved I was going. I got my belongings together and went to the counter to pay. By the time I was done Richard Walmouth was through the door. I watched him make a beeline for his wife. The closer he got, the more she seemed to shrink into herself. If he noticed, he didn't seem to care.

Not a good marriage, I decided as I slid into my car and started it up. The heater wasn't working all that well and I rubbed my hands to warm them. Then I drove to one of the gas stations on Erie Boulevard and filled up, after which I got a Big Mac and looked up Sylvia Stiles in the phonebook.

Carrie Walmouth was right. She was listed and she lived in East Syracuse. I copied the address down on the back of my checkbook. Then I glanced at my watch. It was still early. I had time to take a run out there.

Twenty-Three

S ylvia Stiles lived in a little house on Baggot Street. It was one of two houses on the block. The rest of the structures were warehouses. The house itself was made of cinderblocks and painted a light blue. It looked as if it were no more than three rooms. I wouldn't be surprised if it had been a garage in its past life.

It was surrounded by a white picket fence. Someone had tried to plant cedars by the posts, but they had died. Now they lay there, brown and dried out, a memento mori to good intentions. The driveway was broken up and pieces of asphalt and gravel intermixed. A rusted-out old Taurus sat in the driveway, which meant that someone was probably home.

I got out, rang the bell, and waited. A moment later the door opened and a tiny woman appeared. She was four foot ten inches at most. She was wearing striped yellow-and-purple leggings, a long black turtleneck, and pink ankle boots. Her vermilion hair was in two pigtails. She had on a lot of black eyeliner and mascara and not much else in the way of makeup.

'Yes?' she said, looking up at me.

'Sylvia Stiles?'

She nodded.

'Carrie Walmouth said you might be able to help me out.'

'Now there's a name from the past.' And she cocked her head and waited.

'I'm looking for Janet Gibson. I've been told that your daughter might be able to help me find her.'

She narrowed her eyes. 'And why would she want to do that?'

I could have lied – I thought about it for a moment – but I decided to tell the truth. I had a feeling it would get me further than any story I could invent.

'She accused me of murdering her father and I want to find out why.'

Sylvia's eyebrows shot up. 'So let me ask the obvious question. Did you?'

'Of course not.'

She grunted. 'I don't think so either. You don't give off that kind of aura.' She stopped speaking and surveyed me. 'But you could hurt someone if you had to. In fact, you have.'

'That's true,' I replied.

I was about to ask her why she had said that when she smiled. 'What can I say? I have the gift.' She motioned for me to come in. 'I'll see if I can get Andrea on the phone.' Then she added, 'Janet always did have a flair for the dramatic.'

Sylvia turned and walked away and I followed her inside. I was in her living room. The walls were a bright, pulsing pink. The sofa and chair were a pale orange. Somehow it all worked.

'It's so bleak in the winter here I think one needs some color,' she explained as she went into the kitchen.

That room was ice blue. She picked up the phone and dialed. After a moment she shook her head.

'Andrea isn't answering. I'd leave a message but her message box is full. You can catch her at the coffee place on Marshall Street if you want. She'll be getting off of work in a half-hour.'

I looked at my watch. I still had time. 'How will I recognize her?' I asked.

Sylvia grinned. 'She looks like me only she's three inches taller.'

'So she won't be hard to pick out.'

'Nope. She stands out in a crowd.'

'What do you think of Janet?' I asked Sylvia as she walked me to the door.

'I think she's a girl with issues.'

'What kind of issues?'

Sylvia looked pensive for a moment. Then she said, 'I'm going to let Andrea tell you about them. After all, she knows Janet a lot better than I do.'

'Do you have an idea where she'd go in Las Vegas?'

'None. It's a transient city. People come and go there all the time.'

I wondered if that's why Janet had picked it.

I made it to Marshall Street in ten minutes and spent another ten looking for a parking space. The street was crowded with college kids taking a break from their classes. Just seeing them milling around made me feel like an old lady. College seemed an eon ago. I had been another person then, a person I think I liked better than the one I'd become. I'd certainly been more stylishly dressed.

I went inside and looked around. Andrea wasn't behind the counter. Maybe she was changing in the back room. Of course, she might have already left, but I'd find that out soon enough. I stood in line and I got a medium cappuccino. Then I added two packets of sugar, and took a sip. It wasn't great, but it was good enough. I went outside to wait.

I was leaning against the lamp post sipping my coffee when I spotted Andrea Thompson. Her mother was right. Andrea did look a lot like her. She dressed like her too. She was wearing a bright yellow coat, black tights, and purple suede boots with four-inch wedges. Her hair was dyed a matching purple and she'd pulled it up so it was sticking straight out of her head. The glasses she had on were over-sized tortoiseshell. And she didn't look fat. Not even remotely. If this was what Wendy Walmouth called fat, I'd hate to see what she called thin.

'Andrea,' I called out. 'Andrea Thompson.'

She turned and looked at me.

Then she came over. She took off her headphones. I could still hear the music playing. That's how loud it was.

'Do I know you?' she asked.

'No.' And I told her the same story I'd told her mom.

Andrea nodded her head in time to the music while she listened to me.

'That is so not cool,' she said when I was done.

'Why would she do something like that?'

'Don't know.' Andrea pressed a button on her iPod and the music stopped. 'But I'll tell you one thing. Janet's definitely fucked-up,' she said as I followed her down the street. 'Majorly so.'

She stopped in front of a pizza joint called Augies.

'I'm getting a slice,' she told me. 'If you want to talk to me while I eat it you can. After that I have to go hang a show downtown.'

'You paint?' I asked.

Andrea nodded. 'And how. I'm going down to Brooklyn this summer and working in a gallery.' She grinned. She had the same smile as her mother. 'I'm blowin' this joint, man. I'm outta here.'

I grinned back and grabbed a table. A moment later Andrea returned with her slice of cheese on whole wheat. It looked good and smelled even better. I began to wish I hadn't had a Big Mac. I debated about getting a slice, but common sense finally won out.

Andrea fanned the pizza to cool it off. 'They have the best pizza in here. So what do you want to know about Janet?' she asked.

'For openers, do you have any idea where she is?'

'Well, the last time I heard from her, she was about to go off to some sort of place in Utah.'

'Utah? She told her neighbor she was going to Vegas.'

Andrea took a bite. She wiped a string of cheese off her chin. 'She's interested in becoming a Mormon. I don't think there are any Mormons in Vegas.'

'Mormon?'

'Yup.'

'You're kidding, right?'

'Not hardly. She's been talking about it for a while with me.'

'When did you talk to her?'

'About two days ago.'

Interesting.

'Do you have a number where she can be reached?'

Andrea shook her head. 'She said she'd call when she got a chance. If she calls I'll tell her to get in touch with you.'

'OK.' It wasn't great but it was the best offer I had so far. 'Wendy Walmouth said she did drugs.'

'Now that's a big fat lie,' Andrea cried.

When I first started in this business I might have believed her, but now I could hear the defensive tone in her voice.

'Wendy Walmouth is a preppie loser,' she continued. 'She's never liked Janet.'

'I heard Janet sold E.'

Andrea put her slice of pizza down. 'It really pisses me off when people say things like that.'

'So you don't think it's true?'

'I can't think of anything more ridiculous.'

'Why?'

'Because it's not something she would do.'

'Maybe she's just not telling you.'

'She's my friend.'

I thought about John. 'Sometimes people do things they don't want their friends to know about.'

My comment must have hit home because Andrea frowned. She pulled a piece of cheese off the top of her pizza and popped it in her mouth.

'I refuse to believe that,' she said when she was done chewing. But she wasn't as sure as the first time she said it.

'Would you have believed she would accuse me of killing her father?'

'That's different. She was very upset. She saw you around the house. What else was she going to conclude?'

'How did she see me?'

Andrea's frown grew deeper. 'What do you mean, how? You were there.'

'I mean my friend and I drove by her father's place twice. We didn't stop. It was dark out. I'm asking how she knew it was me.'

Andrea picked another piece of cheese off her pizza and rolled it into a ball. 'What does that have to do with Janet dealing drugs? If she's dealing drugs. Which I'm not saying she is.'

'Nothing.'

Andrea leaned back in her chair. 'But you think the two things are related?'

'Just a theory.'

'Which is?'

'Maybe someone caught her selling stuff and she blew me in to get herself out of it.'

'That's pretty far-fetched.'

'I know it is. On the other hand, she left town pretty suddenly. Why would she do something like that if she weren't in some kind of trouble?'

'She was in shock.' But Andrea didn't sound convinced.

'She was functional enough to pack herself up and leave,' I pointed out.

Andrea broke off a piece of crust and nibbled on it. 'Janet used to eat chocolate all the time . . . She was addicted to chocolate. I haven't talked to her much in the last five months. I've been really busy and so has she . . . I don't know. There was this guy she was going out with. From what she said he seemed kind of sketchy.'

'How so?'

'He was into raves.'

That was probably how Janet got into dealing, I decided.

Andrea smoothed out her napkin. 'He worked as a bouncer in one of the strip clubs.'

'Wonder Women?'

'That doesn't sound familiar.'

'Did you ever meet him?'

'No. But she liked him a lot. I could tell that by the way she talked about him.'

'Do you have a name for him?'

'Jay.'

'Jay what?'

'I think that's his street name.'

'You wouldn't happen to know his real name, would you?'

Andrea shrugged. 'You know how it is. I never had a reason to ask. It wasn't like she was bringing him home to her dad.'

'Given what you've told me, I'm surprised she didn't.'

Andrea reached over, grabbed the shaker full of oregano, and sprinkled some on what was left of her slice. 'She wanted to, but Jay wasn't having any.'

'Anything else you can think of?'

'Like what?' Andrea spread her hands on the table. They were long and narrow, artist's hands.

'If there was one thing I needed to know about her, what do you think that would be?'

Andrea thought for a moment. Then she said, 'She was really conflicted. Her dad wanted her to go into the business with him. He put a lot of pressure on her, but she really didn't want to, only she couldn't say no. So she did things to piss him off.'

'Like dealing drugs.'

Andrea nodded. 'I hate to say it, but when you put it in that context, you could be right.'

'I could see why she wouldn't like real estate.'

'No. She liked real estate. She found it really interesting. That wasn't it at all. It was her father's real-estate company she didn't like. She said she couldn't stand his business practices. She loved him, but hated what he did.'

'In what way?'

'She never mentioned specifics.'

I thought about what Trent had told me about his dealings with Benny Gibson. Then I thought about how the state was getting ready to investigate Gibson.

'Go on,' I prompted.

Andrea took a bite of her slice and chewed. She chewed for a long time.

'That's it,' she said after she'd swallowed.

'It didn't leave her in a good position, did it?' I said.

'No. It didn't at all. One other thing.'

I waited.

'I don't know if this is true or not, but someone told me Janet was getting her Ecstasy from some stripper in Wonder Women.'

Andrea didn't have a name but at least I was beginning to feel as if I were making a little progress.

On the way back to the pet store I called Calli and asked her if she could put me in contact with a reporter on the paper called Otto Cody. He knew all about real-estate transactions in the city and I figured it would be interesting to hear what he had to say about B & J Real Estate, LLC.

'We're on for a late dinner tomorrow night,' she told me when she called me back twenty minutes later. 'Otto suggested Ryan's.'

'Works for me,' I told her.

'Good. We'll meet you there at eight thirty. And by the way, you're buying.'

'I figured as much.'

It would be worth it. Otto was one of those people who knew everyone and everything and after a few drinks he'd tell you all about them. He was also a notorious cheapskate.

Twenty-Four

At eight thirty in the evening Otto Cody shook my hand, gave a slight bow, and slid into the booth opposite Calli and me. We were sitting in the dining room at Ryan's. In New York City, restaurants would just be getting busy, but Syracuse was an early dining city and the place was fairly empty.

Ryan's was an old-style restaurant/bar that had been doing business on the North Side for the past fifty years. It had pressed-tin ceilings, lace curtains on the windows, lots of finished oak, a bartender who knew how to pour a drink, and a cook who turned out tasty food at reasonable prices. In short, it was the kind of place that would never go out of style.

The waitress came over a few minutes later and handed Otto a menu. He handed it back just as fast.

'I only have one thing here,' he explained to us as he ordered a martini, a medium-rare steak with cottage fries, and a house salad with blue-cheese dressing. 'And reserve a piece of the raspberry pie,' he instructed the waitress. 'And don't be frugal with the whipped cream, dear. Glop it on.'

Calli ordered a glass of merlot, the osso bucco, and a green salad, while I asked for a medium steak with a side of garlic mashed potatoes and a Beck's. It seemed like the right beer for a place like this. The waitress left to get our drinks and place our order and I leaned back and studied Otto.

He looked the same as he had eight years ago. He had the same pouches under his eyes, the same salt-and-pepper hair, the same cheap haircut, the same mole on his left cheek, the same brownish teeth, the same white shirt with

the stains on it, the same clip-on bowtie. Maybe his nose
and his gut were a little bigger, but that was about it.

'As you can see my looks haven't improved with age,'
he said to me. 'Neither has my temperament, for that matter.'

'I guess I could say that about myself as well,' I replied.

'Untrue, my dear,' Otto said. 'You're looking less scruffy
than you used to.'

'Scruffy?' I said.

'Scruffy,' Otto repeated. 'It's a perfectly good word.'

'I'm not saying it isn't. I'm just not sure it applies to
me.'

'Well, what would you call someone who wears three-
day-old clothes and doesn't brush her hair?'

'I was never that bad,' I said.

'Maybe I'm exaggerating a bit but there were times when
you came close. My job as a writer is to find the right
words and I am very good at my job. When I want to be.'
He paused while the waitress set down his martini in front
of him. He took a sip and smiled. 'My compliments to the
bar wench,' he told the waitress while she set the drinks in
front of Calli and me. As she turned to go, he gave her a
light pat on the ass. I expected her to turn around and bop
him one. Instead she smiled at him. He winked at her.

'I can't believe you did that,' I said.

'Meg likes that sort of thing, don't you?' he asked our
waitress.

She snorted. 'You're a dinosaur.'

'Which is a good thing to strive for these days,' he replied.
He took another sip of his drink.

'That kind of thing will get you fired at work,' Calli told
him.

Otto sat back in his seat and crossed his arms over his
chest. 'Bring on the white-light Nazis and the politically
correct brigade,' he cried. 'I'm ready for them.'

Calli just shook her head and took a sip of her wine.

Otto took a gulp of his martini.

'I had to give up my typewriter and work on that ridiculous thing they call a word processor. I have to deal with
emails and telephone trees and cellphones with tiny buttons
I have trouble pressing. I have to deal with answering

machines. I can't smoke cigars in public anymore, I can't
have coffee, I'm not supposed to have red meat, a stricture
I reject, or indulge in desserts of any sort. If I can't give
a lovely lady a pat on her fanny from time to time, what
is there left to live for? Besides,' he added, 'Meg and I are
old friends.'

'I figured as much,' I told Otto. I'd forgotten how much
I liked him.

He finished his martini and signaled to Meg to bring him
another.

'Maybe you should slow down,' I told him.

He waved my objections away. 'Years of practice, my
dear. Years of practice have honed my tolerance to a fine
edge. Calli tells me you want to know all about Benny and
Joe Gibson.'

I nodded and took a sip of my Beck's.

'Is this because you were set up?'

'I think it's safe to say that.'

'And also that your friend John was the one who set you
up. And you want to know why he did that?'

I nodded again.

'And you think that finding out about Benny Gibson will
help you in these endeavors?'

'Correct again.'

'But you haven't been charged.'

'Not yet.'

Otto ran a finger around the edge of his martini glass.
'Have they instituted a search warrant on your house?'

'Not yet.'

'That's a good sign.'

'I know, but I'm the only thing they've got and a bird
in the hand . . .'

'Is worth two in the bush,' Otto finished for me.

'Exactly.' I drank a little more of my Beck's. It was
hoppy. Which I liked.

'So who do you think killed Benny Gibson?' he asked
me.

'I don't know.'

Otto raised an eyebrow. 'Surely you have some idea.'

'A general theory. A very general theory. From what I've

been hearing, Benny Gibson's business practices weren't the best. I'm guessing that he pissed someone off.'

'Which is why you want to talk to me.'

I nodded. 'I'm hoping you can point me in a general direction.'

Otto made a steeple with his fingers. 'As you no doubt know, there are two kinds of information: that which is provable and that which is not. I assume you're interested in both.'

'Absolutely.'

'I thought as much.'

Calli and I exchanged looks while Otto took a sip of his martini. I'd forgotten how much he liked to play the professor. He was big on the whole Socratic-method thing. I sat back and resigned myself to a long question-and-answer period.

Meg appeared with the salads. She'd included one for me even though I hadn't asked for it. Otto speared a cherry tomato on his fork and ate it. Then he ate a piece of lettuce.

'What do you know about Benny and Joe Gibson? Specifically.'

'Not too much, really,' I replied. I put a piece of lettuce in my mouth and chewed. Lettuce is one of those things I've never seen any reason for except to hold salad dressing. 'On a personal note, I gather that Benny and Joe didn't get along too well. Benny's wife has problems with alcohol and his daughter has problems with him. On the business side, the firm is in trouble financially. Benny was about to be investigated by the state. And there's a rumor he's linked to a casino that's going to be built.' I tapped my fingers against my teeth while I thought. 'I guess that's it.'

Otto ate one of the salad croutons. It crunched between his teeth.

'That rumor has been floating around for a long time, but the place where the casino is supposed to be built is a protected wetland and they are supposed to be sacrosanct. It's amazing though what the judicious application of cash will do to the hearts and minds of our legislators.'

Otto pushed his salad aside and took a piece of bread out of the basket Meg had just placed on the table. Then

he took out a square of butter, slowly unwrapped it, and
placed it on his plate. Then he began spreading the butter
on his bread. His gestures were short and precise.

'Well,' he said after he'd taken a bite. 'Benny's and Joe's
realty company owns fifteen buildings give or take. They're
mostly residential with a few office buildings. Many of
them are poorly managed; many of them have code violations that I don't think they can afford to fix. Right now,
it's more of a shell game. They use the money from one
building to pay the taxes on another, but they've gotten
further and further behind, so now they're in real trouble.'

I took a piece of bread and started eating. 'Why does
the city let them go on?'

'For the same reason,' Calli said, 'that a bank will go
after you when you can't pay your eight-hundred-dollar-a-
month mortgage, but will let someone who owes fifty thousand a month slide. In fact, they'll even offer them
assistance. The deeper in the hole you are, the more worried
the bank becomes, the more they'll let you skate.

'After all, they don't want to end up holding property.
The same is true of the city. They don't want to take back
buildings. Then they're off the tax rolls. Plus they don't
have the personnel or the expertise to manage them. So
they let things slide, they turn a blind eye to violations.'

'However,' Otto interrupted, 'a group of tenants from
three of the Gibson brothers' buildings banded together and
are suing the company – not that it matters because all the
buildings are owned by different LLCs, Limited Liability
Corporations, and there's no money in any of them. The
same group also went to the New York State Attorney
General and filed a complaint. The AG's office was getting
ready to investigate when Benny Gibson died.'

'OK. But why should that stop anything?' I asked. 'Joe
is still around.'

'True. But a couple of years ago, they split the buildings
up. Benny's are the ones that are being investigated. Joe's
aren't. Smart move on his part.' Otto lifted his martini and
drained the glass. He smacked his lips. 'The question is:
Should I have one more or should prudence prevail? I say
the hell with prudence.' And he raised his hand and snapped

his fingers. When Meg came over he pointed to his glass. 'Another, please.' Then he pointed to me. 'She will tip you handsomely.'

Meg grunted. 'I should have known you weren't drinking on your own dime.'

'Heaven forfend.' Otto folded his hands on the table and smiled complacently. 'I never have and I never will. I prefer to sing for my supper.'

'I prefer to pay for mine,' Meg told him as she left.

Otto leaned in. 'She's bitter because she had to pay for our motel room. Somehow or other I'd forgotten my wallet,' he confided. 'I don't think she's ever forgiven me.'

'Otto, you really are a piece of work,' Calli told him.

Otto took another bite of his bread. 'I've never denied that.'

'In fact you revel in it. Now get to the good stuff.'

'Am I boring you?' he asked Calli.

'No. But you're telling me things I already know,' Calli replied. 'I want to hear things that I don't know.'

Otto grinned. 'Are you telling me I need a better song and dance?'

Calli inclined her head. 'Indeed I am.'

Otto ate another piece of bread. 'Well, there are a couple of other things. All of them are highly speculative, you understand. You can't quote me on any of this.'

'I wasn't going to,' I told him.

'Good. There is one interesting rumor that has been circulating. As you said, Benny Gibson was supposed to be involved in this big casino or maybe big mall project with another realtor.'

'How can he be if he doesn't have any money?'

Otto shrugged. 'That's what I said.'

'And?'

'There's talk he has an account in the Cayman Islands, that he's been socking it away all these years.'

'Who is the developer?'

'Don't know.'

Calli took a sip of wine and put her glass down. 'This is what you consider interesting?'

'Yes, I do, because I heard that this guy hired Gibson to

burn down some of his buildings as well. Does that meet your specifications?'

'That's better.'

'Are you talking about the recent fires?' I asked him.

Otto nodded. There'd been three in the last six months, two on the North Side and one near the Armory. All three were warehouses. All three had been dubbed of suspicious origin by the fire department. In the last one, a vagrant had died.

'Yup,' Otto said. 'Including the one the guy died in.'

Wow. That was a biggie. 'And the police aren't doing anything?' I asked.

'Not at this time. They need something tangible and they haven't got it. They probably never will. Maybe that's because they're not pushing too hard. I've noticed that most police departments don't allocate too much of their resources to investigate the deaths of homeless people.'

I took a sip of my beer. 'I guess Benny Gibson wasn't a very nice guy.'

'And from what I've heard his brother wasn't much better,' Calli added.

Otto turned to me. 'So does any of this help you?' he asked.

'Definitely,' I told him.

I felt as if I was collecting pieces of the puzzle and next I had to see how they fit together.

'Have you talked to Benny's wife?' Otto asked. 'Maybe she could shed some light on the events.'

I drank the last of my Beck's and decided to order another.

'Of course I haven't talked to her,' I told Otto. 'She's in some rehab facility in Connecticut or Massachusetts or Pennsylvania or someplace like that.'

Otto laughed. 'Whatever gave you that idea? She's living off Comstock Avenue.'

'But everyone said . . .'

Otto waved his hand. 'They're wrong. She just doesn't want anyone to know she's returned. Actually, she's been back for the last four months. I'm sure she'll have lots of interesting things to tell you. When you speak to her, tell her that Otto Cody tenders his regards.'

I told him I would. Then Meg came with Otto's drink and our food and the conversation turned to Otto's three Burmese cats. Calli, Otto, and I spent the rest of the meal exchanging pet stories.

Twenty-Five

I drove over to see Martha Gibson the following afternoon. She wasn't listed in the phonebook so calling wasn't an option. And even if she had been I would have driven over anyway. Speaking to someone over the phone is no substitute for doing it face to face. You miss things if you do.

She lived in a plain little house in the outer university area. The house was one-story and painted an unattractive shade of gray. The paint was sloughing off the window frames, giving the place an uncared-for look. Three weed trees had self-seeded in the front yard and been left to grow with no regard to landscaping. A few strands of pastel pink and blue plastic eggs left over from last Easter languished on them, adding to the general impression of neglect.

I parked in front of the house and walked up the path. It hadn't been shoveled in a long time. The snow had packed down into an inch of ice. Footprints, both human and animal, were visible in it. There was a layer of hard pack snow on the three stairs up to the porch as well. I matched my steps to the footprints already in the snow. A shovel and a package of rock salt leaned against the railing. Neither had been used in a long time.

I rang the bell, which sounded out loud and clear. Given the general level of dishevelment, I was surprised that it still worked. A moment later the door opened. A plain-looking woman stood there. She must have been pretty when she was younger – the wide-set eyes and the high cheekbones bore testimony to that – but now the eyes were ringed with dark circles and there were hollows underneath the cheekbones.

Martha Gibson looked tired. More than tired. She looked

exhausted. As if the mere act of breathing was too much for her. She looked to be in her late fifties, although she was probably younger. She was thin and was beginning to get the first signs of a dowager's hump.

Her hair was mostly gray, with signs of light red here and there. It was long and needed a shaping. Her eyes were the color of dishwater. She was wearing an old navy sweatshirt. The collar and cuffs were frayed. Her sweat pants were gray and five sizes too big. When she brought her hands up to her chest I could see they were rough and chapped.

The door opened outward. I took a quick couple of steps into the doorway and leaned against it, effectively blocking her from closing the door on me.

'Martha Gibson?' I asked.

She took a step back, but she looked more annoyed than scared.

'Yes?' she said. There was no recognition of who I was.

I introduced myself. Still nothing. I gave her my best confidence-inducing smile. Contrary to what Ian said, most people actually like me.

'Otto Cody told me you might have interesting things to tell me about your husband.'

'You know Otto?'

'I bought him dinner last night. He said to tender his regards.'

A small smile broke out and was quickly smothered. She licked her lips. They were cracked.

'I don't know why he would have said that,' she complained. Her voice was high and weedy.

'He thought you could help me.' And I explained why.

She listened while I talked. I talked for a long time.

'So you're the person that my daughter accused of murdering my husband?' she said when I was finished.

'She said I was stalking him,' I told her.

'But the police questioned you?'

I nodded. She didn't seem that upset. In fact, she didn't seem upset at all. Interesting. As if she knew I didn't do it. Or she didn't care. Her next words confirmed my latter thought.

'He was a horrible man,' she said. 'And I'm glad he's dead. Does that shock you?'

'Not really,' I said.

After all, I'd felt that way about my stepfather. And I'd said as much to anyone who would listen.

'You know I haven't seen my daughter in years. She doesn't want anything to do with me.'

'I'm sorry.'

Martha shook her head. 'Nothing to be sorry about. I was a drunk. Drunks make terrible mothers. And now she's as screwed up as I was.' She rubbed her shoulders. She was getting cold standing in the doorway. 'Why do you think I can help you?' She sounded puzzled, as if she couldn't imagine anyone coming to her for anything.

'Otto thought you could answer some questions for me.'

She shook her head.

'No one knows that I'm here.'

Her answer was a non sequitur, but I let it go. 'Otto knows.'

'But no one else.'

I was going to say, not even the police, but I thought better of it. She was twitchy enough as it was and something told me that mentioning the police would just add to that.

Instead I asked her if I could come in, which was a formality because I was standing inside the house already. But she didn't seem to notice.

'I guess you can come in for a few minutes,' she said grudgingly.

She turned and padded down the hallway. I followed behind her. The hallway was papered in thick brown-and-white vertical stripes. The floor was composed of chipped brown and gray tiles colored white with salt residue. She led me into the living room. One side of the flowered yellow sofa was ripped to shreds.

'The place came fully furnished and the person who lived here before me had a cat,' she explained.

I looked around. The inside of the house was as bad as the outside. One of the club chairs next to the sofa had a tweed back and a plaid pillow, while the chair on the other side had been mended with duct tape. The coffee table looked as if it was going to fall over, as did the hutch. A giant television sat near the far wall dominating the room.

Martha followed my gaze. 'It doesn't work,' she explained. 'And it's too heavy to move.'

I nodded. So no television. I didn't see any newspapers. Maybe she didn't read them.

We stood still for a moment. I reached for my cigarettes and realized I'd left them in the car. I'd have to do without, because I had the feeling that if I left I wouldn't get back in. Finally Martha jerked her head towards the sofa. I took that as an invitation to sit down. She didn't invite me to take off my coat, but I did anyway and carefully laid it next to me. Martha sat down on the duct-taped chair and jumped back up. She seemed uneasy in my presence.

'I'm not used to being around people anymore,' she said. 'I don't go out much.'

'By choice or necessity?' I asked.

'Choice.' She sat back down. 'People make me nervous.'

'Did they always?'

'I think they did. I just didn't realize it before.'

We were silent for a moment. Then I said, 'Why was your husband a terrible person?'

Martha crossed one leg over the other. After a moment she recrossed them the opposite way.

'He just was.'

I waited. Eventually the silence got too much and she started talking again.

'He was a liar and a cheat. He stole my money and made bad investments. If it weren't for my money there wouldn't be a real-estate company and now I have nothing left.'

She stopped and looked around as if the words she uttered underlined the place she was staying in.

'What else?' I prompted.

'Nothing. Nothing else.'

But it was clear to me from the way her fingers were pulling at the bottom of her sweatshirt that that wasn't true.

'I think there was.'

She clamped her lips together and shook her head.

'Then why are you acting this way?'

'I'm not acting any way.'

But she was. She was acting like a woman with something to hide.

'Did he hit you? Did he abuse your daughter?'

Her fingers got more frantic. I'd hit the jackpot.

'I told you. He was a liar and a cheat. He made bad investments.' Martha's voice was shrill.

'Was he involved with the Mob?'

Her fingers relaxed. It was like she was hooked up to a
polygraph. 'I don't know what he did. I wasn't here. He sent
me away.'

'Why did he send you away?'

Her fingers started in again.

'He sent me away because I was a drunk.'

She acted as if she were reading off a script.

'Why did Otto think you'd have something to tell me that
I'd be interested in?'

'Don't know.'

I looked at her. This wasn't going anywhere. I decided to
change topics.

'What about your daughter?'

'I told you I don't know anything about her.'

'Nothing?'

Martha Gibson nodded. 'Benny said it was better that way.'
The fingers went into overdrive.

'And what did you think?'

'I tried not to think about her. There was nothing I could
do.'

'In what sense?'

Martha Gibson shook her head again. Somehow I didn't
think she was talking about helping her daughter pick out
the right prom dress.

'Nothing,' she repeated. 'Absolutely nothing.'

'So why did you come back here?'

Martha Gibson shook her head again. Her hands collapsed
in on themselves. She began rocking back and forth. Maybe
she knew where I was going with my next question.

'Do you own a gun?' I asked her.

She didn't answer. I watched her for a moment. She was
no longer focused on me. She was rocking back and forth.
I'd seen that kind of motion in small children when they

were very upset and in autistic adults. It's called self-calming. Either that or she was acting up a storm. A possibility I didn't discount.

I wanted to ask her if she'd killed her husband, if she'd come to his house and shot him. It would explain why he opened the door. He saw her and thought he had nothing to fear. It would explain why her daughter ran away. She couldn't deal with what her mother had done. Couldn't face giving testimony. It would explain why her daughter accused someone else. Me. What it didn't explain was how her daughter knew who I was. And the way things were going it looked as if there was a good chance I wasn't going to find out.

'Martha.'

She didn't answer. Just kept rocking back and forth.

'Can I get you a glass of water?'

Nothing.

I didn't feel as if I could leave her in her present state so I stepped out of the room and called Otto and explained the situation.

'I'll be right over,' he said.

He was as good as his word. Ten minutes later he walked through the door.

'She'll be fine,' he said after he'd looked at her. 'She just gets a little overwrought sometimes.'

'Maybe it's something else. Like a guilty conscience.'

'Don't be absurd,' Otto spluttered.

'She certainly has a motive. Wives have killed their husbands for far less.'

'In that case I should be dead. Marriage creates motives.'

'That's not an answer.'

'In the first place I'll testify she was with me at the time of Benny Gibson's death.'

'Was she really or will you just swear to it?'

Otto rolled his eyes. 'Really, Robin. Do you think I'd have given you this address if I thought there was the remotest chance she shot him?'

'No. But that doesn't mean she didn't.'

'I can't talk to you when you get like this,' he said and with that he walked into the living room.

When I let myself out I could see Otto sitting next to Martha on the sofa. He was stroking her hands and talking softly to her.

I got back in the car, turned it on, lit a cigarette, and inhaled. Finally. Addiction is a terrible thing. But what other substance jazzes you up, calms you down, and helps you to focus all at the same time? As I sat there Carrie Walmouth drifted through my mind.

At first I couldn't figure out why I was thinking about her and then I realized what the link was. Both she and Martha Gibson had become visibly upset about their husbands. Carrie had become upset when she'd seen hers, Martha had become upset when I'd talked about hers. The women were at opposite ends of the spectrum in looks and income, but in that way they were alike.

But then lots of women felt that way about their husbands. I pulled out on to the street and headed back to the store. On the way I rang up Detective Keene and shared my thoughts. What do they say about keeping your friends close and your enemies closer?

'So you've decided to confess,' he said.

'Ha. Ha.'

'We have a witness identification.'

'A witness you can't find. Anyway, as you know, witness identification is very unreliable.'

'I don't know anything of the sort.'

'You should read the science section in the *New York Times*.'

'I should read you your Miranda rights.'

'Such a snappy comeback.' I turned on to Comstock. 'We've been through this already. Your timeline for me isn't credible.'

'So you said before.'

'If you thought it was I'd be in custody already.'

'That could happen sooner than you think.'

I stopped suddenly as another car pulled out in front of me. Idiot. Lucky I was going slow.

'Come on. Why the hell would I shoot someone and then come back and drive by his house?'

'People do strange things. Most crime is irrational. Maybe you forgot something. Maybe you wanted to return to the scene of the crime.'

'Right. And I brought someone along for company so he could watch me walk into the house. Not to mention making myself conspicuous to the neighbors.' This time Keene didn't say anything. I debated for a moment and then I said, 'If you're really interested in solving the case you should talk to Benny Gibson's wife.' Despite what Otto had said, I still wasn't convinced of Martha's innocence.

'I'd love to but the department won't pay for me to go to Massachusetts.'

'Would they pay for you to go to Outer Comstock? Thurber Street, to be exact.'

'What's that supposed to mean?'

'Benny Gibson's wife is living on Thurber Street.'

'She's in the Quiet Moments Rehab Center in Quincy, Mass.'

'She moved back four months ago. You should go have a chat with her. She might be your shooter. She really hates him and I have a feeling he did something really bad to her or her daughter.'

'You're nuts.'

'Go check her out.'

'Just let me do my job.'

'That's what I'm trying to.'

A car honked in front of me.

'Are you driving?' Keene asked.

'No. I'm on camel back.'

The car honked again.

'You're definitely on the road,' Keene said.

'No kidding.' And I hung up.

Either Keene would talk to Martha Gibson or he wouldn't. There was nothing more I could say. But maybe there was something I could do. I dialed George. My call went straight to voicemail, which meant his cell was off. I considered calling his house for a moment and nixed the idea. My question could wait. I had no desire to speak to his blonde.

Ian listened to me while I told him about my meeting with Martha Gibson. It was twelve o'clock at night and I was dragging. We'd had a two-hour rush at Shamus's and this was the first chance we'd had to talk. When I was done with my recap Ian pulled his pack of tobacco out from under the counter, put a newspaper down, and tapped a couple of handfuls out. Then he extracted six papers from the pack and carefully placed them on the newspaper as well. I watched him put a large pinch of tobacco on the paper and roll it up.

'So you think that Martha Gibson shot her husband?' he asked.

'It's possible.' Then I added, 'Even though Otto says she didn't. He could be covering for her.'

'And why would he do that?'

'I think they have a thing going.'

Ian put the first cigarette in an empty Chesterfield box and started on the second one.

'Do you have any proof?'

'No.'

A minute later the second one was in the box.

'Let me ask you this: Do you care who killed Benny Gibson?'

I pondered the question for a moment before I answered. 'I suppose I do insofar as it helps me figure out why John did what he did to me.'

'And that's what you really care about?'

'Yes.'

'So why are you so interested in Benny?'

'Because I think that there must be a link to John in there somewhere.'

'And what if there isn't?'

'How can there not be?'

'Easy. What if the guy who killed Benny and the guy who set you up are two separate people?'

'I don't believe that,' I replied.

Ian coughed. 'Your prerogative. But listen to the scenario. One guy, let's call him X, kills Benny Gibson. Now this X is someone Benny knows. The reason? Let's say Benny was running a scam on him so he decides to get rid of him. And he does.'

'Or Benny burns down X's buildings and then blackmails him.'

Ian looked at me. 'Benny Gibson burned down a couple of buildings?'

'Three, according to Otto Cody.'

'Is one of them the warehouse the vagrant died in?'

'Yup.'

'That would be a good lever. Arson is one thing, but someone dying is serious jail time.'

'They're not going to give him a medal, that's for sure.'

'Benny was just your all-around charmer.'

'Yeah, a regular Renaissance man. A little arson. A little soft-core child porn. A little scamming.'

Ian lit a cigarette and inhaled. 'I like versatile people.'

'Me too. But get back to the "two people could be involved in this instead of one" theory.'

Ian took another puff of his cigarette. 'I'm just saying it's a possibility. But there is one thing we know for sure. And that is that Benny's killing was not a spur-of-the-moment decision. We know this because it took a measure of fore-sight to organize your set-up. Correct?'

I nodded. 'Go on.'

'So maybe one guy did it all or one guy killed Benny and another one is covering the first guy's ass.'

'Why involve another guy?'

'Maybe he's already involved. Maybe he has a reason for covering the first guy's ass.'

I went back to Benny's wife. 'How do you like her for the murder?' I asked. 'She certainly has a motive.'

Ian shifted his weight from one leg to the other. From the way he was moving I could tell that his back was bothering him.

'His wife may have shot him,' he replied, 'and she defin-itely has a reason, but from what you tell me about her, she doesn't appear to have the capability to engineer setting you up.'

'Unless she's acting.'

Ian flicked his ash into the paper cup full of water sitting on the counter. 'I suppose that's always a possibility.'

'But you think that's unlikely.'

'From what you've told me I do.'

'And the daughter?'

Ian thought for a moment. Then he said, 'I like her better for this. Evidently she really doesn't like her father. She was the one who discovered the body – always a bad sign. And she got out of Syracuse as soon as she could. And now she's off in some Mormon retreat and no one can get to her. No. I like her a lot better. My only questions to you are: How did she get John involved in this? What did she have on him and how did she get it?'

Those were really good questions. Unfortunately I didn't have the answers.

'And then,' Ian continued, 'we have the brother.'

'Ah, yes. Joe.' I went and got myself a diet soda, opened the top, and took a sip. I would have preferred a beer but this would have to do. Ian didn't allow drinking on duty. 'He and Benny weren't getting along too well.'

Ian took another puff of his cigarette and threw the butt in the cup of water.

'So you said. I assume Joe inherits the business when Benny dies? Or does the wife? What about the daughter? Who benefits?'

'Follow the money,' I said.

'Exactly.'

'Maybe you should talk to your friend and see if she's heard anything,' Ian suggested.

I took another sip of my soda. 'And if she hasn't, maybe Otto has.'

Ian poured a bottle of water into a glass and began measuring out instant-cocoa mix into it.

'It might also be interesting to go back and talk to Melody. See if you can shake anything interesting loose from her.'

Which is what I did.

Twenty-Six

I caught up with Melody as she was walking to her car outside Wonder Women. It was a quiet night in there because there were only four cars in the lot, five if you counted Melody's. She was wearing jeans and a hoodie and looked to be on her way home. The sulfurous lights above the parking lot leached the color out of her skin and hair, giving her a ghastly pallor.

'Can we talk?' I said.

She gave a toss of her head and kept walking. 'About what?'

'The guys Benny Gibson was seeing.'

She smiled. The light made her mouth look like a black hole. 'You got any money?'

'No.'

'Then we can't talk. I told you that before. Two hundred a name.'

I shrugged. 'Fine. I'll just give your name to Keene, the detective who's investigating the case.'

'Whatever.'

'OK, Betty.'

Melody slowed down slightly.

'Betty Heath is a nice name.'

She stopped dead and turned towards me. 'There's nothing wrong with having a stage name,' she hissed.

'I didn't say there was.'

'Don't call me Betty again.'

'Fine.'

She put her hands on her hips. 'Listen, what the hell do you want?'

'I already told you.'

Her nostrils flared. 'I'm not giving them up to you. Period. I have their privacy to protect.'

'Very noble.' I managed to prevent myself from rolling my eyes. 'You mean you're afraid you'll lose their business.'

'Take it whatever way you want.'

'You're going to lose their business if you don't.'

'Not hardly.'

She began walking again. I fell in step.

'I guess I'll call Keene after all,' I told her.

Melody waved her hand dismissively. 'Call away,' she told me. Then she took her car keys out of her bag and clicked her door opener. The lights on the Lexus parked by the Wonder Women sign blinked twice. The girl was obviously doing pretty well for herself.

'Keene will be interested to hear about your little side business.'

'I don't have a side business.'

'Janet Gibson says you do.'

At this point Melody was standing next to her ride with her hands folded across her chest, tapping her foot on the asphalt. 'Right. Janet Gibson isn't here to speak to.'

'That's why God invented the telephone,' I said gambling that she didn't know that Janet was unreachable. Her reaction told me I was correct.

Melody bit her lip. She wasn't looking quite so sure of herself now.

'She was telling me all about how you were selling her E.'

'No she wasn't.'

'Yeah she was.'

I nodded towards her car. 'Nice ride.'

'I like it.'

'Expensive.'

'It's all a matter of point of view.'

'You earn that kind of money stripping.'

Melody smirked. In the light it looked like a death smile. 'Guys like me.'

'They like you enough to give you a forty-thousand-dollar car?'

'Yeah. They do.'

'Keene will probably want to talk to your customers. Make sure that's how you got the car. He'll probably set the tax people on you. You know, to make sure you're reporting your earnings.' I shook my head. 'The IRS can be hell. Much worse than the DA. But you can avoid all of that just by giving me what I want. It's not a big deal. No one will know.'

For the first time Melody frowned. Her shoulders slumped. If I had threatened to beat her up or have her arrested that would be one thing, but being audited was something else. She'd have to give up her clients' names, which effectively meant she was out of business.

'Why are you doing this?' she whined. 'Why don't you go away?'

'Tell me and I will.'

She went back to biting her lip.

'Listen,' I told her, 'I just want to talk to them about Benny Gibson. I have no desire to make trouble for you. I'll lie and say I got their names from a list I found in Benny's file cabinet. I promise.'

'Really?'

'Absolutely.'

She bit her lip some more and tugged at her bag.

'It'll be worse if you don't.'

She sighed. 'I guess you're right.'

'You know I am.'

I was writing them down when out of the corner of my eye I saw Bays step out of the club. He took one look at me and came towards me like a heat-seeking missile that's locked on to its target.

'You,' he said when he was less than a foot away. 'What the hell do you want?'

'World peace.' He was so close that I could smell him.

He glowered at me. I guess he didn't think I was funny, but then I've been reliably informed by Ian that lots of people don't.

He pointed to Erie Boulevard. 'I want your ass off this property.'

'Really?'

'Yes, really.'

'And if I don't?'

'Then I can throw you off or I can call the cops and have you arrested for trespassing.' He folded his hands across his chest. 'So what's it going to be?'

'I'll leave.' After all, I'd gotten what I wanted.

About halfway home I realized I was hungry, so I stopped off at an all-night convenience store for a pint of coffee ice cream.

When I got to my house I walked Zsa Zsa, ate the ice cream, drank a couple of shots of Scotch, and mulled over my next move. I came up with a few possibilities, but by then the Scotch and the ice cream were fighting in my stomach, so I took a couple of Pepto-Bismol and went off to bed.

I didn't feel any better when I woke up the next morning and it took a real effort to drag myself out of bed. But once I got some food in me things began to look up. Before I left for work I looked up the names Melody had given me in the phonebook. Three of them were listed. Two had MDs in front of their names, and the third had an LLD. Two doctors and a lawyer. I was going to have to think about how to talk to them.

It was nine thirty and I was at the shop leaning on the counter and leafing through the local paper when George walked in. He was carrying a Dunkin' Donuts bag in one hand and a cardboard carrier with two coffees in the other. And he looked really good in his black turtleneck sweater, black leather jacket, and jeans. Very sexy. Unfortunately.

He smiled a killer smile. I could feel my anger beginning to melt.

'Just stopped by to say hello,' he said. 'Got you a coffee and a chocolate-peanut donut.'

I'd already had coffee and a donut but I could always find room for more.

'What's the occasion?'

George shrugged. 'None. Just miss talking to you.'

I didn't say anything. I was thinking about his blonde. He must have known because the next words out of his mouth were, 'I love my kid. What am I supposed to do?'

'I don't know.'

'I miss you, Robin.'

I still missed him, but I was damned if I was going to go

down that path. So instead of answering I took my coffee out of the carrier, removed the lid, and took a sip. It was just the way I liked it. Cream and two sugars.

'Wow,' I said nodding to the SUV parked in front of the shop. 'How can you afford to fill that up?'

George laughed. 'It's more economical than it looks.'

'I wouldn't like to drive to Oswego and back every day in that.'

'Fortunately, I just have classes on Mondays, Wednesdays, and Fridays.'

'I thought assistant college professors were supposed to be driving small gas-saving ecologically correct Hondas, instead of big gas-guzzling vehicles. That's so . . . so . . .'

'Suburban.'

'Un-PC.'

'It's leased.'

I took another sip of my coffee and lit a cigarette. 'I must be doing something wrong. I can't even afford to lease a Hyundai.'

'You'd be surprised at the deals you can work out.' George plunked his elbows on the counter. 'So what about it? You want to grab a bite to eat tonight?'

I shook my head. 'I'm busy.'

George took his coffee from the carrier. 'Maybe another time,' he said.

'I don't think so.'

He smiled that killer smile again. Then he caught my gaze and held it. 'I miss talking to you, Robin. I really do.'

I could almost feel myself believing him. What would be so bad about some dinner?

'We'll see.'

George grinned. 'I guess that will have to do.'

'I guess it will.'

A moment later Manuel walked through the door. He grunted at George and continued on into the office. He didn't like George and George returned the favor. Actually they hated each other. When he came out five minutes later George was gone.

Manuel set his energy drink on the counter. 'Was that black Explorer the asshole's?' he asked.

I fed a piece of donut to Zsa Zsa.

'That's what George said.' I'd given up telling Manuel not to call George that a long time ago, although I probably shouldn't have.

'Sweet ride.' Manuel yanked up his pants.

'It's a lease.'

'What's a lease like that cost?'

I shrugged. 'You got me.' Cars have never been my major interest.

Manuel bit his lip. 'Maybe I'll lease one of them.'

'You better start saving your money,' I said. I ate another piece of donut and got to work.

It was a slow day and talking with George had made me restless. I needed to move. So after I cleaned the fish tanks and ordered some crickets and mealworms I decided to go see what Joe Gibson had to tell me.

It was sunny and the temperature was in the high forties. The packed snow by the curb outside the store was melting fast. I got in my car and headed downtown. On the way I passed a carwash. People were lined up waiting to spray the gray salt residue off their vehicles. I cracked the windows open and hummed along in time to the music on the radio. It's amazing what a little sun will do for one's spirits.

Parking downtown was terrible, but this time I got lucky and found a parking spot immediately. The fact that it was on the same block as Joe Gibson's office made me think that the gods were smiling on me for a change.

I went inside the building and walked up the steps. I knew from the plate outside that the building housed three offices, but it was so quiet in there I had a hard time believing it. The door to the realty company was open, so I went in. Like last time there was no one at the reception desk. The only way I knew someone was there was the faint sound of wood scraping across the floor. The overhead lights were off, but the sun shining in through the window showed the streaks on the glass and the dust motes in the air.

I looked around. If anything the place was messier than it had been before. There were stacks of files on the floor, the chairs, and the desk. I spied a carton with two lamps sticking out, another carton full of computer cables, and another one full of phonebooks. It looked as if Joe was packing up.

'Moving?' I asked when he stuck his head out of his office door.

'What does it look like?' He seemed more tired than he had when I'd first seen him a million years ago.

'Spring cleaning?'

He sighed. 'Not funny, Light. What do you want?'

'Not much.' I cleared a spot on the receptionist's desk and perched on it. 'Heard from Janet?'

Joe shook his head.

'I thought you'd be interested, she being your niece and all.'

'Well, I'm not.'

'She's in Utah,' I informed him. 'Wants to become a Mormon.'

'She could become a Baptist for all I care.'

'You should. I hear she wants to repent. Atone for her misdeeds by confessing.'

'And what does that have to do with me?'

'Nothing. I mean I wouldn't like to have someone say they sold E to me, but I guess we're different.'

Joe glared at me. 'I guess we are.'

'I wonder how your brother would have felt if he'd known you were buying drugs from his daughter.'

Joe didn't reply.

'I bet he would have been pretty pissed,' I continued. 'Maybe pissed enough to turn you in to the cops. Maybe you decided you couldn't have that and you shot him.'

Joe shook his head. 'The truth is that he wouldn't have cared if she was – which she wasn't. He was a terrible father, a bad husband, and a worse brother, and he ran our business into the ground.'

'So then you're not inheriting Benny's half because there's nothing left to inherit?'

Joe didn't answer.

'I thought maybe his wife is or the daughter is getting it.'

Joe maintained his silence.

'Of course, it's usually a real pain when that happens.

Businesses tend to go down the drain, so I guess that's one
reason you wouldn't kill him.'

Joe grimaced. 'This is getting tedious.'

'Not for me. I'm having fun.'

'Well, I'm not,' Joe snapped. 'I can't stand here and listen
to your asinine questions. I have things I'm trying to get
done here.'

'Where are you moving?'

'To another office.'

'And where's that?'

'I would like you to go.'

'And if I don't?'

'I'll give you five minutes. Then I'm going to call the cops
and have you removed.' At which point his cell began to ring
and he went in his office and slammed the door. Through
the door I heard him say, 'I don't care what T Rex wanted.
It's what I want that counts.' There was a pause and then he
said, 'That's too bad.' After which he lowered his voice. I
could hear sounds, but I couldn't hear the words they were
forming.

Just to be perverse I decided to hang around for a few
minutes more. That's the kind of mood I was in. OK. So
what had I learned? Nothing that I didn't know before. Joe
didn't like his brother. Joe wasn't being investigated because
otherwise the state AG's office would have swooped down
and confiscated his files. So that reconfirmed that it was
Benny who was being investigated for something else.
Something like tax evasion. Or bribery.

I took my cigarettes out of my backpack and fished around
for my cigarette lighter. I found everything else but that.
Finally I came up with a book of matches. Unfortunately
they were the ones that I'd gotten in my mailbox. They'd
been kicking around in my backpack ever since I'd been to
the casino with Ian. I studied the cover. The letters seemed
fainter, probably because the lead from the pencil was wearing
off. I stared at them for a moment. No, the letters were definitely TG.

I still hadn't figured out what TG was supposed to mean.
I held the matchbook in my hand for a moment. It probably
would be a good idea not to use it, it being evidence and

all. On the other hand, I wanted a cigarette really badly. Finally I said the hell with it – what difference would one match make in the scheme of things – and lit my cigarette.

Then I thumbed through the folders on the desk, even though I didn't expect to find anything of interest, and I was right. I didn't. The first folders I looked through were property valuations. I went through more – surveys, engineering reports, and tax schedules. If there was something germane to what I was interested in I couldn't see it. The next batch contained Benny and Joe's high-school transcripts. Joe had failed advanced algebra, but done well in social studies. Benny had done well in typing, shop, gym, and science survey. The rest of his classes had been a wash, but he'd been on the varsity football team.

After a couple of minutes I restacked the folders and stood up. When I did I knocked over my backpack. Everything came spilling out. I cursed as I gathered my possessions up and threw them back in. I was putting the cigarettes and the matches back in when I made a connection, a connection that had been under my nose all along. I couldn't believe I'd missed it. Sometimes I'm such an idiot.

When I got outside I called John's aunt and got his brother's work address.

It was time to go see Theodore.

We definitely had things to chat about.

Twenty-Seven

Theodore was working for a construction company head-quartered on Teal Avenue. The street was home to a multitude of commercial establishments, low one-story buildings made out of cinderblock or prefabricated parts and painted with whatever paint was on sale that day. Signage was utilitarian. That was because most of the places were strictly for the trade. When you went in you knew what you wanted. They weren't selling you anything.

RCJ Construction was no exception. Long and low, the building was an undistinguished shade of green. It was set back from the road and there was room for eight vehicles on the tarmac out front. Two of the slots were taken up with company trucks. A small sign was mounted to the side. I parked in front of the door and went in. The reception area was big enough for two people to fit in. The floor was covered in linoleum that looked as if it had been around since the fifties. The walls were painted the same color as the exterior ones. A small electric heater wheezed in the background. The front office was separated from the reception area by a glass partition.

I walked over. The guy at the desk glanced up from his computer and asked me what I wanted.

'I'm looking for Theodore,' I replied.

He made a vague waving motion. 'Go through the door, into the corridor and take that all the way to the end. Theo should be in the loading dock.' Then he turned back to his computer. I took a peek. He was playing Solitaire.

I did what he told me. The corridor was long and gloomy. Every other light in the ceiling seemed not to be working. I looked in the offices as I went by. There were five of them. Two were occupied, three weren't, but all of them were stacked with paint cans and flooring and building-material samples. When I got to the end of the corridor I pushed the door open and went in. The area was twenty by thirty feet. At least. Wooden palettes were stacked along the sides of three walls. The fourth had sliding doors.

I spotted Theodore immediately. He was wearing a jump-suit and pushing a broom. I walked towards him. I was about fifteen feet away when he spotted me.

He stopped sweeping.

'What are you doing here?' he asked.

'I think we should talk.'

Theodore rested the broom against his chest and wiped his hands off on his Carhartt suit. He looked more tired than the last time I'd seen him. And there was a sadness about him that seemed to have settled in.

'But I'm working,' Theodore said.

His choice of words was interesting. Most people would have asked what I wanted to talk to them about. But maybe he already knew.

'I'm sure your sweeping will keep for a little while,' I told him.

When I was six feet away I took the matchbook out of my pocket and held it out to him.

'What's that?' he asked.

'A matchbook. A matchbook that someone has written your initials on.'

He shook his head. 'They could be anybody's.'

'They could be, but I don't think they are. I think they're yours.'

'You're crazy,' he said, but his voice lacked conviction.

'Someone put this in my mailbox.'

'Why would they do that?' He seemed genuinely puzzled.

'I think they did it to point me in the right direction.'

Theodore shook his head from side to side.

'Someone from Wonder Women put it in my mailbox,' I told him.

Theodore shook his head more vigorously. 'I've never been in Wonder Women. I don't do things like that.'

'I think this has something to do with some pictures John had in his possession.'

Theodore swallowed and looked down at the floor. 'What pictures?'

'The pictures your cousin Carmella found underneath John's mattress. You mean she didn't tell you?'

Theodore remained silent.

'Because I can call her up and ask her. I just got off the phone with her.'

'Don't,' he said.

'So you do know about them?'

'Yes,' he admitted. He studied a speck of dirt on the floor. 'She told me but they don't have anything to do with me.' The words came out like a plea.

'I'm not buying that.'

He didn't look back up.

'Were they your pictures?'

Theodore remained silent.

'I think they were. They certainly weren't John's. Considering his sexual orientation, he'd never be interested in stuff like that.'

'Neither am I,' Theodore murmured.

'Well, someone had to be, wouldn't you say?'

Theodore shrugged.

'You don't say.' I waited a moment. Then I took out my cellphone. 'Let's call the cops and see what they say. You know what they do to people who have pictures like the ones you gave to John. They throw them in jail and tell everyone what they did. I bet you have more of them on your computer. You know you can never totally erase your hard drive. You have to trash the whole machine.'

'You wouldn't,' Theodore cried.

'What? Call the cops? Why in the hell not? I'm in no end of trouble because of that stunt your brother pulled. I need an explanation.'

Theodore pulled his broom closer to him. 'It's not what you think.'

I snorted. 'Now there's a classic line if ever I heard one.'

'But it's true,' Theodore wailed.

'So tell me what it is.'

Theodore held up his hand. 'Give me a second.'

I held up my cellphone. 'I'm giving you a minute but that's it.'

'Could we go get some coffee?' Theodore asked. 'I need some coffee. With lots of sugar.'

I nodded. 'Sounds good to me.'

There was a Dunkin' Donuts down the road. We walked out of the loading area, down the corridor, and out to the reception area. The guy in the front office looked up. Theodore told him he'd be back in twenty minutes. The guy grunted and went back to his game.

We stepped outside. It was sleeting. Theodore scrunched his neck into his collar. I was half expecting him to make a run for it, but he didn't. He stayed close to my side. I got the feeling he was relieved that he was going to be telling me what had happened.

'I went to St. Anne's when I was in elementary school,' Theodore said to me as he got in my car. 'The nuns always used to talk about the consequences of sin. I never believed them. Now I do.'

He didn't say anything as I pulled back on to the road. He didn't say anything as we drove to Dunkin' Donuts. In fact, he didn't speak until we were settled in the parking lot sipping our coffee and eating our donuts. He looked straight ahead. He didn't want to face me.

'It's all my fault,' he began. 'I like to gamble.'

I took another sip of my coffee and waited.

Theodore fiddled with the collar of his jumpsuit. 'I'm not a good gambler so I ended up owing a fair amount of money. My credit cards were maxed out. People were calling all the time, threatening me.'

I thought of my creditors. 'That's really hard.'

'Yes, it is. They even called me at work. I got really upset and I started popping pills to take the edge off things.' He sighed. 'I thought that if I could get some money and pay people off everything would be OK. Only I didn't want to go to my family. I didn't want to admit that I'd gotten myself in that much trouble. I mean my dad was already upset about John being gay. Just the thought of giving him more aggravation . . . I couldn't do that to him.'

Theodore trailed off. He studied a man walking to his car. I took another sip of my coffee and ate a piece of my strawberry-glazed donut. I hadn't been able to resist the sprinkles on top. I turned the heater to high. It's the only way to get any heat in the car.

'And?' I prompted.

'And I was working for Benny Gibson at the time.'

'Doing what?'

'Cleaning. I'd do his office. Some of his buildings. John got me the job.'

'I thought you two didn't get along.'

'Who said that?'

'Carmella.'

Theodore frowned. 'Typical. No, we got along. We just didn't hang out together. But I always knew he'd be there if I needed him.' Theodore stopped and took a breath. 'I took the job because I was trying to write stories at the time. But I never wrote. I went to the casino instead. And Benny wasn't a nice guy.' Theodore frowned as he remembered. 'He wasn't a nice guy at all. He ripped people off right and left, and he always got away with it. He thought he was entitled to do whatever he wanted. He called me a piece of shit because I forgot to wipe down his desk twice in one week. Said he was going to fire me if it happened again.'

He stopped again. He took a deep breath. 'You know how people don't think that the maintenance man or the maid count. Like they don't notice anything. Like you can do anything you want in front of them?'

I nodded slowly, not seeing where this was leading.

'Well, those pictures I gave to John, I found them in Benny Gibson's trash one day when I emptied the can. They were in a manila envelope.'

'How did you know to open it?'

Theodore looked chagrined.

'Did you go through all of his mail?'

Instead of answering Theodore hunched his shoulders. I had my answer. He went on as if I hadn't asked the question.

'First I was going to go to the cops. And then I got to thinking. It was the middle of the night and no one was around so I sat down and looked at his computer. It was easy enough to get into. The putz had his password taped to the bottom of his laptop. There was more stuff like that in there.'

Theodore stopped for a moment.

'And,' I prompted.

'I made a decision. A strategic decision.'

Suddenly I understood.

'You blackmailed him.'

Theodore grimaced. 'It didn't turn out the way I planned.'

So few things do.

'How did it turn out?'

'I showed him the pictures and asked him for a hundred thousand. I figured ask high, right? I thought he'd bargain. Instead he went to his desk and pulled out a gun. He said he was going to shoot me then and there. I ran out as fast as I could.'

'With the pictures.'

Theodore looked at me for the first time since he'd started talking.

'Yes. With the pictures. I didn't realize I had them in my hand.'

'So what happened then?'

'I drove around, then I went into a bar on LeMoyne Avenue to have a drink. To kind of calm myself down. I had three beers and I'd just about convinced myself that Benny wasn't serious about the gun. That he was going to quiet down. Then Nick, one of the guys that worked for Benny, came into the bar and told me that Benny was looking for me. That he told everyone at the place to call him if they saw me. I didn't know what to do.'

'You could have left the area. Got in your car and driven to another town. Waited until he cooled off to come back.'

'No I couldn't.'

'Why not?'

Theodore lifted his coffee cup and put it back down.

'The hell with that.' Anger crackled through his voice. 'He was the bad one, not me. I wasn't doing that stuff, he was. No way was he running me off. Plus my family is here. Besides I didn't have any money.'

'So what did you do?'

'I made a mistake. I made a big mistake.' His voice was full of remorse. 'I was afraid to go home, so I knocked on my brother's door and asked him if I could crash at his place. Of course he said yes. Then Benny called on my cellphone and I turned my phone off and John wanted to know what was happening. He kept going and going until I told him.'

'Sounds like John,' I commented.

I could see Theodore's eyes beginning to mist over. 'He was a nice guy,' he said. 'He was always willing to help.'

'He was indeed,' I agreed.

'He said he knew someone who would take care of it. Someone he'd met at one of the places he's worked at.'

'Did he give you a name?'

'No. And I was too upset to ask. But I think it was Walmouth's operation.'

'As in Walmouth the developer?'

'Yeah.'

'Why do you say that?'

'Because given all the places John worked at that seems the most likely. I mean who could he meet at the Wind in the Willows Bookstore or the Art Place?'

'True.'

Theodore took another sip of his coffee. He began watching the parking lot again.

'So what happened?' I asked.

'I don't know,' Theodore said. 'The next thing I knew I was watching the news. I heard that Benny Gibson was dead and you were questioned about his homicide.'

'Did you speak to John after that?'

'Once. He said he'd made a terrible mistake. He said he'd made things worse for me. And you. And Benny Gibson. He said he didn't know how he was going to make it up to us.'

Now it was my turn to fall quiet.

'So that's why he killed himself,' I finally said.

'It's all my fault,' Theodore said. 'Everything.'

And he put his hands in his face and wept.

It's hard to see a man cry. I turned and studied the parking lot and tried to think about other things. Otherwise I was going to start crying too and I didn't want to do that. I was afraid that if I started I wouldn't be able to stop.

'I'm sorry,' Theodore said a few moments later.

I turned back. He was wiping his eyes with the sleeve of his Carhartts.

'No problem,' I told him. I mean what else could I say? We sat in silence for a moment. Then I asked him if he wanted more coffee or another donut. I figured I'd give him a couple of minutes to pull himself together.

'A donut would be good.' He still sounded choked up.

I went and got us six donuts. I figured what we didn't eat, Manuel would. Theodore chose a jelly donut, while I had another strawberry.

'You never went to Wonder Women?' I said as Theodore brushed powdered sugar off his chin.

'Never,' he said.

'And you don't know a guy named Bays?'

Theodore licked a spot of jelly off his finger. 'No. Who is he?'

'He's a bartender at Wonder Women.'

'I've never gone in there. Honest.'

I believed him.

'So why did he leave the matchbook with your initials in my mailbox?'

Theodore shrugged. 'Maybe they were someone else's initials. I said that before, remember.'

I remembered.

Every time I thought I was getting someplace, I landed right back at the beginning again.

I kept thinking about that as I drove Theodore back to work.

Twenty-Eight

I should have gone back to work myself, but I was so close to Bays' apartment that I decided to take a detour and see if I could talk to him again. Maybe he could shed some light on why he'd put the matchbook in my mailbox. It had been done for a reason and I needed to know what that reason was. Granted our first two conversations hadn't gone too well, minor understatement, but I was hoping this one would be more successful.

I called the shop first. According to Manuel everything was hunky dory, Zsa Zsa was doing OK, and George had dropped by to say hello. Again.

'What the hell does he want?' Manuel said.

'I think he wants to take me out to dinner.'

'You're not going to go, are you?'

'Probably not, but why do you care?'

'Because he's worthless,' Manuel replied.

'That's fairly harsh.'

'No, it's not. And anyway when you were with him you were always in a pissy mood. You're much nicer now.'

Interesting. I was thinking about whether or not that was true when I heard voices in the background.

'Gotta go,' Manuel said. 'A customer just walked in.'

And he hung up. I took a left and drove over to Bays' apartment. The day had turned dark all of a sudden and there was a promise of snow in the air. According to the weather forecast we were supposed to have warm and sunny weather. Wrong again. This would make the third day in a row that the weatherman had blown it. On the way over I detoured around three squad cars in front of a tumbledown-looking house. It was a more and more frequent sight as gangs and shootings became a way of life in the city.

It took me ten minutes to drive over to Bays' apartment. I spent that time considering what I'd learned from Theodore. I believed his story. I think he was telling the truth as far as he went. However, and it was a big however, why did the person that John contacted shoot Benny Gibson? At least, that was the assumption I was working under. It was certainly the most plausible conclusion.

I couldn't believe it was because he'd threatened to shoot Theodore. Who would care about Theodore except his family? Protecting Theodore might have been a contributing factor, but it was just that. I lit a cigarette and thought about John. Maybe if John had realized that he wouldn't have killed himself. Maybe he would have been able to put things in perspective. I sighed and thought about John some more. He'd always taken things to heart. Way too much so. I was really going to miss him.

I was still thinking about him when I realized I'd gone by Bays' apartment. I put my vehicle in reverse so I could back up. It made a clunking sound, as if the engine was about to fall out. I really needed a new car. One like George had would be nice, but that wasn't on the table. But maybe I could lease a Hyundai. Or get a new used car. When I got a chance I should check out my options before the engine seized up. My mechanic had already told me the piston rings were leaking. He also said it wasn't worth fixing on a car that would go for seven hundred bucks, if that. Oh well. Another thing to deal with. I'd add it to the list.

I went back about twenty feet. There was a parking spot ten feet away from Bays' apartment and I took it. As I walked towards his place I tried to formulate my approach. I couldn't threaten him because I didn't have anything to threaten him with. I couldn't muscle him because I wasn't strong enough and even though Ian had offered to do the honors I didn't want him to. At least not yet.

A cat came down from a neighbor's porch and hissed at me. I gave her a wide berth and continued on. This was going to be interesting. Especially considering that Bays and I hadn't exactly parted on a hospitable note the last time we met.

I climbed up his stairs, took a deep breath, and rang his

bell. I was half hoping that his roommate would answer the door, but he did instead.

'You,' he said.

He looked as if he'd just gotten up. He was dressed in gray sweats. His hair was mussed up. He still had some sleep left in the corners of his eyes. I gave him my most charming smile. He was so surprised he took a step back. And that's when I knew what I was going to do. I was going to be nice. I extended my hand. He looked at it.

'What's that for?'

'Come on,' I said. 'I don't have cooties.'

'I don't shake hands with people.'

'Any people or just me?'

'Any people.'

I put my hand down. This was working well.

'What do you want?' Bays asked.

'I want you to answer a question for me.'

He laughed. Guffawed, really.

'You're kidding, right?'

'Nope.'

'And why the hell should I do that?'

'Because you're a nice guy.'

Bays laughed harder.

'Ian tell you that?'

'No. He said you were an asshole.'

'He's right. I am.'

'No. You're not.'

Bays gave me a curious look.

'Why do you say that?'

'Because that's why you sent me the matchbook.'

'We've been through this before. I didn't send you the matchbook.'

'Let's say that hypothetically you did.'

From the expression on Bays' face I could see I had him hooked.

'What do you mean?'

'I mean let's play a game of let's pretend.'

'As in?'

'Let's pretend you invite me to step inside your house because it's freezing out here.'

He nodded and took two steps back. I took two steps forward which meant I was inside his hallway. I took a quick look around. I don't know what I was expecting but it wasn't this. The words 'squared up and put away' came to mind. There was a coat rack tacked on the near wall. Five jackets were neatly aligned on it. Underneath six pairs of shoes were lined up on a rubber mat. A plastic container sat on a small table. It was filled with hats and gloves.

'Go on,' he said.

'OK. Let's pretend you sent me the matchbook because you didn't like what was going on with Theodore . . .'

I stopped because I saw a confused look in his eyes. And then I realized I'd been wrong. I'd been wrong about the initials standing for Theodore. That's why he hadn't understood.

And that's when the pieces fell together and I finally got it. I'd heard Joe say something about T Rex when I'd been in his office. I'd seen Benny Gibson's high-school transcript. Benny's full name was Benjamin Terrance Gibson. Terry is a common nickname for Terrance, but I'd known a Terrance who'd been called T Rex. I'd be willing to bet anything that that was Benny Gibson's nickname. That's whom Joe had been talking about in his office. I wondered whom he had been talking to. And John had written the word *dino* on the piece of paper I'd retrieved from his wastepaper basket. Under that he'd drawn a picture of a dinosaur and written *T Rex* and underlined it in black.

'It wasn't Theodore, was it? It was Benny Gibson. Only in your place he went by the name T Rex.'

Somehow I'd blundered into the correct answer, even though I'd used the wrong facts.

Bays crossed his arms over his chest. 'That's an interesting story. Go on.'

I nodded. I could tell from Bays' expression that I was right.

'From what I heard, Gibson was a nasty piece of work and who should know better than the bartender of the place he used to frequent? And you must have watched me getting arrested on TV and felt bad for me and decided to give me a helping hand. Only I didn't get it right away. Which must have been very frustrating for you.'

'I don't get frustrated,' Bays said.

I nodded. 'My mistake.'

A white cat with a black mustache came out and wound herself around Bays' feet and meowed. He picked her up and cradled her in his arms.

'This is Perdida,' he said. 'Someone threw her in the dumpster behind Wonder Women.'

I reached out and scratched behind her ears.

'I have a question,' Bays said.

'Go on,' I told him.

'Hypothetically speaking, why didn't I tell you I'd left the matchbook in your mailbox when you found me?'

I continued scratching. Perdida started to purr.

'I don't know.'

'Think about it.'

I did. 'There could be several explanations. The likeliest being that you changed your mind.'

'And why would I do that?'

I thought some more. 'Because it was inadvisable for you to continue with this course of action.'

'In what sense?'

'You were made to see this was a bad idea.'

Bays gave an infinitesimal nod.

I thought about what would make Bays back off. Probably the threat of serious jail time.

'It must have been quite a threat.'

He gave another tiny nod.

'And,' I continued, 'that's why you didn't want to talk to me before. Because both times we were talking in a public place and you didn't want to be seen with me.'

'Not bad,' Bays said. 'Not bad at all. That's quite a story you just dreamed up.'

'Yes, it is, isn't it. So the question is: Who threatened you? Who did John go to?'

Bays corrected me. 'I think the question you want to ask yourself is: Who was Benny Gibson working with?'

'His brother.'

'Beyond that. He had a big project going. Who was it with?'

I thought about the casino. 'Richard Walmouth?'

Bays didn't say anything. Maybe Calli could verify my hunch.

'One last question,' I said to Bays.

'What's that?'

'Did you ever find the person that put Perdida in the dumpster?'

Bays smiled. It wasn't a nice one. 'I certainly did.'

'Good,' I said.

Perdida climbed up on Bays' shoulder and draped herself around him.

'Yes,' Bays said. 'I think it's safe to say the man definitely learned the error of his ways.'

'Works for me,' I told him.

He walked me back outside.

It had started snowing. Little white flakes danced down from the sky. The snow was light and fluffy and wouldn't be around for long. By tomorrow it would be gone. One year we'd had ten inches in May. Hopefully we wouldn't repeat that this year.

I called Calli from my car. She wasn't at her desk so I left a voicemail detailing the information I needed. Then I headed for the shop. On the way I stopped at Augies Pizza and Wings on Marshall Street and got a pie, half sausage and half cheese, and an order of wings for Manuel, me, and Zsa Zsa. I figured we all deserved it.

It took them ten minutes to bake the pizza and fry up the wings. I spent the time calling the numbers I'd gotten from Melody. I left messages with the two doctors and the lawyer. All the receptionists said they'd call back tomorrow. I was curious to see if they would. I returned my cell to my backpack.

By the time I got back in my car the snow shower had stopped. The light dusting of snow on the cars and the ground made everything look brighter.

I could smell the pizza all the way back to the shop. I was really looking forward to a slice and a couple of wings, but I didn't get a chance to eat them immediately because when I walked into Noah's Ark I had a big surprise waiting for me.

Twenty-Nine

I came in the store and put the food on the counter. Zsa Zsa ran out from the back, ignored me completely, and made a beeline straight for the pizza box.

'Don't say hello to me,' I told her as she began barking at it.

Manuel smiled and got off the stool he was sitting on behind the register. 'Thanks,' he said.

'What's going on?'

'Not much. Sold two containers of fish food but that's about it.' Then he nodded towards the aquariums. 'You've got a visitor.'

I slipped out of my jacket. 'Who?'

'The blonde.'

'George's wife?'

'Roger that.'

He'd been watching the old-movie channel again.

'What's she doing here?'

He shrugged. 'You got me. She came in about fifteen minutes ago.'

'Did she say what she wanted?'

Somehow I didn't think she wanted to talk about buying a pet.

'Not to me,' Manuel said. 'But she looks pissed.'

Great. Just what I didn't need.

'I guess I better go say hello.'

Manuel opened the box and peered inside. 'Have fun.'

'I'm so looking forward to this.'

'I told you not to get involved.'

'I'm not involved.'

'I don't think that's what the blonde thinks.'

'Why do you say that?'

'Intuition. You can have my knife if you want.'

'Don't be ridiculous.'

'Just offering.' Manuel turned back to the pizza box, took a slice out, and bit into it. Zsa Zsa began barking and he broke off a piece and gave it to her. I debated eating now, but decided to wait until I was through with George's blonde. I wanted to savor my food not cram it down my throat.

I made my way through the fish tanks. George's blonde was watching the angelfish. She must have heard me coming because she turned towards me when I was about fifteen feet away.

She was one of those tall, big-boned blondes. Before she'd had George's kid she'd been all hard edges and glitz, one of those women who wouldn't dream of going out of the house without her mascara on. But that had been then. Now she looked blowsy. Her hair was done up in a scarf. She wasn't wearing any makeup and I could see that she'd gained about twenty pounds. She was wearing dirty jeans and a stretched-out turtleneck sweater. Not exactly the image of a professor's wife. Somehow I couldn't imagine George being happy with the way she looked, especially since he was so concerned with his appearance.

'I want to talk to you,' she said to me in a loud voice.

'OK.'

'I want to talk to you now.' And she shook her finger at me.

I don't like when people do that. I mean I really don't like it.

'You are talking to me,' I pointed out. 'And I'll thank you to lower your voice. This is a place of business.' Not that we were doing much today.

'Listen,' she began. Her voice was still too loud.

I dropped mine to a low growl. 'No. You listen,' I told her. 'I'm willing to hear what you have to say but if you don't keep your voice down I'm going to call the cops.'

I guess it was my turn to say that. I could see the anger flashing in her eyes and the way her jaw muscles tightened. She was furious at me, but I didn't have a clue as to why.

'OK,' she said. Her voice was a hiss. 'I don't want you hanging around George.'

'I'm not,' I said. 'He helped me out, but that was about it.'

I didn't think it was necessary to mention his dinner invitation.

'That's not what he told me,' she said. 'He told me you've been calling him up and begging him to come over.'

'Hardly.'

'He said he spent one hundred fifty dollars on you because you insisted that he take you out to dinner.'

I laughed. 'You're kidding me, right?'

She took two steps closer to me and put her arms on her hips. I suddenly realized she was four inches taller and probably fifty pounds heavier than I was.

'You think this is funny?' she demanded.

'No. I think this is ridiculous. George and I never went out to dinner.'

Her face got reddish purple. It wasn't a pretty sight. I moved away from the fish tanks and towards the bags of pet food. She followed. I figured if she were going to attack me I didn't want her tipping over a fish tank. Ruptured bags of pet food were one thing, fish on the floor were another. I glanced over at Manuel. He was looking at us and eating pizza as if he were watching a television show and I was his afternoon's entertainment. George's blonde grunted and I turned back to her.

'So you're telling me I'm crazy?' she said.

'No. I'm telling you you're wrong. Maybe you misheard him. Maybe he took his students out after class.'

Her eyes narrowed. She shook her finger in my face. 'Why the hell would he do something like that?'

'Because it's what professors do.'

'Who cares what professors do?'

'Obviously not you. Which is too bad for George.'

She snorted. 'You're as stupid as George said you were.'

'Really?'

'Yeah. He said you think you know a lot and you don't really know anything at all.'

'Somehow I don't believe you.'

And I didn't.

The blonde shook her head. 'I don't care what you think.

Just don't hit on him. You begged him to stay and he left. He made his choice.'

'That's not exactly how things went. I threw him out.'

'George said you'd say that. He told me not to mention the watch.'

'What watch?'

'The Rolex. You said you'd buy him a Rolex if he stayed with you.'

'Are you insane? Do I look like I have money to do something like that?'

'So you're calling the father of my child a liar?'

'No. I'm calling you one.'

Bad comment. The blonde took another step closer. I noticed she was clenching and unclenching her fists. I'd never seen a woman do that before. It was kind of disturbing. I wondered if she'd taken up boxing. I knew that they were offering it at one of the gyms downtown. And then I reasoned that even if she had she probably wasn't very good at it and that cheered me up a little.

'I have a child to raise so do the decent thing and leave my man alone. Stop calling.'

'Hey, I'm not the one that's calling here. He is.'

'No he's not.'

'You know, he cheated on me with you and he's going to cheat on you with someone else. I'm sorry, but that's what men like him do.'

'You just stay away from him,' the blonde cried and she whirled around and strode out of the store.

'Wow,' Manuel said after the door had slammed. 'That was very exciting. I thought she was going to punch you out.'

'I notice that didn't spoil your appetite.'

'I figured you could take care of yourself and if worst came to worst I could always use my knife.'

'No, Manuel. You could call 911.'

'What was that all about, anyway?'

'That's what I'm going to find out,' I said as I reached for my cellphone.

'Who are you calling?' Manuel asked.

'The Pope. George, of course. I want to find out what the hell is going on.'

He picked up on the second ring. I explained what had just happened.

He sighed. 'I'm so sorry,' he said. 'She's on this new medication and it's made her crazy. I've got a call into her doctor right now.'

'How long has this been going on?'

Another sigh. 'Way too long.'

'Aren't you worried about the kid?'

Before George answered I heard a click on the line.

'Gotta go,' he said. 'I have to take this call.' And before I could say anything else he'd hung up.

'So?' Manuel said.

'So nothing.' I put my cellphone down. 'I never thought she was crazy,' I said. 'A bitch, yes. A crazy person, no.'

Manuel stretched. 'I don't know if she's crazy, but she's really pissed.'

'Where did she get this idea from? That's what I want to know.'

Manuel looked at me as if I were a moron. 'From George. He's probably two-timing her with someone else.'

'So he set her on me?'

'Yeah.'

'Why?'

'So she wouldn't find out who he is getting it on with.'

'That's absurd. Where do you come up with stuff like this?'

Manuel rolled his eyes. 'I don't know what planet you're from, but it ain't this one. I know guys who do stuff like that all the time.'

'Then maybe you should get some new friends. George's blonde is having a bad reaction to the meds she's on.'

'That what George told you?'

'Yeah. It is.'

Manuel looked away.

'You don't believe that?'

'I don't believe in the virgin birth either.'

'Why are you saying that?'

'Because I am. Because it's true.'

'You don't have any proof.'

'Fine. Have it your way.' And Manuel moved the pizza box towards me. 'I saved you a couple slices.'

Actually, he'd left me one slice and no chicken wings. I was not happy.

I spent the rest of the afternoon convincing a man that a twenty-foot Burmese python and a three-year-old child shouldn't be in the same house together, explaining to another man why fish tanks need filters, refusing to order a palm viper for a woman who wanted to surprise her boyfriend with a different kind of birthday present, phoning in orders to my suppliers, listening to a sales rep tell me why I needed a new credit-card company, listening to another sales rep tell me why I needed to advertise online with them, dusting, mopping the floor, reorganizing the small-mammal toys, and catching the crickets that had escaped from their bin.

Around five o'clock to my surprise all three of the men I'd called about Benny Gibson returned my call. Their responses were uniform. The litany went like this: I mentioned the name Benny Gibson and they said they weren't acquainted with him. Then I mentioned Wonder Women and T Rex and they all clammed up – not that they'd been very chatty before – and gave me the names of their lawyers and told me not to bother them anymore. They would deem any future contact harassment and would act accordingly.

Somehow I wasn't surprised. From their point of view nothing good could come from talking to me.

'Oh well,' Manuel said.

'Oh well, indeed,' I replied and we went back to work.

We worked until seven. I'd just turned off the store lights and Manuel, Zsa Zsa, and I were at the door when Calli called.

'You treat me like I'm an encyclopedia,' she groused.

'You mean you're not?'

'Ha. Ha. I've had a very trying day,' Calli said.

'Not as trying as mine.' And I told her about George's blonde.

'I hate to say I told you so, but I told you so.'

I shifted my backpack to my other shoulder. 'That's what Manuel said – more or less.'

Manuel nudged me in the ribs. 'What did I say?'

'Nothing.' And I put my finger across my lips to signify

that he should be quiet. He shrugged and went back to zipping up his jacket.

'So what did you find out?' I asked her.

'Actually nothing.'

'I can't believe that.' Zsa Zsa pranced around my feet.

There was a short silence and then Calli said, 'You know, Robin, it's better to let some things go.'

'I'm not that kind of person.'

'Maybe you should think about changing.'

'Are you warning me off?'

'I didn't say that.'

'Maybe not, but it sure sounds that way.'

Static crackled in my ear for a few seconds, then Calli came back on. 'John is dead. He killed himself. He, not anyone else. The direction you're going in has nothing to do with that.'

'How do you know?'

'Because I do.'

'Who told you?'

Silence.

'So you're telling me there's no connection between Benny Gibson and Richard Walmouth?' I continued.

'Robin, I'm telling you for the last time, forget about this.'

'And if I don't?'

I heard a click. Calli had hung up.

'What was that all about?' Manuel asked.

I realized I was standing by the door to Noah's Ark with my cell in one hand and the keys to the shop in the other.

'I'm not sure,' I said. 'But I don't like it.'

And then I punched in the security code and we all skedaddled out of there before the alarm went off.

Ian looked at me. It was twelve thirty at night and there was no one in the bar except me and Zsa Zsa. I was drinking Scotch and Zsa Zsa was having peanuts and a little beer. It had been a long day for both of us.

'And you're telling me this why?' Ian said after I'd told him about what Bays had told me.

'Because I'm trying to figure out what to do and it helps me talk out loud.'

'Forgetting about it seems like a good plan to me.'

'That's what Calli said.' And I repeated what she'd said to me as well.

'But you're not going to follow her suggestion, are you?' Ian said. 'You're not going to forget about this.'

'No. I'm not.'

'Why?'

'Because I owe John.'

'No you don't.' Ian picked a shred of tobacco off his tongue. 'No one held a gun to his head.'

'They might as well have.'

'Leaving a debate about free will aside, if you do find that person, then what?'

'Then I'll turn him in to the police.'

'But he didn't commit a crime.'

'Yes he did.'

'Not in the eyes of the legal system.'

Which was true.

'I'll figure something out.'

Ian raised an eyebrow. 'That's what I'm afraid of.'

'OK. What would you do in a situation like this?'

'I already told you. I'd forget about it.'

'No you wouldn't. You never forget anything.'

Ian snorted. 'We're not talking about me, we're talking about you. I can do things you can't.'

I leered. 'No kidding.'

Ian blushed. 'That's not what I meant. I have connections you don't.'

'I know what you mean and I could say the same.'

Instead of replying Ian went over and fixed himself a hot chocolate, then carried it back to where I was sitting. 'So Bays told you I thought he was an asshole?' he said, changing the subject.

'Yup.'

'He's right. I do. You think he was telling the truth?'

'Yes. But then I also thought that at Turning Stone.'

Ian took a sip of his hot chocolate and pondered what I'd said. I slipped off the bar stool, put some money in the jukebox and punched in the numbers for 'One Night in Bangkok.' When I sat back down Zsa Zsa woofed. I took a

handful of peanuts and fed them to her one at a time while
Ian picked a piece of gum off the edge of the counter and
threw it in the trash.

'Robin, maybe Calli is warning you not to pursue this
because she's concerned for your safety. Have you thought
of that?'

'Of course I have. I just don't believe that's the reason.'

'And if it were?'

'It wouldn't make any difference anyway.' I lit one of my
own cigarettes. 'I can take care of myself.'

Ian pushed the cup he was using as an ashtray between us.

'You know,' he said, 'if a Health Department inspector
came in now, between the dog and the smoking I'd be in
big trouble.'

'Health Department inspectors don't work after five
o'clock.'

'It was just an observation.' Ian tapped his fingers on
the bar. 'OK. So why do you think Calli is acting the way
she is?'

'I think she's covering for Richard Walmouth.'

Ian leaned forward a little. 'Why?'

'Because she's a friend of his wife.' It sounded silly when
I said it. 'She could be getting a pay-off.'

'To do what?'

'To make sure he gets favorable press.' Which also sounded
silly. Maybe Ian was right. Maybe Calli was warning me off
after all.

'They did an article about him not too long ago,' Ian
mused.

'He's supposed to be very community-minded.'

Ian snorted. 'Right.'

'I think I need to talk to him.'

'And say what?'

It was a good question.

Ian took a swallow of his hot chocolate. 'I've always found
that the more information I have the better my questions
are.'

I had another sip of my Scotch and thought about how to
get the information I needed. There was LexisNexis.
Unfortunately I didn't have access to that. I could go do

research downtown, but that probably wouldn't get me that far either.

'Bays might know something,' Ian pointed out.

'I'm sure he does, but he's not going to tell me.'

'He might if it were put to him the right way.'

I thought back to what he said. 'I don't think so. I don't have any leverage.'

'I could persuade him.'

I shook my head. 'Not worth it.'

'Then how about Melody? She might have something to say.'

'She's already said it.'

Ian picked up his cell and punched in a number. Then he walked to the front of the bar. I couldn't hear what he was saying but I could tell from his expression he wasn't getting the result he wanted. He punched in another number, listened for a moment, hung up, and walked back towards me.

'She's down in Florida. Something about her sick mom. And her cell is disconnected.'

'How could you be talking to her if her cell is disconnected?'

'I was talking to her roommate.'

'Oh. Have you noticed there seems to be a lot of leaving town going around?'

'Yeah, I have.' He began tapping his fingers on the counter again. 'You should forget about this.'

'You know I'm not going to.'

Ian was silent for a moment. Then he said, 'So where else can you get the information you need?'

I thought about the two docs and the lawyer. I could keep at them, but what would be the point? I believed them when they said they'd get an order of protection and have me arrested if I got within sixty feet. It's one thing to talk to someone like Bays and it's another thing to knock on the door of a $500,000 house and demand to speak to the person inside. No. They were a bad road to go down.

'I could use the direct approach and go through Benny Gibson's files.'

'Cut out the middle man.'

'Exactly.'

'So where do you think these files would be?'

'Probably in the office.'

'Not in Benny Gibson's house? You said Benny and Joe had a fight. Maybe Benny took his files to his house.'

'He certainly could have, but I saw a lot of boxes in the office. I'm betting that even if Benny took his files to his house Joe brought them back again.'

'That makes sense.' Ian grinned. 'It would also be a good thing because Benny Gibson's house would be difficult to get into, with the neighbors being so close and all.' Ian looked at me and I looked at him. 'What about the alarm system?' he asked.

'I don't think there is one. I didn't see a key pad by the door.'

Ian scratched his chin.

'Doesn't mean there couldn't be one. It could be located someplace else.'

'Doubtful. They're usually located close to the entranceway. Otherwise they're too inconvenient.'

'True.' Ian ran his finger around the rim of his hot-chocolate cup. 'Could anyone see you from the street?'

I closed my eyes and visualized the layout. 'The front office looks on to the street, but the back offices look into the alleyway. The walls of the other buildings that face the alleyway are solid brick. No windows.'

'I see,' Ian said. He fell silent.

'So what do you think?'

'If you were actually telling me about this I'd tell you it might work, but since you're not telling me I'm not saying that. Of course, if you were telling me, I would also have to point out that this is not the kind of thing someone like you is suited for. However, since you never listen to what I say I wouldn't tell you that anyway.'

'Having a sensitive moment, are we?'

'Yes, I am.' Ian put his hand to his chest. 'I'm a very sensitive person.'

'Yes, you are.' And he was. But he was also someone who was capable of hurting someone really bad and never giving it another thought.

I finished up my drink.

'Go home,' Ian called to me as I left.

'I am.'

Which was true. I just wasn't staying there.

I gave him a goodbye wave and headed out into the night. I wanted to change my clothes and drop Zsa Zsa off at the house before I went out again.

Thirty

It took me fifteen minutes to drive down to the Armory. During that time I saw three cars and four people out walking, plus a stray dog ripping a plastic garbage bag to shreds. The city was buttoned up for the night. The streets were quiet down at the Armory as well. Unlike New York or Chicago, Syracuse isn't big on nightlife during the week. Especially in the winter and early spring. Most people are home by ten and in bed by eleven. The weekends are a different story, with lots of people in their twenties and thirties dining out and bar-hopping. Then there are cops all over the place making sure that nothing happens. But not tonight. Tonight nothing was happening.

Tonight bartenders leaned against cabinets and watched TV. Tonight customers leaned on their elbows and nursed their drinks. Tonight you could put your car anywhere you wanted to. Even the panhandlers were off the streets. They were probably holed up someplace smoking an eight-ball. Pools of light from the street lamps reflected on to the sidewalks. Onondaga Creek rolled along black and silent within its banks.

A photographer would have loved it. Very Edward Hopper. But not me. I wanted the streets to be busier. That way my vehicle wouldn't stand out. After a minimal amount of deliberation I decided it would be safer to park my car in one of the nearby lots. The one I had in mind was used by the wait staff from the nearby restaurants and bars and hence would remain half full until those establishments closed. Hopefully, I'd be gone long before then.

I parked my car next to a black SUV, got out, put my money in the meter, got a ticket, walked back, put it on my windshield, locked my door, and left. Normally, I'm prepared to take my chances with the parking gods, but the last thing I needed now was to get towed from the lot because I'd been too cheap to pay the three bucks.

The lot was a block from Joe Gibson's office and I took it at a medium pace. If anyone saw me I didn't want anything about me to stand out. I was probably being paranoid, but I did it anyway. It beat thinking about what would happen if I was wrong and the office was alarmed.

I encountered one couple on my way to the office, but they didn't see me, or if they did they weren't paying attention because they were too busy arguing. Their voices followed me all the way to Joe's office. The street in front was deserted. No cars were driving by. I took a quick look up and down, stepped into the alley that ran next to the building, and put on my gloves. They were black, like my jeans, jacket, and turtleneck sweater.

The alleyway was narrow and curved around the building's back end. Out of the corner of my eye I caught two rats disappearing behind a garbage can. I was sure there were many more that I wasn't seeing. Probably a whole colony. The creek and the garbage cans would attract them.

I stepped over a couple of empty beer bottles and a garbage bag spouting crumpled-up newspaper as I followed the alley. It was dark, which was good in one regard – no one could see me – and bad in another because it was difficult to see where I was going. When I got to the back I looked up. There was the ladder to the fire escape. It was about six feet off the floor, which is what they usually are. If the alley was wider I could have driven my car down it and stood on that. Unfortunately it wasn't. I looked over towards the back wall and spotted a large plastic toter. It was sturdy enough to do the trick.

I dragged it over and managed to get it on its side. Then I climbed up on it and got hold of the ladder and climbed up the rungs, just like I used to do at my aunt's apartment in the Bronx when I was a kid. I guess you never lose the knack for certain things. In two seconds I was on the second floor.

There was an air conditioner in the window that Joe hadn't bothered to remove. Obviously he wasn't paying the utility bill. It took all my strength but I managed to push the window frame up slightly. Then I pulled the air conditioner on to the fire escape and shimmied into the opening I'd created.

I pulled the blinds down and looked around. I guessed I was in Joe Gibson's office. A look at a handful of junk mail left on one of the cartons confirmed it. There were stacks of files on the floor and the chairs, as opposed to the desk, which was an oasis of calm. Since I didn't know what I was looking for I was going to have to go through as much of the material as I could.

I started with the files on the two chairs. They were records of old deals made in the thirties and forties. I scanned each of them and put them aside. Then I hunkered down and looked at the ones on the floor. There were three piles. All the information dated back to the fifties and sixties. There were old tax records, insurance forms, deeds, bills of sale, and inspection reports. Most of them had to do with properties in Liverpool and were of no interest to me.

I got up and sat down behind the desk. Unlike the chairs and shelving in the office, Joe Gibson's desk had the aura that expensive pieces of furniture project. It was made of rosewood. It gleamed. You could tell that whoever was polishing it loved it. In contrast to the rest of the room the top of the desk was immaculate. The only thing on it was a hand-tooled leather calendar.

I thumbed through it and learned that Joe Gibson had an appointment with the dentist in two weeks and with his doctor tomorrow. Other than that the calendar was bare. I was guessing he was the kind of guy that kept track of his important stuff in a PDA.

He didn't live in an expensive housing development but he bought a lot of high-end accessories. And of course, I reflected, all that plastic surgery had cost him a pretty penny as well. He certainly wasn't shy about spending money on himself.

And on that thought I went back to work. I started with the left-hand side of the desk. The first drawer was full of pens and pencils. Costly ones. I picked up two Mont Blanc pens and put them down. The man had good taste. The next drawer was even more interesting. There were two nine-by-twelve manila envelopes. Both were fastened with clasps.

I opened the first envelope. It was filled with hundred-dollar bills. I opened the other one. It was as well. I did a rough count and came up with eighty grand.

Not bad. Was someone paying Joe off? Or was it just his walking-around money? Or was it the rent from the buildings the realty company owned? Was everything off the books? It wouldn't surprise me if it were.

For a moment I thought about keeping say ten grand or so, but my conscience got the better of me and I returned the money to the envelopes, put the envelopes back in the drawer, and closed it. Then I started on the upper right-hand side. There was a thin manila envelope sitting on top of a bunch of tax returns.

I opened it up. In it was a prospectus from a company that sold gaming equipment. I turned it over. It was addressed to Richard Walmouth. He had scrawled a note across the back. *TG. Does this work for you? R.* TG as in 'T Rex Gibson'? So it was true. Walmouth was going to build a casino. Or at least he was thinking about it. And Benny Gibson was along for the ride. What did Walmouth need him for? According to Trent, Benny had been broke.

But Otto had intimated that he wasn't. Maybe he'd been scamming Trent. Maybe he'd been busy accumulating money to pour into this venture. Maybe that's why he wasn't paying his taxes. Maybe that's why he wasn't fixing up the buildings. Maybe he just wanted to empty them so he could apply for Federal grants, something he couldn't do if they were still occupied, and put the money into the casino. Or it could be that Walmouth was returning the favors Benny had done for him. Nothing like a spot of arson and manslaughter to put a man in your debt.

Another question: How come the paper hadn't mentioned this, at least not in any substantive way? Last year, if I remembered correctly, there'd been a couple of lines in a real-estate column speculating on the possibility of a new casino, but that had been that. I hadn't seen anything else. It was hard to believe that people didn't know about this. We were talking big money here.

I could see where Gibson being investigated might be inconvenient for Richard Walmouth. Especially if anyone started looking at the pictures on Gibson's computer. But inconvenient enough to kill him? Doubtful. But holding him up for the dead vagrant? That was a different story. I realized I was tapping my fingers on the desk.

And now Joe was involved. Had he been involved all along or did he just come on board after his brother had died?

The casino was what Benny and Joe were discussing with the doctors and the lawyer at Wonder Women. They were trying to get them to invest. And then something else occurred to me. How were they hoping to get this deal through the legislature? They had to have a Native American connection. That was the only way casinos opened up these days. Was it with the Mohawks? The Onondagas? I wondered if Manuel's friends Chad and Jellybean had heard any rumors. My money was on the Mohawks. The Onondagas were more traditional. I was wondering what the timeline for this endeavor was when I thought I heard a noise. It was very faint.

I listened hard. There it was again. Possibly a door closing? Now the sounds were different. Muffled thuds one right after the other. I closed my eyes so I could hear better. It was the stairs. Someone was coming up the stairs. Then I heard voices. A burst of laughter. Two men I thought, although I wasn't sure. Of course, whoever it was could be going to the third floor. Maybe they were having a late-night business meeting. Maybe they were going to have sex on one of the desks.

Unfortunately since they had to pass Gibson's office to get to the stairs that led to the third floor there was no way to tell before it was too late where they were going. Once they walked through Gibson's office door I wouldn't have time to get back out, replace the air conditioner, and shut the window. As it was I was cutting it pretty close now.

I quickly closed the desk drawers, grabbed my backpack, and slipped out the window and on to the fire escape. Then I wiggled the air conditioner back into the window. It was heavy and my shoulders began screaming in protest, but I ignored them because by now I could hear voices. Definitely two men. I recognized Joe Gibson's voice right off. The other one sounded familiar but I couldn't place it.

I wasn't listening to what they were talking about because by now I was leaning on the window to shut it. The window wasn't going down. I pushed as hard as I could. The right side wasn't giving an inch. It was stuck. I looked around the fire escape. There was nothing I could use on it.

I studied the molding around the window. It had been patched several times with wood putty. Sometimes if the molding was warped the window wouldn't come down. I hoped that was the case now. I took my knife out of my backpack and opened it up. I was going as fast as I could but my fingers were clumsy from the cold and everything took longer than it should have. I pried the top part of the molding up, then ripped the rest of it off.

The window crashed down on top of the air conditioner. Or at least that's what it sounded like. I expected everyone to come running. No one did. A crack snaked its way across one of the glass panes. Two seconds later I heard the door open. I snugged up against the wall.

'I could swear I heard the window slam,' Gibson said. I recognized the falsetto in the voice immediately.

'I didn't hear anything,' a second voice replied.

I heard a grunt then Gibson said, 'It's cold in here. It feels as if someone left the window open.'

'The baseboard heating probably isn't working,' the second voice suggested.

I heard the drag of something across the floor then Joe Gibson said, 'No. It's fine.'

A moment later the other voice said, 'These old buildings have funny air currents.'

The other voice sounded so familiar. But I couldn't place it. I was trying to figure out who it was as I rubbed my arms to keep warm. The wind had kicked up and I was blinking snowflakes out of my eyes.

'Funny,' Gibson said. I could tell from the sound that he was right at the window. 'I don't remember this crack being here.'

I held my breath. I was now so close to the wall I couldn't get any closer to it without being in it. This, I decided, had not been one of my better ideas.

'I'm sure you just didn't notice it,' the second man said.

And then I recognized his voice. It was John's pal, Trent Goodwell. I was positive. God. What an idiot I'd been. I'd believed everything he'd told me. Now I wondered how much had been true and how much had been lies.

There was a moment of silence then Gibson said, 'Thanks.'

I wondered what Gibson was thanking Goodwell for as I made out the rustle of papers being moved. I caught the words 'how soon' and 'good shot' and 'next year', then the voices moved farther away. I took a chance, sidled up towards the window, and peeked in. I saw Trent Goodwell's back as he went through the door. There was no way I could mistake him for someone else.

I felt a strong urge to speak to him now. I had a moment of satisfaction as I fantasized about dashing into the room and seeing the expression on their faces. But that wasn't going to happen. I listened for a moment. I could make out Gibson's and Goodwell's voices rising and falling. Now was the time to leave. It probably would have been prudent to wait until after they left, but I was losing feeling in my fingers and toes and my cheeks had gone numb. If I waited much longer I wouldn't be able to climb down the ladder at all because I wouldn't be able to feel the rungs. When I finally made it down the ladder and through the alley to the sidewalk I looked out. The street was deserted. I stepped on to it. The light in Gibson's office was on, so they were still up there. I cupped my hands together and blew into them as I made my way to my car. I was going to wait for Trent Goodwell at his house. It was time we had another chat.

Trent arrived home half an hour later. I almost missed him because I'd fallen asleep but the sound of his vehicle pulling into his driveway woke me up. He got out of his car and hurried towards his house. He walked with a peculiar bobbing motion. His head was stuck out in front of him and his eyes were planted on the ground. I could see his mouth moving. He was talking to himself.

He must have been lost in his thoughts because he didn't become aware of me until I put my hand on his arm as he was turning his key in his front door. He spun around. I

smelled wine on his breath. He'd probably been out celebrating his good fortune.

'You and I need to talk,' I said.

'What are you doing here?' he sputtered. 'It's late.'

'Believe me, I know what time it is. Let's go inside.'

'Why?'

'So we don't wake the neighbors up. And anyway, it's
cold out here.'

At my words Trent tightened his scarf around his neck. It
was one of those long ones, the kind that English school-
boys wear.

'What do you want?'

I guess Trent didn't care about the neighbors. Oh well.

I told him I wanted an explanation of what he was doing
in Joe Gibson's office tonight.

His eyes widened. 'I wasn't in Joe Gibson's office.'

'I saw you there.'

'How could you have?'

I lied and told him I'd been driving by.

'But I didn't see you,' he protested.

'Maybe you should have your eyes checked.'

He studied one of the slats on the porch floor.

'Tell me,' I said. 'Was anything that you told me when
you came to my house true?'

'I have to go inside,' Trent said, still avoiding my eyes. 'I
have to go to sleep. I have a long day tomorrow.'

'Don't you care about John?' I asked him. 'Don't you care
at all?'

Trent looked up at me. 'I was doing it for him.'

'Doing what?'

'Investing . . .'

'In the casino?'

Trent went on as if I hadn't said anything. 'I wanted to
make a lot of money so we could go live somewhere like in
Greece or the Azores. Somewhere warm. Someplace where
people would leave us alone.'

'I thought it was a question of you leaving other people
alone.'

'That's cruel.'

'No. That's true.'

'You don't know what it's like,' he cried.

'The only thing I do know is that you're a fuckin' liar. Is anything you told me the truth?'

Trent wrung his hands together. 'I loved John.'

'You had a funny way of showing it.'

'I wasn't sleeping with Benny Gibson. I swear.'

'Maybe you were and maybe you weren't.' I raised a hand to forestall his comment. 'Right now I'm interested in the stuff you told me about Benny Gibson and his buildings. Why did you lie?'

Trent massaged his forehead with the fingers of his right hand. 'Because this is none of your business.'

'Fair enough. What were you doing with Joe Gibson?'

He shrugged.

'Giving him money?'

He stuck his chin out. 'I'm being a good businessman.'

'Even though he might have had something to do with John's suicide.'

Trent's voice rose in protest. 'He didn't have anything to do with John's suicide, his brother did. And anyway that was John's decision.'

'I don't buy that.'

'It doesn't matter whether you do or not.'

'So you're still going into business with Walmouth.'

There was the tiniest twitch below Trent's left eye. I'd scored a hit. It was all I needed to know.

'You know, you're not a good friend to John. You're not a good friend at all,' I told him.

Trent pushed his door open. 'Well, neither are you. He wouldn't have wanted you poking around, making a fuss. He would have wanted you to forget about this. He didn't like scenes. He didn't like being the center of attention. Or have you forgotten?'

'What a load of crap,' I said. 'Is there anything you can't rationalize?'

Trent stepped inside and slammed the door. I stood there for a moment, then turned and went back to my car. I probably could have handled that better, I reflected as I drove home, but I really didn't see how. Nor did I care.

To cap the evening, when I got home I found a note pasted

on my door. Right in the center. It would have been hard to miss. It said, 'Drop it.' Very succinct. The paper was white printer paper, the type was probably sixteen point, and I guessed the font was Times New Roman. In other words, it was something anyone could have printed.

I tore the note up and went inside. I was tired, I was disgusted, and the only thing the note had done was make me even angrier than I already was. Which was saying a lot.

Thirty-One

It was about nine thirty the next evening and Ian had switched on the local news. Zsa Zsa and I watched as the announcer mentioned that a Chester Jacobs had just been found with a gunshot wound to the leg. The injury was not considered life-threatening and he was being treated at University Hospital. People with information about the crime were urged to call the police hotline. Then they flashed his picture on the screen.

'Wasn't that one of the guys in here looking for Chad?' I asked Ian.

'Yup.' Ian lit a cigarette. 'His real name is Chester. Wow. No wonder he doesn't want anyone to know.'

I took a sip of my Scotch and was listening to the weatherman tell us we were going to enjoy two mild days when the door flew open.

'Robin,' Manuel cried. 'You gotta help.'

I took one look at his face and ran outside. Ian followed. Chad was in the front seat of Manuel's car. He was moaning. There was blood coming from his forehead and pouring out of his nose. I went to open the door, but Ian pushed me out of the way.

'I take it this is the second moron in tonight's little adventure,' he said to Manuel as he opened the car door.

Manuel gave him a blank look. 'I don't know what you're talking about.'

'They announced C.J. was shot on the news about three minutes ago,' Ian explained as he squatted next to Chad.

I heard Manuel curse. 'But he's OK, right?'

'He has a bullet in his leg,' I said. 'The police want anyone who has information to call them.'

'He won't talk,' Manuel said.

'You better hope not.'

'I have a broken nose,' Chad mumbled.

Ian grunted. 'You're lucky you don't have more than that.'

I think Chad told Ian he was in serious pain, but it was hard to understand him with the blood coming out of his nose.

'Put your head up and pinch the bridge of your nose,' Ian instructed. 'That should stop the bleeding. And for your information you didn't break your nose, you tore your cartilage. You can't break your nose because it's not made of bone.'

Somehow I don't think Chad cared about that particular piece of information. Instead he pointed to his side. 'I think I broke a couple of ribs too and my head hurts.'

'Getting kicked in the head will do that to you,' Ian said.

'How do you know what happened?' I asked Ian.

'Because I've seen enough of this stuff.' Then he turned and asked me to get him some paper towels. When I came back he took the roll out of my hands, ripped off a handful, and blotted off the blood on Chad's forehead. There was a good-size gash on his left temple.

'Here.' Ian handed him the roll of towels. 'Use these to clean yourself up.'

Chad took a wad and held them under his nose. The bleeding was beginning to slow down.

'So did you or the other guy start it?' I asked.

'C.J. just came at me,' Chad muttered. 'I didn't see him coming or nothing. He kicked the crap out of me.'

'Guess he wanted his money,' Ian said.

Chad didn't say anything.

'So how did your gun go off?'

'It fell out of my pocket.'

'You didn't have the safety on?'

Chad remained silent.

'I bet C.J. was shot in the back of his leg,' Ian guessed.

Chad pressed the wad of paper towels closer to his nose.

'That's what I thought,' Ian said. 'Where's the gun?'

'It's in the car.'

'Give it to me,' Ian ordered.

Manuel looked at me.

'Do it, Manuel.'

'But, Robin . . .'

'Now.'

He went around to the driver's side, reached under the seat, came back with a brown-paper bag, and handed it to Ian.

Ian peered in the bag. 'Nice. A Glock. This should be worth something.'

'Hey,' Manuel squawked, 'that's seven hundred bucks.'

'I know what it's worth,' Ian said, 'and I know who would like it.'

'You can't do that,' Manuel cried.

Ian snorted. 'I most certainly can.'

'Robin, make him give it back.'

'Absolutely not,' I told Manuel. 'You're in enough trouble as it is.'

'I didn't do anything.'

'You just happened by.'

'More or less. I drove up just as it was happening.'

I rolled my eyes.

'What? Don't you believe me?'

'No. I don't. Now what do you want me to do.'

Manuel hitched his pants up.

'Tell me!'

'Chad needs a place to stay for a couple of days,' Manuel muttered.

'So take Chad home with you.'

'I can't. My mom would kill me.'

'Forget it,' I told him. 'The answer is no.'

'But he has nowhere else to go.'

'I'm sure he has friends.'

'Not anymore.'

'I have to work.'

'That's all right,' Ian said. 'Go home. It's going to be a slow night tonight, anyway.'

'Thanks,' I told him.

He grinned. 'Any time.'

Manuel tugged at my jacket. 'Come on, Robin, it's just for a couple of nights.'

I don't know why I said yes, but I did, just like Manuel knew I would. I hate the fact that I'm so predictable. Manuel helped Chad into my vehicle and we drove out to Wegman's. Chad stayed in the car while I ran in and got Advil, Neosporin, tape, and butterfly bandages for the gash on his forehead. Then I threw some milk, cereal, bread, and peanut butter into the cart as well. Chad would probably be hungry later. And anyway, it's always good to have food in the house.

As I got back to the car Zsa Zsa moved to the rear seat. She'd been cleaning Chad up. It was a job that would take a while. Right now he looked like a poster child for a fright show. Chad's eyes were swollen and ringed with black and purple and the gash on his forehead was still dripping blood.

'Thanks,' he said. 'I'll be gone by tomorrow. I promise.'

'Where will you go?'

'The Rez. I should have stayed up there.'

'How come you came down?'

'It was a stupid idea. I wanted to make some money so I could pay those guys off. I figured I'd give them maybe half and make them happy.'

'Only it didn't.'

'That's for sure.'

I started the car and Chad collapsed back in his seat and closed his eyes.

'What do you know about the casino that Walmouth is trying to build?' I asked. I was betting that Chad would have heard some gossip about it.

'Word is Albany is supposed to give the OK next year. At least that's what Benny said.'

'Benny Gibson?'

'Yeah. He was going down to Albany and talking to people. I guess now his brother is.'

'You knew Benny Gibson?'

'He used to come into Wonder Women.'

'What were you doing in Wonder Women?'

'I bar-backed there for a couple of months.'

'What happened?'

'The owner kept cutting back my hours so I quit. You got a smoke?'

I fished two cigarettes out of my pack, lit them both, and handed one to Chad.

'Thanks.' He took a long drag and put his head back on the seat rest.

'So tell me more about Benny Gibson.'

'He was a pervert.'

'How d'you know? Did he have it written on his forehead?'

'I saw him one day in the mall and I had one of my cousins with me. She was nine. The way he was looking at her wasn't good.'

'Go on.'

'That's it.'

'That's it?'

He put up his hand. 'I swear. Some things you just know.'

'And you didn't do anything?'

'What was there to do? He didn't do anything. And anyway, he was helping with the casino. Which was a good thing. It's going to make us rich.'

'Us?'

'Yeah. Like my people. My tribe.'

'That isn't what happened with Turning Stone.' At Turning Stone there'd been no end of controversy within the tribe. The people for it. The people against it. The people who got rich. The people who didn't.

'Yeah. But this is different.'

I moved on to East Genesee and braked for a stoplight.

Chad winced. 'Take it easy.'

I apologized. 'How is this going to be different?'

'Because we're going to do it right.'

'So who's the front man?'

Chad mentioned a name I hadn't heard of.

'And who is he?'

'One of the chiefs.'

We stopped at another light. 'And Walmouth is the behind-the-scenes guy?'

'I don't know.' Chad groaned. 'My head is killing me.'

'Chester really kicked the shit out of you.'

'I thought I could talk to him, but he just got really pissed when I showed up without all the cash. I tried to explain to him.'

'Then why'd you show up? I wouldn't have.'

Chad grimaced again. 'I thought I'd have backup.'

'Manuel?'

Chad didn't say anything.

'Don't you know he's always late?'

'He got caught in a traffic accident.' Chad groaned again. 'It hurts to breathe.'

'I got bad news for you. It's going to hurt more tomorrow.'

We drove in silence for a while. I spent the time thinking about how little sense Chad's story made.

'So how were you going to make the money?'

'What money?'

'The money that you were going to give Chester.'

Chad groaned louder. 'I feel like I'm going to puke.'

I pulled over to the side of the road.

'What did you do that for?'

'You said you had to throw up.'

'No I didn't.'

'Yeah you did.'

Chad looked at me. I looked at him.

'I repeat, how were you going to make the money to give Chester?'

'I had some.'

'How'd you make it?'

'We . . . we . . . worked installing car alarms,' Chad stuttered.

'What did you do?'

'I told you.'

'You told me something.' And suddenly I knew. There was only one thing that made sense.

'You were going to rob Chester, weren't you?' I asked. 'That's why you set up the meeting. But things got out of hand.'

'No, Robin. You're wrong,' Chad answered. But I could tell he was lying.

'I don't think I am. Was Manuel the driver?'

'It wasn't like that.'

'Then what was it like?'

Chad looked straight ahead.

'Not talking, huh?' I asked.

'My head hurts.'

'At least if you're going to set up a scam do a good job.'

'That's cold.'

'I suppose it is,' I replied.

We finished the rest of the ride in silence. Which was a good thing because I needed time to get myself under control. I was seething. Not about Chad. From him I expected this kind of behavior, but I didn't expect it from Manuel. Maybe I should, but I didn't. Once we got home Chad went off to clean himself up and I called Manuel.

'This is it,' I said when he picked up.

'What are you talking about?'

'I'm talking about the fact that Chad tried to rob C.J.'

There was a few seconds then Manuel said, 'That's what he told you?'

'Yes,' I lied.

'It was a dumb idea.'

'It certainly was. So why did you go along with it?'

'I didn't think things would go down the way they did.'

'That is not an excuse.'

'Hey,' Manuel squawked, 'he's my homie. He needed my help. What else could I do?'

'You could have not gone.'

'He has a kid with my cousin.'

'The one you've been babysitting?'

'Yes.'

'Lovely.'

'I promised my cousin I'd keep Chad safe, OK?'

I couldn't think of anything to say.

'So I'll see you in the morning?' Manuel asked tentatively.

Instead of answering I studied the curtains in my living room. They needed to be cleaned.

'Robin . . .'

'Yes, Manuel?'

'Please.'

I relented. 'Fine. I'll see you in the morning.'

'Thanks. Thanks for everything.'

I hung up. One part of me wanted to brain Manuel for his stupidity while the other part wanted to hug him and keep him safe. I was thinking that I was glad I didn't have kids when I heard Chad and Zsa Zsa walking down the stairs. Zsa Zsa scratched at my pants legs and I bent down and rubbed behind her ears. Then I turned around to study Chad. The gash on his forehead looked even nastier with all the blood cleaned off it. I went and got the Neosporin and the butterfly bandages and closed it up as best I could.

'You're going to have a nasty scar,' I said.

'I know.'

I sighed. Here I was harboring a known felon. I couldn't even imagine what George would have said. Well, I could. He would have picked up the phone and called the cops. Mr Straight Arrow. But I couldn't do that. There was Manuel to consider and Chad looked so pathetic I felt bad for him even though he didn't deserve it.

So I made up the bed for him and gave him some clean towels. He ended up staying two days before one of his friends picked up him and drove him back to Canada.

'I owe you,' he told me when he left. 'If you ever need anything tell Manuel and I'll do it.'

The next day the local television news said that Chester had been released from the hospital. Guess the wound wasn't that serious. The police were still looking for leads in his shooting: the victim had refused to aid them in their investigation and no witnesses had come forward. Fancy that.

I wasn't worried about the police finding Chad or Manuel. I was worried about Chester's friends finding them. But after a couple of days I figured that if they were going to do something they would have done it already and I went back to thinking about Richard Walmouth. I can only think about one thing at a time and Richard Walmouth was it.

No matter where I turned everything seemed to end with Walmouth.

I figured it was time we had a talk so I called Walmouth's office and left a message with his personal assistant. She said she'd pass it on. I wasn't hopeful that she would or that if she did I'd hear from him, but as it turned out I was wrong.

Thirty-Two

I was spared the trouble of going to see Richard Walmouth because he ended up coming to see me. I had just closed up the shop for the evening. Manuel's mom had picked him up and Zsa Zsa and I were walking to our car which I'd parked a little way down the block when a black Hummer cruised to a stop by the curb in front of the store. The Hummer loomed over the street, making everything around it look small and shabby. Not that the street needed any help.

Normally I would have figured that the vehicle contained Walmouth or one of his cronies. Had to. I mean who else could it be, right? None of my friends would own a car like that. And a Hummer wasn't the type of ride you typically saw in this kind of neighborhood. My neighbors tended to drive rusted-out hulks. However, the last time I'd seen Walmouth he was driving a Cadillac Escalade. I lit a cigarette and waited.

A moment later the rear door opened and Richard Walmouth leaned out. I guess the man had a thing for expensive cars.

'You want to talk to me?' he said.

'That's what I told your personal assistant.'

He jerked his head towards the inside of the vehicle. 'Then get in.'

For a moment I thought about not getting in. What had my grandmother always said about not accepting rides from strange men in cars? But then I figured that if someone like Richard Walmouth wanted to do something bad to me he'd turf it out. People in his position don't like to get their hands dirty. Especially not in a brand-new expensive car – although given his income bracket he could probably trash it and go pick up another one from the dealer without putting a dent in his bank account.

I put my cigarette out and walked to the car. Zsa Zsa ran ahead of me.

'The dog doesn't get in,' Walmouth said.

'Then forget it,' I told Walmouth. 'If Zsa Zsa doesn't ride neither do I. Understand?'

'Yeah. I understand but let's remember you were the one that wanted to talk to me,' Walmouth said.

'Well, you must want to talk to me as well,' I told him. 'Otherwise you wouldn't be slumming in this part of town.'

He stared at me for a moment. The streetlight emphasized his weakening jawline. I could see the beginning of jowls. Something I hadn't noticed when I'd seen him getting out of his ride at the cafe.

'I don't like dogs,' he announced. 'They shed and they smell.'

No wonder his wife had looked the way she had at the sight of him, I thought. This man was a real charmer.

'Well, this dog doesn't shed and she's just had a bath.' I mean the nerve of him.

Walmouth was quiet for another moment and then he said, 'Go around to the other side of the car and get in.'

'And Zsa Zsa?'

'Her too. But so help me if she pees or poops in the car I'll throw her out the window.'

'That's insulting. She hasn't done anything like that since she was eight weeks old.'

Walmouth slammed his door shut and I walked around to the other side and got in. Zsa Zsa followed.

'What,' I said as I sat down, 'no one to hold the door? Where have manners gone these days?'

Walmouth grunted. Then he nodded to the driver and he took off. The driver was a large, generic bodyguard type with a shaved head. He was wearing a black shirt that cut into his fat neck and a black leather jacket. But there was something familiar about him. I knew I'd seen him before. I just couldn't figure out where.

Walmouth was doing suburban high-end casual. He was wearing a chocolate-brown suede jacket over a small-checked brown shirt and a pair of corduroy pants. When he moved his hand I could see his watch. It was an expensive Piaget.

I'd seen one similar to it advertised in the *Wall Street Journal* recently for $20,000.

I sat back in my seat and touched the leather. It was like glove leather. There was a large storage/table-like structure between Walmouth's seat and mine. I half expected the Hummer to start taxiing down the runway. Zsa Zsa looked at me and woofed. I picked her up and put her on my lap.

'So what do you want?' I asked Walmouth.

'It isn't what I want,' he said. 'It's what you want.'

'What I want to know is simple. I want to know why John set me up and then went and killed himself.'

'So I've heard.'

'How did you hear?'

Walmouth rubbed his chin with his right hand. I could see the beginnings of bags under his eyes. He looked like someone who had had a long day and wanted to be home.

'People talk. I hear things.'

'What people?'

He gave an exasperated sigh. 'Do you want to hear what I have to tell you or do you not?'

'Yes. I do.'

'Good. John was very fragile. He had a wealth of psychological problems.'

'So you knew him?'

'Not really. I'm repeating what the human-resources officer told me.'

That struck me as a strange comment for an HR person to make, but I didn't say anything.

Walmouth continued, 'He worked in my office for two months a couple of years ago.'

That was before I knew him. 'What did he do?'

'He was an administrative assistant.'

'Meaning?'

'He ran errands, answered e-mails, took care of packages. He did what needed to be done.'

'And then?'

'And then we reorganized the office and eliminated his job. He was offered another position with our office down in Utica but he wasn't interested so he quit.'

'May I see his record?'

Walmouth clasped his hands together. 'I'm afraid that that wouldn't be appropriate.'

'Why?'

'Because those records are private.'

'But he's dead.'

'It doesn't make any difference. We could get sued.'

'So what was the link between John and Benny Gibson?'

Walmouth bent over and straightened out one of his socks. 'As far as I know there wasn't any.'

'I find that hard to believe.'

Walmouth shrugged. 'Believe what you want.'

I realized we were cruising the neighborhood. 'And between Benny Gibson's daughter and John?'

'None that I know of. There. Are you satisfied?'

'Not even remotely.'

Walmouth put his hands on his legs. 'I've been very patient with you.'

'In regards to what?'

'You've talked to my wife. You've talked to my daughter. That's enough. I want you to stay out of my business. I will not have my life disrupted by the likes of you.'

I let the 'likes of you' part go. 'I'm not going away until I find out what happened to John.'

'I have nothing to do with John. I have nothing to do with Benny.'

'Benny worked for you.'

Walmouth's mouth compressed itself into a thin line.

'Benny worked for you unofficially.'

'Prove it.'

'Don't worry, I will. Every time I talk to someone your name seems to come up. You want to explain that?'

'I've already told you, I don't want to explain anything to you. I don't have to explain anything to you.'

'Then why did you come looking for me?'

'To tell you that I've had enough. I'm in a very delicate business negotiation and I don't need anything to disturb it.'

'I'm flattered you think I have that power.'

'I don't, but the rumors you're starting could be annoying and I don't like annoying.'

'You mean the rumors about Benny Gibson?'

Walmouth looked at me, but didn't say anything. I noticed that his neck was wrinkly. Even though his face didn't show it he was older than he looked.

Zsa Zsa shifted on my lap. I moved her paw off my stomach. 'The rumors saying you had him killed,' I continued.

'And to what end would I be doing this?'

'How about because he was blackmailing you about the fires he set for you. About the fires he set for you in which someone died. That's manslaughter. And then there's the kiddie-porn factor. Not good. Not good at all.'

Walmouth raised an eyebrow. Mr Cool. 'And where did you get this information?' he demanded.

'A book I read.'

Walmouth leaned forward. I could see his hands clenching and unclenching. The car started slowing down. I was aware of the sudden tension in the back of the driver's neck. Some people would have taken that as a sign to shut up, but I figured if I pushed hard enough maybe Walmouth would lose his temper and say something.

'So why did you have him killed? Was it the fire? That was careless on his part. It could have raised lots of problems for you. Or was it because he liked little girls? I can understand why you might consider him a liability.'

Walmouth opened his mouth and closed it. He rested his hands on his knees. I could see from the way his hands looked that he'd gotten himself back under control. Instead of answering my question he studied me for a moment. Then he said, 'Do you have good legal representation?'

'What do you mean?' It wasn't the question I'd expected.

'It's an easy question. Do you have good legal representation?'

'Yes,' I lied.

'Good. Because you're going to need it.'

'How so?'

'Simple. If I hear that you've been saying things like this around town I'm going to sue you for defamation of character.'

'That's not going to change the facts.'

'There are no facts. This is a product of your imagination.'

'No. It's not.'

'Can you prove it?'

I didn't say anything.

The corners of Walmouth's mouth turned up. 'I thought not. And even if what you're saying is true – which it isn't – it doesn't matter because no one will believe you anyway. You have no proof. You have nothing. You will never have anything. I'll make sure of that. And most importantly, no one is interested in what you have to say.'

'Don't worry. I will have something.'

Walmouth laughed. 'Now there's a triumph of wishful thinking. By the time I'm through with you, you won't have a business, you won't have a house, you won't have a car, you won't have anything but the clothes on your back. You'll be collecting cans on the street and living in a shelter.'

'You forgot to add "you and your little dog too".'

'What are you talking about?'

'It's a line from *The Wizard of Oz*, when the Wicked Witch is threatening Dorothy and Toto.'

'I'm serious.'

'So am I. Did you tack a warning note on my front door?'

Walmouth sniffed. 'I'd hardly resort to such juvenile tactics. *This* is my warning to you. If you're smart you'll pay attention.'

'Otherwise you'll bankrupt me?'

'I'll do a lot worse than that.'

'Is that a threat?'

'No. It's a statement of fact.' Then he signaled for his driver to stop.

'What?' I asked. 'No return trip?'

'Get out,' Walmouth said.

'I guess chivalry is dead.'

The driver turned and put his hand on the door handle. As he did I realized where I'd seen him before. It was Bays' roommate. No wonder Bays had acted the way he had.

'Hey, Carl, nice seeing you again.'

'You better be going.'

'You know him?' Walmouth asked.

'Yeah. He and I are best buddies.'

'Really?' It wasn't a happy 'really'.

'Yeah. Really. Ask him.'

'She's a lying—' Carl began, but Walmouth cut him off.

'We'll talk later,' he told him.

Carl growled at me and I threw a kiss back at him. I mean what the hell. A girl has to have some fun sometimes. Carl started to get out of the Hummer.

'Stop,' Walmouth said.

'You listen better than Zsa Zsa,' I told Carl. 'Did he take you to dog-training school?'

Then before he could answer Zsa Zsa and I got out of the Hummer. The trick with this kind of thing is knowing when to stop. I barely had the door closed when Carl gunned the Hummer and took off. I looked around. Fortunately we'd only gone ten blocks, but it was cold and a bad neighborhood and I wanted to get out of there as quickly as possible. Which I did. On my way back to my car I impulsively called Carrie Walmouth and told her I needed to speak to her.

To my surprise she agreed to see me if I could meet her in a half an hour. She was catching an early plane tomorrow for India and she'd be there for the next six weeks, she explained, but if I wanted she could give me a half-hour of her time. I told her I wanted. We settled on Pat's Steak House, which was ten minutes away from her.

When I got to my car I made another phone call because I wanted to confirm a suspicion. I called Otto Cody and asked him if Richard Walmouth owned Wonder Women. He confirmed that he did indeed own it, along with another strip club on the North Side.

'But according to what I read in the paper he's supposed to be Mr Model Citizen.'

'What can I say,' Otto remarked. 'Money trumps morality every time. And anyway, you should know better than to believe what you read in the papers.'

As I drove over to the steakhouse I couldn't help thinking about how Wonder Women kept on popping up. Only John had never gone there and I didn't think that Theodore had either.

I killed the time before I met Carrie Walmouth sitting by the fireplace, sipping a Scotch on the rocks, and staring at the flames. Pat's was cozy and relatively quiet this time of night. It was best known as a steakhouse, but it had a nice-sized bar with a circular stone fireplace in the center. A copper hood in the center drew off the smoke, but the place still smelled like campfires. I was one of ten people here tonight. The others were a couple on what was obviously their first date and a large group of people dressed in office clothes who looked as if they were celebrating someone's promotion.

While I waited for Carrie I thought about my strategy for the meeting. The truth was I didn't have one. I was going by instinct pure and simple. I wouldn't have called her except I kept remembering the look on her face when she'd seen her husband. I was hoping I could use that feeling to get her to tell me something that would let me help her . . . and myself. Because as of now I had nothing concrete on Richard Walmouth. A fact he'd been kind enough to point out.

Carrie came into the bar ten minutes later. Her cheeks were flushed. She was wearing jeans and a white Irish fisherman's sweater. The clothes suited her. She stood at the door for a moment glancing around. Then she spotted me and hurried over.

'I can't stay long,' she said as she slid into the seat next to me. 'I have to finish packing.' The waiter came over and she ordered a glass of red wine. I put my hand over my glass to signify I didn't want a refill on my Scotch.

'What does your husband think about your going?' I asked.

Carrie combed her hair with her fingers. 'He's in favor of it. In fact he's the one that suggested it.'

'I was just talking to him.'

She smiled. 'He said he had a meeting he had to go to. I didn't realize it was with you.'

I started to reply but just then the waitress came over and set down Carrie's glass. I waited till she was gone to resume speaking.

'He's not a nice man,' I told Carrie.

She gave me a bright, brittle smile.

'He threatened to bankrupt me and throw me out in the street. Actually, he threatened worse.'

I'd expected Carrie to say something, but she didn't. She just took a sip of her wine. 'Not bad,' she commented after she'd rolled it around on her tongue. 'New York State wines have come a long way.' She leaned forward slightly. 'I can hardly wait to get to India,' she confided. She was all breathy, like a college girl talking about her new date. 'I'm going to live in an ashram. I've been dreaming about it for months.'

'Didn't you hear what I said about your husband?' I asked.

Carrie took another sip of her wine. Then she ran her finger around the rim of the glass.

'What did you think I wanted to talk about?'

Carrie shrugged.

'I saw the way you looked at him the day we had lunch together. You really don't like him.'

She tried to smile again but her smile faltered. I was getting to her.

'It must be hard living with a man like that,' I observed.

Carrie took a big gulp of her wine. 'You have no idea,' she murmured.

'I think he had Benny Gibson killed. I think he had me set up. But I can't prove it.'

If I expected that what I was saying would shock Carrie it didn't. That was a message in itself. She looked at me matter-of-factly and said, 'Take it from me. You'll never be able to. He's too smart for that.'

'So you think he's capable of doing things like that?'

She thought about her answer for a moment. Then she said, 'People are capable of many different kinds of actions.'

I took a sip of my Scotch. 'That's nice to know.'

Carrie shrugged. 'We are what we are.'

Somehow I found that no help at all.

'Is there anything that you can think of that might help me?'

She looked genuinely puzzled. 'Do what?'

'Point me in the right direction.'

She threw back her head and chortled. 'So you can turn my husband in to the police. I don't think so.'

'But he abuses you.'

She gave me a defiant look. 'So what if he does?'

'That's not a good thing.'

Carrie shrugged. 'Everyone has to put up with something in their life.'

'Don't you want to get back at him?'

'No.' She ran her hand through her hair again. 'He's the instrument of his own destruction.'

'I don't get it.' I watched the office party break up out of the corner of my eye.

'There's nothing to get,' Carrie said. 'He makes his own world. Eventually it'll destroy him.'

'That's very nice theoretically, but I think what's needed here is something a little more concrete.'

Carrie took another sip of wine and carefully set her glass down on her coaster. Then she gave me a benign smile, the kind of smile the enlightened bestow on the less enlightened.

'I might be wrong,' I continued, 'but I got the feeling you wanted to help me.'

'No. You weren't wrong,' Carrie said. 'I did.'

'But you don't want to help me now?'

Carrie shrugged. 'You have to help yourself.'

This had started out OK and was going south at a rapid rate. 'What made you change your mind?'

'I was at Diksha.'

'Diksha?'

'How can I describe it?' Carrie's hands fluttered around her glass. 'It would be like a prayer meeting. Only it's so much more. I was in the presence of my satguru when I saw everything clearly for the first time.'

'About not helping me?'

'About attaining the kundalini force. The more I concern myself with the things that my husband is involved in the more I mire myself in this world. He must finish his own path. And I came home and told Richard I thought it was a good thing—'

'I thought he suggested this trip to you?'

Carrie waved my objection away as if it were too minor to consider. 'As I was saying, he thought it was a good thing for me to go to the ashram. He's even donating money. He said I could stay in India as long as I want.'

'I just bet he did,' I said. 'Bribery works very well.'

Carrie finished her wine. 'Negative energy is a bad thing.'

'So is bullshit. Why did you agree to come to meet me if you weren't going to help me?'

Carrie put her hand on my arm. 'But I am helping you,' she said earnestly. 'I'm helping keep you out of harm's way.'

'How do you figure that?'

'Because if I told you what you wanted to know you might come to harm. This way you won't.'

'Or maybe it's because you wouldn't get your trip to India.'

'I didn't have to come,' Carrie said. Which was true. 'My husband is a bad man. You should stay away from him.'

'That seems to be the universal consensus,' I said.

Carrie stood up. 'Calli told me you were extremely stubborn.'

'And she's right. One last question.'

Carrie glanced at her watch. 'My flight to JFK is taking off at six o'clock tomorrow morning.'

'All I want to know is did you know John Gabriellas?'

Carrie thought for a moment. 'I can't say I did.'

'He worked for your husband.'

'So do a lot of people.' And with that she left.

I gulped down the last of my Scotch, paid the tab, and left as well. I should have just gone straight home after Walmouth dropped me off and saved my money.

Thirty-Three

When I got to the store the next day, just for laughs I called up Detective Keene and told him what I'd found out about Richard Walmouth and Benny Gibson and Theodore Gabriellas.

He listened to me and then when I was done he said, 'And your point is what?'

'Obviously, that you should investigate Richard Walmouth. He seems to be at the epicenter of this thing.'

Keene laughed. It was more of a cackle actually. 'The only way that is going to happen is if I find Richard Walmouth standing over his victim with a gun in his hand and even then it would be problematic. Given his connections, I wouldn't go near him. No one will.'

'How about the "equal justice for all" thing?'

'I didn't think you went in for weed.'

'Ha. Ha.'

'You know what they say to first-year law students, don't you?' Keene asked me.

'Never confuse justice and the law.'

'There you go, then. I say no more. Gotta go,' he said. I heard a click as he hung up.

'Lovely,' I said to Zsa Zsa.

She looked up from the bone she was chewing on and wagged her tail. Sometimes I envied her. I took a couple of sips of my coffee and got down to work. But it was hard to concentrate. I couldn't sit still. I felt as if I had to move. At this point any movement was better than no movement.

I was pretty sure I knew who was responsible for Benny Gibson's death. I was also pretty sure I couldn't do anything about it. At least nothing legal. Because I didn't have any proof and I didn't see how I was going to get it, although maybe that wasn't true. Walmouth wouldn't have warned me off if there wasn't something to find. But what? I didn't know.

Everything I'd dug up about Richard Walmouth was circumstantial. What did they say about Ronald Reagan? He was the Teflon President because nothing stuck to him? Well, I felt that was about Richard Walmouth. And the truth was that Joe Gibson and Martha Gibson had equally good motives for killing Benny Gibson. So did the daughter. Maybe it was a family affair.

All three of them did really, but even if I could prove it I was left with the same question. Why had I been set up? Why had I been picked? What had made John do what he had? I was as far away from answering that now as I had been when I started. All that talking to people and I still couldn't come up with the answer to the question I wanted answered. It was very frustrating.

It was so frustrating that when Manuel came into the shop I decided to take a run out to Martha Gibson's house again and see if she would answer a question that was bothering me. That is if she'd let me in the door. Given the way our last meeting had ended I wouldn't be surprised if she didn't.

But she did. This time she came to the door in a fleece caftan over which she'd put a large man's sweater. Her gray hair was in two braids. On her feet were a pair of rabbit slippers. Her eyes had a vacant expression in them that hadn't been there before. It was as if she'd gone off on a trip and wouldn't be coming back for a while. I was guessing that whatever new kind of meds she was taking were flattening her out.

'Martha,' I said gently. 'Do you remember me?'

She nodded. Her movements were jerky.

'Can I come in for a moment?'

She just looked at me.

'I need to ask you a question.' I realized I was speaking slowly and distinctly the way you would to a small child.

She moved out of the way and let me pass. I walked into her house. As I entered her living room I could see that the whole place looked more cared for. Although the floor was still chipped, there was a bright hook rug on the floor. Someone had put a cover over the chair that was held together with duct tape, thrown a comforter on the sofa, and removed the television. In its place was a smaller model, tuned to the cooking channel.

'It's nice that you can watch TV now,' I commented.

She gave a vague nod and sat down on the sofa. Her eyes were riveted on the set. I sat down next to her. I took the picture of John Gabriellas I had in the shop out of my backpack.

'Martha, does this man look familiar to you?'

She shook her head. She hadn't even glanced at the picture. I got up and turned off the television.

She looked as if she were going to cry. 'Why did you do that?' she whimpered.

'Just for a moment,' I reassured her, and I handed her John's picture. 'Have you ever seen this man?'

Martha squinted at it. She turned it to the left side and then to the right.

'Well?' I said after thirty seconds or so had passed.

Martha nodded. 'He used to come to the house sometimes.'

'And do what?'

'Bring stuff.'

'What kind of stuff?'

'Sometimes messages for Benny. Once Carrie sent him over with some stuff that Janet had forgot at Carrie's house.'

'I didn't think the two girls were friends.'

'They used to be. A long time ago.'

'But you told me you were away.' Away. Now there was a nice euphemistic term for you.

'Yes. But I'd come back on the weekends lots of times.'

'I don't mean to be rude but the neighbors said they never saw you.'

'That's because I'd be at our house on Sandy Pond. I liked it there. It was nice and quiet. Benny let me come. Most of the time he wasn't there.' She looked at me earnestly. 'You know the weekends don't count. They're not real time.'

'When did this happen?'

Martha shrugged.

'Try and think,' I urged.

She looked at me. Her eyes were full of nothing. 'I can't,' she said in the kind of matter-of-fact voice she'd use to discuss the weather. 'The medicines make me not remember things. Now can I go back to my show?'

'Sure.' I'd gotten as much as I was going to get. I took John's picture out of her hand and got up and turned the television back on.

When I left she was sitting exactly the way I'd left her. On the way out I ran into Otto. He was carrying two bags of groceries.

'You're doing a nice thing,' I told him.

He scowled at me. 'You shouldn't have called Keene.'

'I didn't feel I had an option.'

'People always have options.'

'You're right. It was unnecessary, but I didn't know that at the time. I'm sorry if I caused Martha trouble.'

Otto's eyes lost their fierce look. 'It's all right,' he said. 'She's gotten past it.'

'Good.' And I shut the door and left. I really wanted to think about what I'd just found out.

Carrie had lied to me. She knew who John was. She'd used him for errands. At least once. So had Richard. I wondered if there was a way to get John's work sheet from Richard. Not that that would prove anything. But still it was something to do and at this point I needed a task.

George would know. And if he didn't that was OK too, because the truth was I wanted to talk to him. I felt as if I could think more clearly after I did. First I tried his cell. His voicemail came on immediately and I left a message asking him to call me. Then I thought: Dumb. He was probably teaching. Maybe he had office hours. Possibly I could reach him there. I called the college and got the number of the History Department. I dialed that.

The phone rang twice before an elderly female voice said, 'History Department. How may I help you?'

I gave her George's name and told her I'd like to leave a message for him.

'I'm sorry,' the secretary said, 'but there's no one here by that name.'

I laughed. George had always complained about how incompetent the departmental secretary was and I guess he was right. 'I think you're mistaken,' I said, and I repeated George's name.

'No,' the secretary replied. 'I'm not mistaken. This is a small department and I'm responsible for putting through all the paperwork. Believe me when I say he's not here.'

'He's a new hire. He used to teach adjunct.'

There was a short pause then she said, 'Perhaps he's teaching in another department. Why don't I connect you to the operator?'

Only the way she put it, it really wasn't a question. She obviously wanted to turf the crazy lady off to someone else.

'Fine.' A moment later the operator came on and I explained what I needed.

'Let me check for you,' she replied. 'I'm going to put you on hold.'

I lit a cigarette while I waited.

'No,' she said when she came back on. 'I'm sorry, but we have no one here listed by that name. Perhaps he's teaching at one of the other state schools. Sometimes people get them mixed up.'

'Is there anyone else I can talk to?' I asked her.

'You could try personnel,' the operator suggested. She sounded dubious.

I told her I'd like to do that. I spent the next ten minutes on the phone with them. The first five minutes were taken up with convincing the man on the other end of the line that he wouldn't be violating the privacy act if he told me whether or not George was working there. The second five minutes were taken up with him looking through the files while I waited.

'Nope,' he said when he came back on the line. 'I'm sorry. But according to our records he never worked here. At least not as a professor.'

'What was he?'

'A security guard. But that was only for three months. Maybe it's someone with the same name. Without his social-security number it's hard to tell.'

'Thanks,' I said.

The man told me it wasn't a problem and hung up. I was stunned. I didn't know what to make of this. All the stories George had told me about his classes. Were they all lies? Had I misunderstood? Was I going crazy? I must have misunderstood.

I could feel my guts tying themselves into a knot. I lit a cigarette, took a couple of drags, and flicked it out the window. Then I lit another one and smoked that. There had to be an explanation. I'd ask George when I saw him. He'd explain. The explanation would make sense and then everything would be fine. It would be better than fine. It would be hunky-dory.

I started driving. It felt good to be moving. It gave me something to do. I went up one street and down another, but somehow I got to the place where George lived with his blonde and the kid. I guess I must have been heading there all along without realizing it.

I sat in the car and looked at the house. It was small and nondescript. It wasn't old and it wasn't new. It wasn't in bad shape, but it wasn't in good shape either. The laurel bushes on either side of the steps were strung with old Christmas decorations. The lopsided remains of a rotting-out Halloween jack o' lantern leered at me as I walked towards the front door. I rang the bell. A few minutes later the blonde answered. She had rubber gloves on. I assumed she'd been cleaning. Her eyes opened wide when she saw me. I could see her jaw muscles tightening.

'I thought I told you to leave us alone,' she said.

'You did,' I agreed.

She took her gloves off and laid them on the small table off to the side of the door. 'So why are you here? What will it take? A court order to get you to stay away from us?'

'I'm sorry. I know I'm intruding, but I have a question for you.'

She looked puzzled. This was clearly not what she was expecting from me. Her curiosity must have outweighed her animosity because she asked me what I wanted.

'I want to know where George is working.'

The blonde stared at me. 'What kind of question is that?'

'A straightforward one. Please,' I begged.

The blonde studied an empty soda bottle that was standing on the railing for a moment and then she said, 'He's head of security for Richard Walmouth's operation. Why?'

I lifted a finger. 'Stay with me for one more second. So he's not a college professor?'

The blonde laughed. 'Of course not. Whatever gave you such a ridiculous idea?'

'He told me he was.'

Two furrows creased her forehead. 'Well, I don't know why he would say something like that.'

'Does he have his Ph.D.?'

'Does he look like someone that would have that?'

'When he was living with me he told me he was going for his Ph.D. in history. I saw the books. He'd leave them on the table. He used to go to the library to work.'

The blonde shook her head. 'I don't know what to tell you.'

'How long has George been working for Walmouth?'

The blonde thought for a moment. 'I'd say a couple of years.'

'And you know this for a fact?'

'I've dropped him off there once in a while.'

'And before that?'

'I think he worked as a security guard for S.U.'

I just stood there. My throat felt as if it was constricting. I was having trouble speaking.

'He really said that to you about being a college professor?' the blonde asked.

I nodded. It all made sense.

She took a couple of steps backwards and beckoned me in. She closed the door behind me. We were standing in a small hallway that was probably four feet by two feet at the most. 'I was getting cold outside,' she explained. I nodded again. My eyes fell on one of the baby's hats. 'She's at the sitter. I have to get her in a little while.' The blonde stooped down and picked up a stray leaf on the floor tile. Then she straightened up and said, 'Can I ask you a question now?'

'Shoot,' I said.

'Remember how you said you threw George out of your house?'

'Yeah. I remember.'

'Was that true?'

'Absolutely. He didn't want to go. He kept telling me that he'd work things out with you. I finally changed the locks on my house and put his stuff in the garage. He just wouldn't listen to me.'

The blonde absentmindedly wiped her hands on the front of the sweatshirt she was wearing. 'Did you call him up for dinner and beg him to come over?'

I shook my head. 'Never.'

'Is he the one doing the calling?'

'Yes.'

'Does he call a lot?'

'Not really. But he drops by the shop every six weeks or so and asks me out. In fact, he tells me how much he misses me and how he wants to get back together with me.'

'I see.' The furrows on the blonde's forehead became more pronounced. 'Did he lend you money so you could fix your roof?'

'No. Is that what he told you?'

'Yes. Five thousand dollars.'

'Wow. That's a fair chunk of change. I wonder what he did with it?'

'I wish I knew.' The blonde bit her lip. 'He's been lying to me all this time.'

'Me too,' I said. 'And I never even suspected.'

'Me either,' the blonde said. 'I wonder what else he's lying about?'

'Probably a lot of things.'

'I think so too,' the blonde said.

'So what are you going to do?' I asked.

She stuck her jaw out and put her hands on her hips. 'I'm going to go upstairs and pack. Then I'm going to pick up the baby, and go stay with my parents for a while until I figure this out.'

'Seems like a good plan,' I said.

The blonde shivered. 'I don't know why I have the chills,' she said.

'Probably for the same reason I do,' I told her. Then I wished her luck and left.

Thirty-Four

Normally when something bad happens to me I'm the first one on the phone. I broadcast it all over town. But not this time. This time I didn't want to talk to anybody. I didn't want to admit what a fool I'd been. I didn't want to talk about how George had lied to me. And for what? For the sheer fun of being able to do it? And then I wondered what else he'd lied about. Was anything he'd told me real? It was a disturbing thought.

I felt as if I'd been dropped down the rabbit hole. I'd known this man for a long time. He'd been friends with my husband. Then when my husband had been murdered, George had stepped up to the plate and helped me. We'd been friends and then we'd become lovers. Granted, it hadn't been an easy relationship. He was an inveterate womanizer. And he'd lied about that all the time. But that was different. That was like someone lying about his gambling or his drug use. I understood that kind of lie. I didn't understand this kind of lie.

These lies had no reason. These lies were gratuitous. And then it occurred to me that maybe George's blonde was lying. A faint hope stirred in my chest. There was one way to check. I pulled over and called Richard Walmouth's company. After a minute of pressing buttons I finally got to a live person and asked for the head of security.

'I'm sorry, he isn't in,' the operator said. 'Would you like his voicemail?'

'That's all right. I just want to send him a letter. His name is George Samson, right?' I asked.

'That is correct.'

'I just wanted to make sure.' Then I asked for the zip code to make my request seem more authentic.

The receptionist gave it to me and I hung up. I felt numb.

Pancaked. I drove back to the store. At one point I went
through a red light without realizing. I was just glad I didn't
hit anybody.

When I walked in Manuel was leaning on the counter.
'What?' he said. 'No donuts? No KFC? No Chinese?'

'Sorry,' I said.

Zsa Zsa came running out to say hello. I bent down and
scratched her rump. She wiggled to one side and then to the
other. Then she licked my hand and ran through my feet. I
petted her some more and walked into my office. I was
hanging up my jacket when Manuel came in.

'What's wrong?' he said.

'Nothing.'

'No. I know you. Something's definitely wrong.'

'I don't want to talk about it.'

'What is it?'

'Didn't I just say I really don't want to talk about it?' I
could hear my voice rising.

Manuel threw up his hands. There was a hurt look on his
face.

'Fine,' he said. 'Don't tell me. I don't care.'

I put my hand on his arm.

'I'm sorry. I'll tell you later. I just can't talk about it now.'

'It's pretty bad, huh?'

'Yeah. You could say that.'

'Does it have anything to do with me?'

I shook my head. 'Nothing at all.'

Manuel shuffled his feet and yanked up his pants. 'You
know if you need me . . .'

'I know. Thanks.'

'I mean it.'

'I know you mean it.'

'You want me to get you something to eat? I can go to
the corner and get you a candy bar or something like that.'

I laughed. His concern made me feel better. 'I'll be fine.
Honestly. I just need to be alone for a few minutes and then
I'll come back out and we can start putting away the new
shipments we got in this morning.'

Manuel walked to the door. Then he turned and stood
there. I told him to go and shut the door behind him. I leaned

back in my chair when he was gone. Zsa Zsa went over to her bed, lay down, and started gnawing on her bone. Somehow being in here made me feel calmer, more centered. I took a deep breath and then I took another. When I felt calm enough I picked up the phone and called Ian.

'What do you want?' he growled.

'Nice greeting.'

'I had a bad night. I had to throw Electra's son out.'

'You're always throwing someone out.'

'True. But then Electra jumped on my back and scratched my face.'

All I could think of was I was glad it wasn't me.

'That's not good.'

'No. It's not good at all. So are you coming in tomorrow?'

'Why wouldn't I be?'

'I don't know. I thought that's what you were calling to tell me.'

'No. I was calling to ask you a question.'

'OK,' Ian said after a pause. 'I'm waiting.'

'Hypothetically speaking you find out that someone has been lying about themselves.'

'What's new about that?'

'I mean on a massive scale. He's saying he's one thing and he's another.'

'He's a scammer.'

'No. Much worse. He's not getting any visible gain. And he lies to everyone about everything.'

Ian was quiet for a moment. Then he said, 'I once knew this girl who told everyone she had cancer and she didn't, but even when you knew that she didn't, even after you'd learned that she was lying, you could have sworn she was telling you the truth. I remember watching her eyes fill up with tears when she told me she needed to have a bone-marrow transplant or she would die immediately. Then three weeks later I saw her on the street and went over and asked her how she was doing and she told me she was fine. The transplant had been a success. You know those things are a six-month ordeal.'

'Yeah. I know.'

'Later one of my friends told me she was a pathological

liar. It's a personality disorder. These people lie to get attention. They lie to feel in control. They lie because it gives them
a sense of power. Lots of times they keep the people in their
personal life separate from each other, because that way they
can't compare notes. Is that what you're talking about?'
    'I think so. And what do you do with someone like that?'
    'You stay as far away from them as you can.'
    'Thanks,' I said.
    'So who are you talking about?'
    'It's just . . . I . . .'
    'You really are a bad liar.'
    'I don't want to talk about it now,' I snapped.
    'Hey. That's all you had to say. Call me when you do.'
    I promised I would and clicked off. Then I lit a cigarette
and thought about the implications of George being head of
security. It meant that George knew Benny Gibson. It meant
that George knew John. John probably went to him for advice
about his brother's predicament. It meant that George probably knew Janet Gibson. Knew what she did. He certainly
knew Richard. He certainly knew how to kill someone. Being
an ex-cop he knew how things were done. He certainly knew
me. But why had he chosen to set me up? What purpose did
this whole thing serve? *Cui bono?* Who benefits? I couldn't
see it in this case. Or maybe I just didn't want to.
    I thought George loved me. Or at least cared for me. Why
do something like this to me? I couldn't understand it. I just
remembered all the times we'd spent together. This wasn't
the George I knew. This was a different George. One I
couldn't even begin to comprehend. And even worse I didn't
know what to do about it. I felt paralyzed. I had no proof.
I couldn't call Keene and tell him. He'd have me committed.
    I remember reading once that there was love and there
was hate and there was indifference, but the worst thing of
all was hate masquerading as love. It seemed as if that's
what George was doing to me. I was wondering where I'd
read it when Manuel knocked on the door.
    'Robin,' he said, 'we got a guy out here who wants to buy
three of the baby Burmese pythons.'
    I told him I'd be right there.

*   *   *

I spent the rest of the day working in the shop. It was unusually busy so I managed not to think about George. Instead I ran to the bank to get change and to Sam's club to get plastic bags and the aluminum containers we use to contain the gravel in the tortoises' cages. Then I put together a pricing sheet for a restaurant on Marshall Street that wanted to buy a tropical-fish tank from us as well as a maintenance schedule. By the end of the day, Manuel and I had also managed to unload and stack our fifty-pound bags of dog food, cat food, and litter. Nothing like physical pain to take your mind off problems, I always say.

By four o'clock business had died down and by five no one was out on the street. A storm had blown in from the west and everyone was hunkered down. The sky was dark and it had begun to sleet. The newsman on the radio came on every ten minutes or so to announce another accident in or around the city and to suggest we drive with extreme care.

Manuel's mom called him and asked if she could pick him up early. I told Manuel to go ahead. There was no point in his hanging around. I couldn't see anyone else coming in. I'd close up the shop. There wasn't much more to do anyway. Manuel left around six. I could have done some bookkeeping and filing, but instead I opened the day's paper, spread it on the counter, and began to read.

The words blurred in my brain. I couldn't seem to focus on what I was reading. I guess the day was finally taking its toll on me. Even though I wasn't thinking about it consciously I was still thinking about what I'd discovered in some corner of my mind. I was reaching under the counter to get the scissors to cut out an ad for a new furnace that I wanted to look into when Zsa Zsa started barking. I glanced up as the door opened. George was standing in the doorway.

'We have to talk,' he said.

I could feel my breath catching in my throat. 'No. We don't.' He was the last person I wanted to see.

He advanced towards the counter. He looked big. His white sweater shone under the lights. There were speckles of sleet on his skull.

'I just got home,' he told me. 'And my wife and my baby weren't there.'

'I'm sorry.' I just wanted him gone.

'She left a note. She said she'd gone down to her mom's house. So I called her and she said you and she had had a conversation. She called me a liar.' By now he was at the counter. 'Why were you at my house?'

'I had a question,' I whispered.

'What kind of question?'

'George, I have to go.'

He pointed to the newspaper I'd been reading. 'You weren't in a hurry before.'

'I wasn't aware of the time,' I stammered.

He smiled. It wasn't a nice one. 'What's the matter, Robin?'

'Nothing.'

'No. Something is. I can tell. You should never play poker. You'll always lose.'

'You're wrong.'

'Don't you have any questions for me?' His voice had taken on a coaxing quality.

'No, George,' I whispered. 'I don't.'

He cocked his head. His smile grew wider. He stroked the edge of the counter with his finger. 'But you always have questions, Robin. You always have lots and lots of questions.'

I cleared my throat. 'I really have to go,' I said. 'I have to get to work. Ian is waiting for me.'

'No, he's not. You don't work until tomorrow night.'

'The schedule has changed. And anyway, I have to go home and feed the cat.'

'Home. Now there's an interesting word, don't you think?' He gave 'home' a twist.

'In what way?'

'Everyone wants a home, but you threw me out of mine.'

'No, George. It's my house. Not yours. You moved in with me.'

'Yes. But I gave up my place to be with you. I helped paint the bedroom. I shoveled the driveway. That made it mine. And you just threw me out. Just like that.'

'Is that's what this is about? My throwing you out of my house?'

'Our house,' George corrected as he moved closer to me.

'Our house. And then you made me go to the garage to pick up my things. Like I was some kind of bum.' He shook his finger at me. 'You shouldn't have done that, Robin. That was a bad thing to do. But I was nice to you anyway. I kept coming around. I offered to take you out to dinner. I offered to help you with things. But all you did was refuse me.'

'That's because you had a child with another woman,' I told him as I walked to the space between the counter and the wall. But George was faster. He had gotten there before me.

'So what. I have enough love in me for several women.'

I wanted to leave, but I couldn't. George was blocking my way. I was trapped behind the counter. I glanced outside. The street was empty. Nothing was moving. Except for George. Who was coming closer. His anger was palpable. Zsa Zsa must have felt it because she started growling.

'Robin,' George said sorrowfully. 'You abandoned me.'

'No. I didn't.'

He took another step towards me.

'You left me. I never would have left you.'

'Is that why you set me up, George? Because you were angry at me?'

He shook his head. A bemused smile played around the corners of his mouth. 'I've never been angry at you. I just wanted you to come to me for advice. For help. The way you used to do. I've been watching over you all the time. I'm your guardian angel. I never would have let anything bad happen to you.'

'Well, it certainly happened to John.'

George shrugged. 'He was a fag. A pussy. What do you expect from someone like that?'

'What about Benny? Did he deserve what he got?'

'He was a perv. He got exactly what he deserved.'

'That was your personal judgment?'

'That was my boss's, but I concurred. After all you can't stand in the way of progress. Or maybe a more apt expression would be: the good of the many outweighs the good of the few.'

'And what about me?'

'You're just stubborn. You'll come around. You always do.'

'Not this time, George. You need to leave.'

He grinned. 'See. You keep saying that, but you don't mean it.'

'I most certainly do.'

He took another step towards me. 'Here. Let me show you what you're missing.'

'No, George.' I held my hand out. 'You keep away from me.'

'Or you'll what?'

'I'll hurt you.'

'That's not possible.'

'Let's not find out, shall we?'

He shook his head again at my stubbornness and stupidity. 'You used to like me inside of you.'

'That was then and this is now.'

I took a step back and grabbed for the phone, but before I could get it George reached over and yanked it out of its connection. I dove for my backpack and grabbed my cell out of it. I saw him swing his hand. It was like it was in slow motion. He connected with mine and the cell flew out of my hand and landed on the floor in front of the counter.

'George, I'm going to call the cops when this is done.'

His smile grew wider. 'No you won't. You won't want to after we're done. And anyway they won't believe you. I'll just tell them we had a lovers' quarrel. It'll be strictly a "he said, she said" thing.'

Then George reached out and grabbed my wrist. I should have been expecting it but I wasn't. I tried to wiggle out of his grasp. It was useless. His grip was too strong. I went to kick him, but he jammed his leg between mine and lifted me up till my ass was on the counter.

'George. Stop.' I tried to push him away from me but he was too heavy.

'It's going to be fine,' he murmured in my ear. 'Everything is going to be fine.'

'Someone is going to come in.'

'Don't be silly. No one is going to come in on a night like tonight.'

Then he leaned me back, pinning my upper body with one of his arms. I tried to kick, but I couldn't. I didn't have the traction. And then I saw the scissors. They were right where I'd left them. Maybe I could get them. Maybe I could stab him in the back with them before he got them out of my hand. But if I didn't succeed it would just make him madder.

I decided I didn't care. He was tearing at my pants now. Trying to get the zipper down. But his eyes were still watching me. I didn't have a chance now. I'd have to wait and hope. And then he howled in pain. His grip on me eased. He looked down. I remember thinking that Zsa Zsa must have bitten him as I reached over and grabbed the scissors. He looked up. He saw the scissors.

'What do you think you're doing?' he said.

He grabbed for them. But I brought my hand up and around in an arc and stabbed him in the neck with all the strength I had. He screamed and staggered back.

Then he reached up and pulled the scissors out of his neck. Blood started spurting out of the wound. The world turned into red mist. His eyes widened and he put his hand over the wound to stem the blood, but the blood spurted between his fingers and ran down his neck. Nothing he did could stop it.

He held out a red hand. 'Robin.' He coughed. A froth of pink foam edged his lips. I remember the rational part of my mind thinking that I must have hit one of his carotid arteries. That's why there was so much blood. He lurched towards me. I wanted to move, but I couldn't. My legs didn't seem to be working. I could see George's skin. It was turning ashy. He made a gurgling noise. It seemed to go on forever. He collapsed on the floor. His arms and legs started twitching. A dark stain spread along the front of his pants. Then he was still. The parrots were shrieking and I put my hands over my ears to blot out the noise.

I became aware of Zsa Zsa's whimpering. And of my breathing. I was panting. I was hot. I was cold. I looked at my hands. They were covered with blood. So was my sweater. I touched my face. My cheeks were wet. At first I thought it was blood, but then I realized I was crying. It took me a moment before I could summon up the courage to step over George's body. For some reason, I expected him to reach out and grab my leg.

Everything in the room seemed distant. Off kilter. The birds kept squawking. I wanted to go to sleep, but a voice in my head told me I had to call Ian. My legs wobbled as I walked across the floor. When I picked up my phone my hands were shaking so badly I could hardly hold on to it. Somehow I managed to dial Ian's number.

'What?' he growled when he answered. 'Don't you have anything better to do than annoy me?'

'You have to come now,' I cried. 'Something very bad happened. I . . .'

'Shush,' Ian said. 'Don't say anything else. I'll be right over. Where are you?'

'At the store. I . . .'

'Lock the door and wait for me and for God's sake don't call anyone else. You hear that?'

'Yes.'

'You think you can do that?'

'Yes,' I whispered.

'Good.' And Ian clicked off.

Thirty-Five

It took Ian an eternity to get to the shop. I spent the time with my back against the counter, staring at the fish tanks, and wondering what it would be like to be an angelfish. I felt so tired I could hardly move. I didn't even have the energy to wash my hands. I just wiped them off on my jeans. When Ian knocked I got up and let him in. He took one look at me and his jaw went slack. I gestured towards the counter. He went behind it and then came back out.

'I should call the police,' I said.

'What happened?'

I told him everything.

'Anything else?' he asked when I was done.

'No. I really have to call the police.'

'No you don't. What you have to do is go home.'

'I can't leave . . . this.'

'I'll take care of it.'

'The police . . .'

Ian took me by the shoulders. 'Do you want to go to jail?' he asked.

I shook my head.

'Because that's what's going to happen.'

'No. He attacked me.'

'There's only your word. You thought he was harassing you. You lost it, picked up the scissors, and that as they say is that.'

'No,' I protested. 'He was trying to rape me.'

'Listen, Robin, George is an ex-cop. He's Walmouth's head of security. Do you think they're going to want to have what this guy was really like broadcast around?'

'But—'

Ian raised his hand. 'He made your friend kill himself, he

probably killed Benny Gibson or if he didn't he arranged
for it to happen, he set you up to take the fall, he almost
raped you. Did I leave anything out?'

'No.'

'And anyway if you wanted to call the police you would
have done it already.'

I didn't answer because it was true.

'One moment,' Ian said. Then he took out his phone and
dialed. I heard him telling Manuel to get over here and to
bring Chad and Jellybean with him.

'I didn't know they were back,' I said.

He ignored my comment. 'You have a change of clothes
at the shop, don't you?' he asked me instead as he slipped
his cellphone back in its case.

I nodded. 'In the office.'

'And shoes?'

'An old pair of sneakers I use for painting.'

'Good. I want you to go in there and change. Then I want
you to take the clothes and the shoes you're wearing and put
them in a plastic garbage bag and give them to me. Can you
do that?'

'Yes.'

'Excellent. After that I want you to go into the bathroom
and wash your face and your hands. And then you and Zsa
Zsa are going to get in your car and drive home and I'm
going to follow you to make sure you get there OK. After
which you're going to give me the keys to the shop and I'm
going to come back and clean things up. Tomorrow when
you open it'll be like nothing ever happened.'

'How is that possible?'

'All you have to know is that it is.'

'I'm not sure I can do this.'

Ian gave me a gentle push towards the office. 'You'd be
surprised what you can do when you have to.'

As it turned out Ian was right. I really did surprise myself.

I slept very well that night. I expected to have nightmares,
but I didn't have any. I crawled into bed and went right to
sleep. And my conscience didn't bother me. At all. Maybe
it should have, but it didn't. Once I had time to get over the

shock I figured I only gave George what he had coming. And from what I could tell no one really cared that he had vanished. Certainly his blonde didn't. Last I heard she'd taken the baby and moved to Tucson, where she was working in a flower shop.

Thirty-Six

Five months later I was sitting in Shamus's with Ian and Zsa Zsa, having a beer. It was the end of summer, but you couldn't tell that from sitting in the bar. It was as dark and dingy now as it was in the winter.

We were listening to the local newscaster recapping the latest story. It seems Richard Walmouth was being arrested for tax evasion. According to the reporter his wife had finally had enough and turned him in to the IRS. I guess all that time in the ashram hadn't helped Carrie disconnect after all.

'See,' Ian said, 'that's why I'm never getting married again. You tell your wife something and the next fight you get into she's running to the lawyers.'

'I didn't know you were married.'

'A long time ago.' And he turned back to the television. 'Well, it's nice they got Walmouth for something,' he added.

'A homicide charge would have been better.'

Ian took a sip of his bottled water and lit a cigarette. 'Don't worry. You know what they say. What goes around comes around.'

'Don't tell me you really believe that?'

'Sure I do.'

I looked at him. He was serious. Although sometimes with Ian it was hard to tell. He took another drag on his cigarette. By mutual consent we hadn't discussed the night George had died since it had happened. I didn't want to know about it and Ian didn't want to tell me about it, so it was a good balance. But listening to the reporter brought everything back. Suddenly I wanted to know what had occurred, or rather I wanted to know the Cliff Notes version.

'Are you ever going to tell me what happened that night?'

'No.'

I didn't say anything.

Ian took another sip of water. 'But I'll tell you a story instead,' he informed me.

I leaned forward a little. 'Go on.'

'Now this is fiction.'

'That's what a story is, isn't it?'

'Exactly. Once upon a time . . .'

'Ian . . .'

'OK, I'm gonna tell you some background, so you gotta bear with me.'

'I'm listening.'

'There were these two punk-ass Indians who spent a fair amount of time dealing.' Chad and Jellybean, I thought. 'Mostly things worked out, but occasionally they didn't. Occasionally they or one of their crew would get ripped off by one of the pussy-boy niggers on the street.

'Now this involved a loss of product and like any good businessmen they tried to minimize this occurrence whenever possible. If it happens once you don't want it to happen again. In the business they were in, you get ripped off you gotta teach the person that ripped you off a lesson otherwise this is going to continue, right?'

I nodded. I wasn't sure where this was going.

'And that would be a bad thing because they'd lose their cred and everyone would be doing it. So one night they grab the little bitch who had been ripping them off right from his block and take him out to the Rez and –' Ian made a motion with his right hand pretending he had a knife, slicing from left to right across his throat – 'they toss him in the garbage dump, which is a deep pit, and then they throw some more garbage on top of him and they leave. And people are still looking for him, because the Rez is sovereign land and no one can go on it without permission and no one is giving permission to the white man. And these two Indians are good at this because they've done it lots of times.'

I took a sip of my beer. I was beginning to see where this was heading.

Ian picked a piece of tobacco off his tongue. 'Do you understand what I'm saying?'

'I guess it was a good thing I was nice to Chad,' I observed.

'Like I said. Karma. So when someone called them up and asked them to do a certain kind of favor they knew the drill. Only this time when they went around to the dump it was closed. Locked up tight. So they had to go around to a different hole, one that was farther away.

'You couldn't see the bottom of the hole in the dark so they just tossed their package in and covered it with a lot of garbage. Lots of stuff down in the dump. Tires. Old chairs. Stoves. It all went down the hole. And then when they were done they got a little shack, kind of an outhouse deal, and moved it on top of the pile. They thought it was pretty funny. You know, putting a crapper on a piece of shit, although it's always seemed stupid to me that they would mark a grave with a shack that could eventually be identified by comparing aerial photos.'

'Four people did this?'

'Three people.'

'What did the other person do?'

'He felt an overwhelming urge to clean.'

'Sovereign land, huh?'

'That's what I said. No one's allowed in except the Indians.'

'I believe the correct term is Native Americans or First People.'

'Like I give a fuck.'

I took a sip of my beer. 'Do you believe in ghosts?'

Ian laughed. 'Not in the slightest.'

'Do you believe in justice?'

'God's or man's?'

'Certainly not man's.'

'So you believe in God's?'

'When he's watching, which isn't often.'

'No. He's always watching, which is why you have to be careful.'

'Do you think justice and vengeance are the same?'

'Why are you asking?'

'Because I can't decide.'

'I can.' Ian threw his cigarette in a cup half filled with water. 'I guess you could say, I'm an Old Testament kind of guy.'

'So you think he got what he deserved?'

'Yes. I do.'

'I'll drink to that.' And I finished my beer.

I'd like to tell you I feel differently after that night, but I don't. I'd like to tell you my life has changed in some dramatic way. It hasn't. Keene came around a couple of times and asked some questions, but then he stopped doing that. In fact, I haven't talked to any representative of the Syracuse Police Department in months.

I'm still running the shop and working at Ian's bar two nights a week. Manuel is still helping me. Jellybean and Chad drop by the shop once in a while, but they're still on the low-by up on the Rez. The last time they came in they brought a litter of puppies with them that they wanted me to find homes for. Which I did.

As Ian would say: life goes on.

Some people just aren't with us anymore. That's all.